# CRIMINAL TRESPASS

# CRIMINAL TRESPASS

HELEN HUDSON

*G. P. PUTNAM'S SONS*
*New York*

Published by G. P. Putnam's Sons
200 Madison Avenue
New York, NY 10016
Published simultaneously in Canada by
General Publishing Co. Limited, Toronto

*The text of this book is set in Baskerville.*

Library of Congress Cataloging in Publication Data

Hudson, Helen.
Criminal trespass.

I. Title.
PS3558.U29C7   1985      813'.54         84-17923
ISBN 0-399-13055-1

*Printed in the United States of America*
1   2   3   4   5   6   7   8   9   10

*TO CANDIDA DONADIO*

*. . . that things are not so ill with you and me as they might have been, is half owing to the number who lived faithfully a hidden life, and rest in unvisited tombs.*

GEORGE ELIOT, *Middlemarch*

# CRIMINAL TRESPASS

A public library, like a railway station, gets all kinds. They come in groups, like packaged tours. The old men, waiting patiently for the doors to open, come for warmth and company and the daily news clamped to long wooden rollers. Later, the housewives come, between marketing and manicures, for cookbooks and Gothics and biographies of the wives of famous men. At lunchtime, the office workers rush in for travel books in summer and how-to books in winter: *Brew Your Own Beer, Construct Your Own Computer, Cure Your Own Cancer.* At exam time, huge high school students crowd the reading room, smelling of sweat and hair spray.

They hardly notice me, a thin, middle-aged white woman behind the loan desk in a sweater set—I have two, one beige and one pearl-gray—and a pencil like a feather in my hair. I watch them all, these people who borrow my books. I read their faces like texts and their gestures like punctuation marks: the way they eye the spines and yank down the volumes and riffle the contents like the Yellow Pages. They leave gaps on my shelves but hand me—along with their cards to be stamped— hints of their lives to stir my curiosity and fill my mind.

Rannee is different. She belongs to no group. She travels alone. She is a handsome young black woman with smooth skin and soft features and a "calm so deep" I used to think of her as Serena. She has been coming for years. Now, of course, she comes every day. She treats the library more like a church than a depot. She walks silently between the shelves like pews and slides the books gently from their niches. She is reading her way through Fiction. History, she tells me, will be next. It is *her* history that interests me.

# THE
# QUARTER

# 1

The name on her birth certificate is Saryanna Clorinda Simms, but no one ever called her that. "What an interesting name!" the white ladies up North said, though they called her Sara. "Where did you get it?" But she didn't know. Even Grandma Sukey who named her didn't know. Mama wanted to call her Tallahassee, where her favorite cousin lived, but Grandma Sukey said that was no name for a colored child, though she never called her Saryanna either. She called her simply Girl. To Mama she was Sister and to the other children she was Tink. Daddy, whose pet she was, called her Shoo. She was most like him, with the same syrup-colored skin and the same way of holding herself, as if looking over the heads of a crowd. To her husbands and lovers she was Sweetie and Peachers and Doll. Her friends in the North called her Lyle, the name bequeathed to her by her second husband, who disappeared long ago. She thought of herself as Rannee, a name she had given herself when she was very young. It was as close to her real name as she could get.

She was born in Simms Quarter in the middle of the Depression, in the middle of the night, in the middle of a southern summer that boiled the water in the well and curled the edges of the roofs. Until she went to school, Simms Quarter was her whole world, a closed world made up of Grandma Sukey and Grandpa Vernon with their sons and families. All the other black people around her lived in family settlements too: the Johnsons in the Johnson Quarter and the Burnses on Burns Hill. The white people lived far away in Chawnee at the end of a long dirt road.

Simms Quarter was a wide stretch of fields and streams and trees with gashes of red clay leading to the cabins and oozing into the grass. The dust was everywhere, coating the tongue and the eyeballs. In summer, the heat came down like a wet towel. Farther along the road, enormous vines grew up and over the trees and bushes, covering them like paint, imprisoning them all. It frightened Rannee to think of the trees shut up inside those enormous leaves. She wondered if the vines would keep on growing, moving slowly up the road and cover Simms Quarter too.

The land had originally belonged to Grandpa Vernon, but now it was divided among his eight sons. Each brother farmed his own land but they all helped each other. They raised each other's roofs and took in each other's crops and shared each other's equipment. Daddy had a wagon and Uncle Doc had a mule and Uncle Lester had a bull. The wagon could be used to haul cotton or wood or people. On Sundays they put chairs and sides on it to take the grown-ups to the Chawnee Immanuel Baptist Church. The children took the short cut through the fields and woods, careful not to tear their Sunday clothes. They were warned to be careful.

One Sunday, climbing a fence, Rannee tore her dress. When she got home, Mama frowned. "I 'member this," she said. "I lay it on the shelf."

The next Saturday, Mama told Rannee to fetch the switch. "You 'member when you tore your dress?" Mama said.

"Yes, ma'am." Rannee began to cry.

"You *tole* to be carefer?" Mama said.

"Yes, ma'am."

"You *warn* to be carefer?"

"Yes, ma'am."

Mama raised the switch.

Mama did all the whipping in the family. She was a tall, heavy woman with smooth black skin who filled the cabin and ruled their lives as if she absorbed knowledge through the soles of her bare feet. If any of the children went to bed without a bath or ran outside without shoes or cussed under his breath or sneaked a fig from the tree in the front yard, Mama would say, very quietly, "Fetch that switch." Mama always knew.

Mama's mama was Grandma Tilder and her daddy was Popper, but they lived way over on the other side of Flat Rock and Mama almost never saw them anymore. Mama could read and write a little and, once in a while, on rainy days during lay-by, she would read aloud to the children: from a magazine Daddy found in the trash at the general store, or Bible stories from a book called *The Busy Businessman's Companion* left by the mailman instead of the Sears Roebuck catalogue years ago. But Mama didn't have much time for reading. She hardly even had time to smile. She cooked and cleaned and worked the patches and even went up to the field; and, sometimes, she put on her hat and shoes and walked the five miles to Chawnee to help out in some white lady's house or fetch some white lady's wash. She taught the children to be very careful, always, how they talked to grown-ups. They must say "Yes, sir" and "Didn't hear you" or "What did you say?" instead of just plain "What?" Otherwise Grandma Sukey or one of the aunts would tell her: "You should bring up that chile to mind," and Mama would be very angry. "You so cute," she would say. "Didn't I tell you to be carefer how you talks to grown peoples? You stay home from Homecomin an study your manners."

Her own brother, Clarence, had not been careful. He was a tall, handsome young man who worked as a bellhop at the Magnolia Hotel. He could part his hair on one side or the other and could read right through the newspaper every day. He was in the churchyard one Sunday morning when the sheriff and two deputies drove up. They were looking for a man who had stolen ten dollars from one of the hotel guests. They stood staring at Clarence with their stomachs out and their guns, nose down, on their hips.

"Don't know nothin about it," Clarence said. He put his foot on a tombstone and bent over to tie his laces.

"Hey, you nigger," the sheriff said. "We talkin to you."

Clarence straightened up and smiled. "Yes sir, Mr. Sheriff, sir," he said. "I hear you. An I answered you. I don't know nothin about it. I didn't know nothin about it Friday when you aksed me. I didn't know nothin about it Saturday when you aksed me. An I don't know nothin about it today, Sunday, twenty-third of June, when you aksed me." He bent down to tie the other shoe.

"Sound like this nigger evadin the law," the sheriff said. "Can't leave him in no churchyard evadin the law." The deputies picked up Clarence by the armpits and dumped him in the road. "Resistin arrest," the sheriff said, drawing his gun. "Next time we won't be so petikkiler *where* we do it." They left him in the dust with blood all over his shirt and his laces neatly tied.

Mama rarely spoke to her children about Clarence, her favorite brother. But she trained them never to talk back.

Mama herself hardly talked at all, as if, Rannee thought, she wanted to pretend she was alone all the time. At meals, she took her pie tin, the jar she used for a cup, and a can of sugar to the back porch and ate by herself. She sat in her rocker, filling it like dough in a pan, and poured sugar over everything. If she wanted more, one of the children brought it to her. Rannee always jumped when Mama called. She liked to fetch things for Mama. She liked to be alone with Mama in the kitchen in the early morning, before the others were up, watching Mama's strong, quick fingers, listening to the tune she always hummed, a strange tune that nobody else knew. It was always the same tune, hummed so softly, first thing in the morning, as if she had slept with it held tightly in her mouth all night.

Daddy was different. "Outa the rut," Grandma Sukey said. He was tall and slim and lighter than Mama and very formal, very "dainty," perhaps from being around white people so much. He worked at the saw mill in Chawnee and said "Scuse me" and "Beg your pardner" and talked very gently. He wore neat blue pants and a blue shirt that he got from the company store and a hat that Mama said must have been born right along with his head. It wasn't a big straw hat like the uncles' but a small city hat with a tiny brim and a ribbon around the crown. He was never without it. Once, when Rannee was very little, she ran into the kitchen early one morning and saw a strange man standing by the stove, drinking coffee out of a tin can. For a moment, she was frightened. But it was only Daddy without his hat.

Rannee never saw Daddy read and she knew he couldn't write, except his name. But he knew all kinds of things—like how to take out splinters and where to get the best raspberries and where to find her after a whipping. He knew how to make White Lightnin out in the back woods where the whiskey still was. The children were never allowed out there. But, sometimes, Rannee saw Daddy and the uncles drinking under the trees.

Daddy never did any whipping and he always disappeared when he heard Mama say, "Fetch that switch." He liked to hug and kiss his children and take them with him whenever he could: to feed the cows or the pigs or go fishing, just to have them around. Especially Rannee. When she was very little, he stood her between his legs or sat her on his shoulders or his lap. He always gave her something to hold—a bottle of water, an ear of corn, a sweat-stained bandana—so she felt she was really helping. When she was older, he even took her riding on Uncle Doc's mule, just like a boy.

But he was at the mill all day. When he came home, he went straight to the field, which was like another room in the house where Mama and Daddy lived much of the time. It was terribly big. It swallowed them up. They got smaller and smaller whenever they went there. Rannee loved to go to the field with Daddy when she was little. She sat in the wagon, staring at Daddy to keep him from disappearing, humming to herself, and waiting to bring him things: seed and hammer and water and little buckets of fertilizer. She learned to drive the wagon as soon as she knew left from right. Sitting high on the seat, she could see the fields poured out all around her and the sun sizzling like a skillet in the sky.

She was the second of eleven children, a sober, sturdy child with spikey little braids sticking up all over her head and large hands and feet. "To mind your step an earn your keep," Grandma Sukey said. Beet, whose real name was Bethulla, was the first. She was quick and long-legged and always missing, leaving Rannee to face the younger children coming up. They were all squeezed into a three-room pine board cabin Daddy had built himself. It had a front porch and a back porch and flowers out front, wherever Mama could stick one: wild roses and zinnias and touch-me-nots and morning glories. In the back there was only the dust in summer and the mud in winter and a barrel of rainwater screened over for washing.

In the beginning, Rannee liked to help around the house. She swept the porches and picked the vegetables from the patches and stacked the wood, singing hymns softly to herself, the only songs she knew. She was always trying to comb Mama's hair or polish Daddy's boots with half a biscuit. "Thank you, Miss Shoo," Daddy would say, grinning and tipping his hat. "Is most obligin." Sometimes he gave her a penny for grinding or parching the coffee, which meant putting the beans in the oven. But she had to be very careful. If she burned them, she got a whipping from Mama instead.

When Mama didn't need her, she played in the yard, making biscuits and pies, cutting dolls from the Sears catalogue, singing "Fix me, Jesus, fix me right." One morning she was playing house under the "scaffer" Daddy had built around the china-berry tree. The children used twigs for dolls and stones for furniture and the roots of the tree for walls dividing the rooms.

22

"I gonna have to give this Liza Dee chile a whippin," Rannee told Marbelle, her favorite cousin, a skinny little girl with a big round face like an all-day sucker. "She done broke my kerosene lamp. She *tole* to be carefer. She *warn* to be carefer. But she a slow learner." She reached into her pocket for the little plastic stick Uncle Floyd had brought her from a bar in Montgomery, but found a chinaberry instead. She left Liza Dee sniffling in the bedroom, lay down on the "scaffer," and ate the chinaberry, studying the sky through the branches, licking the foam off the clouds. She put the pit up her nose and blew it out. Then she picked another chinaberry, ate it, put the pit up her nose, and blew. It was something she had been told not to do but she enjoyed it: swallow, push, blow; swallow, push, blow. One pit didn't come out. She kept blowing through one side and trying to breathe through the other. But the pit stayed right up there. She lay flatter, breathing and blowing, wondering what would happen if that pit never came out at all and she had to walk around with little branches growing out of the hole in her nose.

"Why you makin that funny noise?" Marbelle asked.

"Got a chinaberry pit up my nose."

"Why you put it up there? You better git it out quick."

"Can't."

"Then you gonna swell up an die."

Rannee knew she would have to tell Mama. Mama would know what to do. But Mama would give her a whipping too.

Mama was sitting in her chair on the back porch with Baby Jupe standing on the floor beside her, chewing on her. He stopped eating and turned to look at Rannee. She could see a piece of Mama flopped outside her dress looking all sore and puffy. Mama covered it with her arm. "What you want?" she said.

"Got a chinaberry pit up my nose, ma'am," Rannee said.

"How it git there?"

"I put it there, ma'am."

Mama stuffed herself back into her dress. "Fetch the switch," she said. But before the lashing, she took Rannee's head in her

23

hands and shook it like a bush. The pit fell out and Mama reached for the switch. As soon as it was over, Rannee ran to her favorite spot in the woods under the sweet gum tree.

The woods were up on the hill behind the back house. They were dark and full of tall stern trees with their heads together. Even Beet, who was older, was afraid to go there. But Rannee was never afraid, except of thunder and crawling things. "Ain't nothin in those woods but what the good Lord put there," Daddy had told her, and she believed him. She liked to go there early in the morning to watch the sun come up and to pick wild berries and nuts. Now she took off her shoes and lay down and stared through the branches. After a while the sun disappeared and the sky turned sooty with clouds like enormous thumbprints. It was very quiet, as if the trees and leaves were holding their breath, waiting for her to leave. But she didn't want to go home. She didn't want to see Jupe eating Mama and Mama just sitting there and letting him.

She would go see Uncle Floyd, she decided. He was her favorite uncle, a short, thin man in overalls with a big head stuffed with chapter and verse, and a sweet singing voice and a great rubbery scar, like a third lip above his mouth, where he had been knifed for cussing a white man. He went all the way to Flat Rock to work in the fertilizer factory where he swept the floors and stoked the furnace and scrubbed the latrine and often brought back old newspapers he found lying around. Sometimes he went to Montgomery to get a wife, but he always came back alone.

"On accounta his wildness an his cussin," Mama said each time. She hated cussing. Whenever any of the children said anything "from the bottom a their tongues," Mama made them chew sacking dipped in vinegar.

"That'll draw it out," she said.

It was true that Uncle Floyd was a big swearer but he was a big singer too. Rannee loved to hear him sing. He sang at church and at Homecoming and Revival meetings. When he was alone he whistled. There was always some kind of music coming out of Uncle Floyd. Rannee loved to sing too, but most of the time she kept it inside, except when she was alone, working in the house or the fields, or when she sang duets with Uncle Floyd. Then she let her voice go very high and skip and swoop and bounce as it pleased, with Uncle Floyd's voice, deep and steady and strong, right below. It was like holding hands with their voices.

Uncle Floyd kept a second chair on his front porch just for her. He answered her questions and told her stories about the cities of the North that glowed all night, with the dirt all covered up so your feet never touched the ground, cities that grew way up into the sky and way down into the earth where it was always light. People walked and ate and read the newspapers down there and rode on trains that shrieked and rushed back and forth and never stopped. These cities had so many people that you could never see them all and the living had to travel for hours to find an empty spot for the dead.

"Who live in those cities, Uncle Floyd?" Rannee said.

"White folk. Rich white folk. Ridin aroun in big shiny cars an eatin an drinkin an playin their radios. Seem like everyone up there got a radio. Music comin out all the time."

It sounded wonderful. "Think you might be goin up there sometime, Uncle Floyd?" she said.

He grinned. "Mebbee. Sometime."

"Think you might take me with you?"

He grinned wider so that his scar seemed to be smiling too. "Mebbee," he said. "Sometime."

So even though Mama told her to stay away from his cabin, Rannee often wandered up there, early in the morning or late at night when no one was watching. And whenever she went, Uncle Floyd was always up, dressed in his blue overalls, reading his newspaper or whittling and whistling "Only Believe," with his feet on the rail, as though he never went to bed at all. "Don' like sleepin in that bed all by myself," he said. Rannee, thinking of the cold, wet, crowded bed in the back room at home, could hardly believe him. He always stopped reading or whistling when he saw her and started cussing instead.

"Well, Holy Moses an Revelations an Second Samuel," he would say, nodding and smiling.

"What all that mean, Uncle Floyd?" she asked him once, sitting down beside him with her feet on the rail too. He was the only grown-up she dared to question.

"Tha's good Ole Testamin Bible words," Uncle Floyd said. "They's all right there in the Lord's book along with the Psalms and the Proverbs and the Prophets. An don' you forget it."

"No sir, Uncle Floyd," Rannee said. Though watching that scar wiggle around under his nose, she thought that maybe Mama was right about cussing. But it didn't keep her away from Uncle Floyd.

Now, lying under the sweet gum tree, she felt the wind begin to rise. She would go and see Uncle Floyd, she decided, sitting up and putting on her shoes. But suddenly, there was a terrible crash. It seemed to shake the woods. She looked around and saw a huge tree lying down, right across her path. She was terrified. There was no one else there. It must have been the Lord, she thought, leaning over and blowing down that tree. But why? For growing too tall, for sticking its head too far up into the sky and looking in at Him? He had blown it down right in front of her.

She turned and ran the long way out of the woods so she would not have to pass it. At the edge, she stopped, panting. There was no one in sight. The whole Quarter looked deserted with an enormous sky swooping down around the cabins. Behind her she felt the trees getting ready to tumble down the hill. Suddenly, the Quarter with its rickety little cabins looked small and pitifully exposed between the white men at the end of that straight, dusty road and the trees bunched up just behind. For the first time in her life she was afraid of the woods. God lived in those woods, she thought, not in the Chawnee Immanuel Baptist Church which was small and smelled of babies and Preacher Brown's talcum powder.

She began to run, past Uncle Lester's and Uncle Link's and Uncle Doc's. Uncle Floyd was sitting on his front porch with his feet on the rail, whittling and whistling "Only Believe" as usual. She ran up and sat down beside him. "Tree fall down in those woods, Uncle Floyd," she said softly, clasping her hands between her knees. "An there weren't nobody there at all."

Uncle Floyd's knife stopped whittling. "That so?" he said. He turned and looked at her. "Hurt you?" he said.

"No, sir," she said.

"Scare you?"

She didn't answer.

He closed his knife, stood up, and took her hand. Together they walked back into the woods. Uncle Floyd, still holding her hand, walked right up to that stretched-out tree. It looked enormous lying flat on its back like that, long as the road into town.

"How come it fall down?" Rannee asked, holding his hand. "How come, Uncle Floyd?"

"Drop dead," Uncle Floyd said. "That tree jes ole an tired an dead. Ain't nothin to be scared of."

She looked down and saw the wrinkled bark and the stiff naked branches and the twisted roots. She had never known that a tree could get old and tired and die. "Poor ole tree," she murmured. But she held tight to Uncle Floyd's hand as they climbed over that huge trunk.

"God livin in these here woods, Uncle Floyd?" she asked.

"God livin everywhere," Uncle Floyd said.

It was a terrifying thought: that big strong white man following her around, bigger and stronger than the "rollin store" man and the candy man and the fish man and Mr. Junius from the general store—the only white men Rannee ever saw—all put together. She imagined Him with a hump like Mr. Junius, stuffed with dimes and quarters, and a wandering left eye like the "rollin store" man who could watch both sides of his truck at once, and a rusty old scale like the fish man for weighing up her sins. She imagined Him driving around in a huge black car

27

with curtains and artificial flowers in the windows like the candy man, the back piled high with fancy boxes. She wondered why the grown-ups bothered to sit in church every Sunday, spoiling their one day of rest, with the babies peeing on their laps and Preacher Brown shouting at them till dinner, when all the time He was right there, in the kitchen or on the front porch and even in the back house. But she couldn't believe He was really there *all* the time. He probably went to Montgomery once in a while, like Uncle Floyd. She wondered if He had a wife. She had never heard of a *Mrs.* God.

When she got home, the house was very quiet. She could see Mama's chair on the back porch with its arms around Mama. Rannee was still very angry at Mama, who never got whipped or told what to do or kept away from Homecoming. Rannee longed to be grown-up too.

Suddenly, she noticed the smell of candy in the kitchen, a rich chocolatey smell. One of the candy man's boxes was lying on the table. He often left boxes of candy for the older children of the Quarter to sell around the neighborhood. They never got to eat any of it or even to see it or smell it. All they could do was feel the stiff white paper. But this box was unwrapped. She stared at it. There was no one around but Baby Jupe drooling into a crack in the floor. Rannee hurried to the box and lifted the lid. It was completely empty except for that sweet chocolatey smell. She put the lid on again and carried it—on tiptoe—to the back room and hid it in a hole in the floor under the bed. But first she took one more long, delicious whiff. Then she went to the back door and stared at Mama.

She was sitting all alone, sewing bloomers out of sacking with a pan of peas at her feet. She didn't jiggle her feet or rock her chair or get up to pick a fig hanging right there on the fig tree. She just kept sewing. Nothing moved except her hand and that needle going in and out, in and out. Rannee thought of all the things Mama had sewn: all the pillows out of flour sacks and the sheets out of feed sacks, with Mama's beautiful colored embroidery covering the seams; all the spreads with the fringes

28

around the edges and the quilts and the "Big Muffie Gowns" and the dresses and the shorts. When she wasn't sewing, she was cooking or cleaning or washing or ironing. Mama was always doing something. She never just stood around in the woods like Daddy and the uncles, or rocked on the porch like Grandpa, or played under the "scaffer" like Rannee. Rannee thought that maybe she didn't want to be a grown-up like Mama or Grandma Sukey or any of the ladies of Simms Quarter after all. She wondered if Mama would get old and fall over and die like that tree. But Mama's face was still as smooth and clear as the water in the well.

"Sister," Mama said without looking up.

"Ma'am?"

"Those peas needin shellin."

Rannee smiled. "Yes, ma'am," she said happily, and hurried to sit down beside Mama.

Sometimes Mama sent her up to Cousin Travers with a bowl of "lights." He would be sitting on his back porch, surrounded by children.

Cousin Travers wasn't really a cousin. He wasn't a relative at all, just an old man who had been born in slavery and lived in a one-room shack by himself. He had short, white hair fizzing up all over his head and no teeth, and his lips were all pleated as if he had tucks in them, now that his mouth was so empty. He walked all hung over with his head down as if looking for something in his left pocket. He was a "piddlin" man who "fitted in." Rannee never knew where he came from or how he landed in Simms Quarter but, as long as she could remember, he had been there, working around the settlement, picking beans, collecting eggs, weeding patches, and waiting for Death to come riding up like a Yankee soldier in the Civil War. The Quarter gave him his shack and his food. He ate at Grandma Sukey's or Uncle Doc's or wherever he happened to be at mealtime. Sometimes he bought the children peanuts from the "rollin store" man. The children helped him clean his cabin and brought him cigarette paper from Mr. Junius's general store. They loved to sit on his steps on Saturday afternoon and listen to his stories about slavery.

"How come that white man own you, Cousin Travers?" Marbelle said.

"Cause he bought my mama an my daddy. He own them an everythin they got. He own they cabin and they clothes an they babies." Rannee wondered who had sold them and why.

Cousin Travers's daddy had run away before Travers was born, so the white people watched Travers and his mama all the time. They watched him when his mama took him to the field, a tiny baby tied to her back. When he was older, they put him in a collar and tied him to a tree in the yard or made him lie down on the floor of the shack and tied him to the doorknob.

"It cole an damp in there," Cousin Travers said. "Tiny, like a smokehouse with jes one room goin roun an roun. My whole life goin roun an roun. An that one room all empty. Nothin in it. Nothin at all. Not a chair or a taber or a bed or even a winder. We slep on the floor an wash in the stream an shat in the woods. That cabin full a crawlin things skittlin all over me." Rannee shivered. Once, Cousin Travers felt something creep into his ear. "It never come out," he said, spitting into a red handkerchief. "I still tryin to git it out. But it never come. Never heerd right in that ear to this day." He blew his nose hard and examined his handkerchief and shook his head. "A lil somethin left over from slave days, livin inside me all the resta my life," he said.

He and his mother ate whatever scraps the white people brought them, shoved in through a hole in the door. "Lotsa days we have nothin to eat at all. That Mr. Kincaid one mean, ugly white man." He wiped his mouth. The children sat perfectly still, holding their breath.

"Had a lil whip he carry everywhere," Cousin Travers went on. "You always know he comin by the sounda that whip, slappin agin his boot. Always had to be whippin somethin. But that jes a *lil* whip, what they call a crop. That whip for *horses*.

That whip never use for peoples. For peoples he got a big long stingin lash. Make the skin boil clean up offa your back." He paused and squinted across the yard. Rannee held on to her elbows. "I still hearin it," he said. "I be workin my patch or settin on my porch or sleepin in my bed an I hear that lil whip goin slap, slap, slap." And he would think, for a moment, that he was back in slavery again, with Mr. Kincaid coming to tie him up in the hot sun of the yard, or on the damp dark floor of the hut, and make the skin foam up on his back. The children poked inside their noses and scratched their knees and stared.

Rannee wondered if the grown-ups in Simms Quarter had learned about whipping from Mr. Kincaid. She felt sorry for Cousin Travers who had been a slave when he was little and now had trouble just putting his hand into his pocket himself. She always ran to the window as soon as she woke up to make sure he was all right. But no matter how early she got up, Cousin Travers's light was always on and there was always a little feather of smoke floating out of his chimney.

At supper time, Mama stood over the kitchen table and said, "Someone here seen a empty box from the candy man settin right here on my kitchen taber? Settin right here, an now it gone." The children stared. Beet felt around in her nose as she always did when she was frightened, and Bay put both thumbs in his mouth. Baby Jupe, kneeling on Daddy's lap, tried to put his head in Daddy's shirt pocket. Rannee stared at the back of Jupe's neck with the little rolls of fat waiting to be stretched out.

"How come that box move isself?" Mama said.

"Magic," Daddy said. "That there a magic box."

Mama stood leaning on her palms, looking at them all a bit longer. Beet pushed her finger farther up her nose until Rannee thought it would go right through the back of her head. No one said anything and, after a while, Mama picked up her supper and carried it out to the back porch.

Later, when no one was watching, Rannee ran up to Uncle Floyd's to tell him about the candy box. But, for the first time,

31

Uncle Floyd was not there, was not sitting on his porch as always after supper. The chairs were still firmly on their rockers, not tilted, heads down, against the rail the way Uncle Floyd always fixed them before going to bed. "Settlin them for the night," he called it. The door to his cabin was closed. It was too late for him to be still at work and too early for him to be visiting any of the other uncles. Everyone at Simms Quarter ate his meals at home except on special occasions. Maybe he had gone to Montgomery, she thought, but he hadn't mentioned it that morning. She walked slowly around the cabin, though she knew it was empty. Maybe he had gone to Montgomery after all. But she felt slightly uneasy.

At home, before getting into bed, she knelt down and took one more long, deep sniff from her candy box.

# 2

Rannee was fast asleep with Bay's heels on her chest and Beet's elbow in her neck when she felt someone shaking her. It was Daddy with his face in pieces from the light of the lantern. She felt scared. He didn't say anything but just woke the other children and hurried them all up to Grandma Sukey's. He didn't tell them why and they didn't ask. He carried the little ones and the lantern. The older children clung to his arms. It was very dark. The lantern swung back and forth and the sky rolled around and the night poured down all over them. Rannee could feel crawly things on her hands and face and even inside the sacking of her "Big Muffie Gown." But she didn't cry or say anything. She just hung on to Daddy's right pocket. He left them all at Grandma Sukey's in a small room that had a bed and several pallets.

Beet and the little children began to cry. Rannee lay stiffly on her back all alone on a nice dry pallet with no one's feet in her face. But it was very dark at Grandma Sukey's, with no cracks in the roof letting in the sky, just the blackness stuffed into her eyes and up her nose. She couldn't breathe. She wondered if Daddy had left them there for good.

"Daddy give us to Grandma Sukey," Beet wailed.

"Why he do that?" Rannee said.

"He tireda havin us roun all the time. Bay messin like he do and Jupe screamin an you actin so fierce. I wanna go home. I scared. I scareda Grandma Sukey."

"What *she* wan us for?" Rannee said.

"She gonna sell us," Beet moaned. "Like Cousin Travers."

The next morning, after breakfast, Grandma sent them home. "Your mama sick an peoples comin to see her," she said. "She wan a nice clean house. I keepin Jupe. He too lil. But the resta you git on back there an clean up that house."

Near the yard, Bay shouted, "There go ole witchy woman!" Rannee looked up and saw Miss Martha Jane riding her mule up the path.

She was an old colored woman in a long dress and a very long white apron and a skull cap. She brought all the babies around Chawnee in a little black bag. She brought colored babies to colored people and white babies to white people. Rannee wondered where Miss Martha Jane got all those babies, but she never asked. Children were not allowed to ask questions in Simms Quarter. "Mine yo manners," Mama would say. "Is so," Grandma Sukey would say.

Children were not even allowed to listen when the grown-ups talked. "Don' be settin there lookin in grown people's moufs," Mama would say.

Mama's door was shut and, later, Aunt Effie and Aunt Lovey came out. They had their hats off as if they'd been there for a long time. "Miss Marfa Jane brung your Mama a nice new baby boy," Aunt Lovey said.

Oh no, Rannee thought. They didn't *need* another baby, and she certainly didn't *want* another baby. But she didn't dare say so.

"Got too many babies already," Beet muttered. Luckily, the aunts did not hear her. They were too busy putting on their hats.

The children swept the floor and washed the dishes and

made up the double bed in the back room. They dragged the wet mattress out in the sun and washed the heavy sheets and stacked the wood and carried in the water. When they were all finished, Rannee sat on the front porch and thought about that new baby. She was angry at Miss Martha Jane for bringing so many.

Mama had to stay in bed for ten days. Aunt Effie or Aunt Delsie came over to take care of her and the baby, and sometimes one of the other aunts put on her hat and came just for a visit. But if Mama tried to get up, one of the aunts would say: "Don' be flouncin aroun here, Lucine. You gonna catch your pneumonia. Your body ain't back to proper function yet. No flouncin till your body back in safe channels agin." The children took care of the house and the patches. In between, they stood in the doorway and stared at Mama. But they weren't allowed to see that new baby for nine days. "Don' you be tryin to see no new baby," Grandma Sukey said. All Rannee saw was a little lump in the bed next to Mama. He was all covered up, even his face, as if Mama didn't want him to see where Miss Martha Jane had left him.

Rannee envied that new baby sleeping in the double bed in the front room all alone with just Daddy and Mama. Baby Jupe had been moved to the back room where all the other children slept, crowded together in that double bed with someone's urine always soaking the sheets. Lying on her back, Rannee stared through the holes in the roof at the stars nailing up the sky.

After ten days, Mama was allowed to get out of bed and sit in a chair and hold the baby. One morning, Grandma Sukey said, "Your month up, Lucine," and Mama put on her shoes and walked out the back door. She walked around the house once and came back in through the front door. She walked very slowly, as if examining everything, Rannee thought, to make sure that Miss Martha Jane had brought that baby to the right place. Rannee kept hoping that she had made a mistake and that Mama would give the baby back. But she didn't. She just kept going out every day and staying out a little longer and walking a little farther. Gradually, she was doing more and more.

No one brought any presents for the new baby and there was no celebration of any kind. It was just colder and wetter and more crowded in that double bed in the back room, and it didn't smell of chocolate any more. It smelled of urine.

One morning, Mama was back in the kitchen again, as usual, in her long, loose dress like Father Abraham in the Sunday school coloring cards, with her breasts squashed down by binders and her lips tucked under, holding in that secret tune, making hoecakes. She nodded at Rannee coming in for breakfast and went on stirring.

Rannee got an old pie tin and helped herself to stewed rabbit and mustard greens left over from supper which had been left over from dinner. While she ate, she thought of that woman up North who had no food at all. "Not a lick, not a crumb," Preacher Asa Brown had said in church. But she set the table anyway and made her children sit down around it. They sat down to knives and forks and empty plates, and said grace anyway.

Rannee's family never said grace, maybe because they never sat down together. Daddy never got home from working in the field till after dark, and in the morning he ate before anyone else, standing up alone in the kitchen. Sometimes, on Sunday, he sat down to dinner with the children. But Mama never ate anywhere except on the back porch, alone.

Rannee finished eating, washed the pie tin, and started for the door.

"Where you goin?" Mama said.

"Jes up to those woods, ma'am." She liked to go to the woods in the early morning when He was still resting—she knew He never slept: "Slumbers not nor sleeps," the hymn said. Too busy spying, she thought. But He would certainly be resting now with His head on a cloud and His feet on the sun ready to kick it into another day.

"What you doin in those woods all the time?" Mama said.

"Jes lookin, ma'am."

"You hangin aroun with Uncle Floyd?"

"No, ma'am."

"Floyd's a deacon in the church, don't forgit," Daddy said, hurrying in with his hat and his big morning smile. "An a student of the Bible."

An the best singer in the whole choir, Rannee thought.

"Don' give him no right to cuss like he do and carry on so wild."

Rannee got a clean can and poured out Daddy's coffee.

"Thank you, Miss Shoo," he said, extending his cheek.

She pressed her lips against it, hard enough to make a dent. She liked to kiss Daddy. She wondered why Mama never kissed him. But Mama never kissed anyone except the newest baby until he went into the back room. Then she didn't bother.

Rannee ran out into the dark yard where the chinaberry tree still leaned against the sky. She slipped off her shoes, tied them around her neck, and ran up the hill. She ran softly into the woods, past that big tree still lying down with its head toward the Quarter as if trying to crawl its way out. She climbed the sweet gum quickly and sat watching the sun come up: just a tiny spot at first, like a single note in church, and then the whole sky breaking into color like the rest of the choir joining in. Soon, she was singing too, loud and high and happy, green and purple and yellow and red, enjoying the sunrise.

She sat there for a long time, watching the day shouting down at her, until the colors began to fade. Suddenly, she remembered the new baby and prayed to the Lord not to let Miss Martha Jane bring any more. Rannee promised to be good all the time. She would never lie or steal or sniff inside Mama's candy box, if only Miss Martha Jane would leave those babies somewhere else. After a while, the colors grew fainter, stretched, split, and disappeared. Soon it was just an ordinary sky again with a few ordinary clouds floating around in it like suds in a pan.

Rannee walked the four miles to the Chawnee Primary School for Negroes—a short cut through the woods and fields—with Beet and the cousins. She wore her shoes tied around her neck and carried her dinner in a syrup can. The black school stood beside the black church with the black cemetery in between. Weekdays or Sundays, the children stared out the window into a graveyard. School, like church, began with psalms and hymns and scripture reading and the Lord's Prayer. The school was a single room divided by a partition, with one teacher on each side. The only heat came from a potbellied stove. Two old colored men came sporadically to cut down the trees in the woods behind the school. The boys split the logs and the girls stacked them. If the wood ran out, the school was closed.

The children sat on backless benches, ten or twelve to a bench, and wrote on their laps. They brought their own pencils and paper and took turns sharing the books. Most of the work was put on the board to "take off." Rannee sat between Marbelle and Odette Peters and felt scared.

The teachers were two old colored ladies named Miss Dora French and Miss Nora French. They were twin sisters who looked exactly alike and wore long black dresses with long sleeves and their hair pinned up like inverted teacups. There was no difference between them. The children lived in a state of constant confusion.

They were harsh old women who swatched the children regularly and pinned notes to their sleeves so the children were whipped again at home. Every morning, they sent one of the big boys out to the woods to cut new switches. Sometimes they made a child do his lessons standing in a corner on one leg with his face to the wall. If he put his foot down, he might have to stay there all day, every day, for a week. Sometimes, they made a child go without dinner. Beet almost always had to go without dinner for missing a spelling word. Then she would go all faint and miss her "times tables" too. Then she got swatched. Walking home, Rannee would carry Beet's dinner in front of her while she ate it with both hands. One day Rannee had to feed her because of the pain in Beet's palms. Near home, Beet began to cry. "I not workin in no field today," she said. "Not with all this hurtin in my hands."

"You don't go to that field," Rannee said, "Mama gonna whip you."

"She gonna whip me anyway," Beet said. She began to cry again. "Wisht I was all growed up right this second," she said.

"Why?"

"Why? So's I could git outa that ole school and this here ole Simms Quarter."

"How you gonna do that?"

"Dunno yet. But I will."

"Where you gonna go?"

"Dunno that yet neither. But I will. Soon's I growed."

Rannee did her homework crouched under the "scaffer" beneath the chinaberry tree, and then went up to the field as always. Beet lay in the grass under a tree and studied her face in a pie tin. Rannee worked up and down the rows alone while her back ached and her fingers throbbed and her sweat dropped like seeds on the ground. She thought about all the things she hated to do—like wearing shoes and going to school and working in the field and emptying the babies' slops and sleeping in that cold, wet, crowded, smelly bed. And she hated all those people around her all the time: the mean people who beat her like the Misses French and Grandma Sukey and even Mama; Daddy who just looked sad and walked away whenever Mama said, "Fetch that switch;" the children always needing something; and the selfish people like Beet, lying on her back and admiring her cheekbones.

Suddenly Rannee wished she were grown-up too. She knew exactly what she would do. She would go to Montgomery with Uncle Floyd and find him a wife, and sing at his wedding, and *never* come back.

# 3

One morning, Rannee couldn't see any light in Cousin Travers's cabin or smoke coming out of his chimney. She ran to tell Mama. They found him lying on the floor, half-dressed and staring at the ceiling as if he had fallen down all of a sudden like that tree in the woods and hadn't even had time to close his eyes.

He never got up again. The people in the Quarter brought him his meals and washed his clothes and the children cleaned his cabin. Everyone took turns sitting up with him. Someone stayed with him all the time. Mostly, it was Mama, padding around on bare feet, silent as pillows. Her hands were quick and firm with sharp fingers to feel out the sickness. She got leaves from the Johnny Quill plant and baked them in the oven and wrapped them around Cousin Travers to cook out the fever. She fed him "tea" made of leaves and pine needles boiled with hogs' husks and sweetened with molasses. She put cobwebs mixed with chimney soot on the cut on his head where he had fallen. She examined his fingernails regularly. But he went on lying there just the same, moving nothing but his eyes, closing the right one for "yes" and the left one for "no."

He got terribly thin, as if most of him were sliding out the bottom of the bed, except for his chin, big as a doorknob, and his hair bubbling up, and the extra folds in his lips. Rannee wondered what he was thinking about, lying there so still, staring at the ceiling with that scared look on his face. Was he thinking of Mr. Kincaid and listening, again, for the slap, slap, slap of his crop? Finally, a doctor came, a squat white man with a thick white neck spurting up over the top of his collar. Rannee saw him in front of Cousin Travers's shack one morning, brushing his trousers and wiping his hands on a handkerchief as big as a towel. He had a big shiny car like the candy man's that made a special noise to scare the chickens off the road. "He the smartest doctor in the whole county," Grandpa Vernon said. "Cut a piece right outta Mr. Junius and sewed him back up agin so you'd never knowed nothin was missin."

But the next morning, Cousin Travers couldn't even move his eyes. They were both wide open, staring at a crack in the roof. Staring straight into heaven, Mama said, closing them down.

They put him in a box Uncle Lester had made, a plain box with the lid up, set out on two chairs on his porch. Everyone came to see him. Rannee stood on tiptoe. He was wearing a shiny black suit she had never seen before with his head propped up by a stiff white collar. But his feet must have grown from being in bed so much because they wouldn't fit into his shoes. They had to bury him in a pair of Uncle Doc's shoes with the laces tied around his ankles. They closed the lid over his face and put the box on the wagon and took it to the graveyard beside the church. Rannee walked with the other children, taking the shortcut as they did every Sunday. In the cemetery, they all stood around and watched while some of the uncles dug a hole and Preacher Brown read something from the Bible. He looked terribly sleepy, but perhaps it was just that he had forgotten his glasses. " 'He shall return no more to his house, neither shall his place know him any more,' " he read. He teetered back and forth beside that empty hole. Rannee watched in fascination. If he fell in, would *he* return no more? But they put Cousin Travers in his grave and covered him up and Preacher Brown read. " 'God will wipe away all tears from their eyes.' " Rannee waited breathlessly. In the end, she wiped her tears away herself with her clenched fist.

Then the grown-ups got back into the wagon and the children cut back through the woods to get on with the chopping and the cleaning and the cooking, leaving Cousin Travers all alone in that box in the ground.

"How long Cousin Travers have to stay there?" Rannee asked Uncle Floyd that evening, sitting beside him with her feet on the rail.

"He lef there already," Uncle Floyd said.

"Where he at?" Rannee said.

"Heaven. That ole man in heaven right this minute, enjoyin the Lord."

Rannee thought of him, sitting down with the Lord at the kitchen table, offering him tobacco and peanuts and White Lightnin from the uncles' still, distracting His attention from Rannee. "Thank you, Cousin Travers," she whispered.

But his grave was still there, she noticed the next Sunday, with a vase of dusty wax flowers on his head. She wiped them clean with the hem of her dress. She wondered who was living there now.

In the church, the other children were already seated for Sunday school in the four corners of the one-room building. Rannee hurried to her place. Aunt Billie was reading from the Bible in a loud, angry voice: " 'Behold, I will bring evil upon thee,' " she warned.

She was the superintendent of the school, a small, shrivelled woman with a sucked-in face. She had spent a year in Birmingham working in the kitchen of the Sacred Heart School for Girls before she married Uncle Asher and came to live in Simms Quarter. She always wore a green hat and a string of skinny black beads from Birmingham which she called a "Rosemary." "After that sweet Sister which give it to me," she said. She spent most of Sunday morning tiptoeing around the room, plucking at her bosom and her neck and her lips, listening in corners. The children were afraid of her. It was rumored that she had learned strange and terrible things in that convent school in Birmingham, though no one knew what a convent was or anything at all about Birmingham. But Marbelle had seen Aunt Billie in the graveyard once, lashing one of the Johnson girls with her skinny black beads.

Aunt Billie lifted her head now, frowned at Rannee, and raised her voice. "'And I will cut off from Ahab him that pisseth against the wall,'" she read. Rannee was fascinated.

After Sunday school she sat in the back pew, turning her eyes from the sight of the women nursing their babies right out in public with pieces of cloth over their naked breasts and their knee-babies stretched out on the seat beside them. She never paid attention in church except to the hymns. Instead of praying and listening to Preacher Brown telling what the Lord said to Abraham and Isaac wandering around in the Land of Canaan, she thought about the cities up North. She thought about going there with Uncle Floyd someday to sing in the choir with him and maybe even sing on one of their radios. With so many radios they must need lots of people to sing on them.

She looked up front and saw Daddy and Mama and the spot where Cousin Travers used to sit with a long length of neck sticking out of his collar and his head bent way over to one side, as if he were listening to his heart instead of Preacher Brown. She was glad he was in heaven now, walking and talking to the Lord, and didn't have to wink his eyes any more.

But the next morning, she found herself looking out of the window as usual. Cousin Travers's door seemed to be open and she thought she saw a tiny finger of smoke waving to her out of the chimney. She ran up to his cabin but the door was closed.

She went on slowly, past the empty porch where he had been set out like a cake to cool, and on past Grandma Sukey's and up into the woods. Straight ahead, in a clearing, she saw Uncle

Doc, squatting under a pine tree with the other uncles in a circle around him. She wondered what they were doing.

Uncle Doc was the oldest of the brothers, and the biggest. They got smaller as they got younger, as if they had all been lined up before birth, according to size. So Uncle Doc, who was the oldest, was also the biggest and had Grandma Sukey looking out of one eye and Grandpa Vernon out of the other. It made him careful and crazy both, Daddy said. Uncle Doc was always very quiet in the mouth and very quick in the feet and very particular with his hands. He could fix anything, which was why he was called Doc. He did all the slaughtering in the Quarter—four or five a day, in season. The children helped cut out the chitlins. But Rannee could never stand the sight of the blood spurting out or the sounds of the pigs squealing or the sight of their dead little eyes staring. She always stood behind the chinaberry tree till it was over.

Uncle Doc was a good hunter. He hunted rabbits and squirrels and possums and coons in the woods up behind the old Sutcliffe place. There were wild turkeys and wild ducks in that woods too, but they were for white men to shoot. Colored men weren't allowed to hunt anything but possums and rabbits and squirrels and coons. Sometimes when Uncle Doc was creeping around, looking for something to hunt, he stumbled on a wild turkey or a wild duck sitting there all alone, waiting. But Uncle Doc didn't mess with it. He knew that one dead turkey could mean one dead nigger. Uncle Doc always moved on.

But this morning was different. This morning he was squatting on his haunches and smiling at his brothers and saying, "He jes settin there waitin. Settin there all by hisself, lookin at me and waitin. Waitin to be killed by a colored man on Thanksgivin. A distinction. A real distinction. Weren't nothin else I *could* do." Rannee was frightened. For now she knew what they were doing. They were plucking a wild turkey and burying the feathers.

There was wild turkey for dinner that day. That one turkey was divided among eight families, so the children didn't have more than a whiff of the tail. "That there a *Thanksgivin* turkey," Daddy said proudly.

"What that?" Rannee said.

But Daddy was too busy making everyone sit down to dinner together, with the littlest children on pieces of paper on the floor and Mama right beside him. She kept her plate in her lap as if she were still out on the back porch, and sweetened everything, meat and vegetables and biscuits and greens. Daddy, watching her, ate very slowly, cutting everything into tiny pieces as if he wanted to go on sitting beside her for the rest of the day.

Suddenly, it began to thunder, a thrashing, crashing sound that rolled around all over the sky. "You all be quiet now," Mama said sternly, "an *listen*. That the *Lord* talkin now."

The thunder came closer and closer as if it were about to crash into the cabin. The little children began to cry. The Lord sounded *very* angry, Rannee thought, like most grown-ups, only worse. He was going to punish them all, because of Uncle Doc. The wind stuck a tongue beneath the door, a long tongue, that chilled the back of her neck and blew out the lamp. The cabin began to rock as if someone were pushing it back and forth like a cradle. Rannee thought of the words Preacher Brown had shouted out in church last Sunday: "And there were lightnings and voices, and thunderings, and an earthquake, and great hail."

She jumped up and ran into the back room and knelt beside the bed with her head under the mattress. But the thunder followed her there, shouting at her. She wondered what it was saying. She wondered if Mama knew. Mama always knew. But she never told. Rannee would have to ask Uncle Floyd.

But when she went up to see him the next evening, he wasn't there again. His chairs were still standing on their rockers as if waiting up for him. Where was he? She knew he wasn't visiting any of the other uncles because all the other cabins were dark too. No one in Simms Quarter went anywhere at night except to church during Revival, but that was in summer. And Uncle

45

Floyd never went to Montgomery on a weeknight, not when he went to work the next day. She knew he had to go to work tomorrow. So where was he?

The ground grew hard and the trees turned stiff. The days were dark at both ends and the house was stuffed with babies and noises and smells. Several weeks before Christmas, the children of Simms Quarter began to hunt for shoe boxes or paper bags. On Christmas Eve, each child put his name on his box or bag and left it near the fireplace.

"All ready for Santa Claws comin down that chimney," Daddy said.

"Why he come down the chimney?" Bay said.

"Cause the doors in this house all stuck," Rannee said, and grinned at Daddy. She didn't really believe in Santa Claus. She had been smelling apples all over the house for days, apples she knew Daddy had sneaked in and hidden. She even knew what the presents would be—they were always the same, every year—and had a little paper dress, cut from the Sears catalogue, in her pocket, all ready for that little naked doll. She loved Christmas, even without Santa Claus. She preferred to think it was Daddy bringing the presents instead of some strange fat white man who would never know what she wanted and would certainly never fit down their crooked chimney.

On Christmas morning, she sang "Merry Christmas to You" to everybody, beginning with Baby Jesus right down to Aunt Effie's last, the newest baby in the Quarter. She made up the tune and words herself. It was beautiful, she thought. Some day she might even sing it on the radio, like the lady she heard that Saturday when she was waiting in Mr. Junius's shop for a pound of sugar for Mama. She always had to wait in Mr. Junius's shop, waited while white people came and went or just stood around talking to Mr. Junius. But that day, she didn't mind.

She finished scrubbing the table and sweeping the floor and went to open her box. But when she lifted the lid, the box was empty.

46

She was kneeling on the floor and she went on kneeling there with her head bent, staring into that empty box. Finally, she turned to Mama. "Why?" she said. "What for? What I do?"

Mama looked very big to Rannee, kneeling on the floor, looking up over the great hill of Mama's breasts. "You member that candy man box?" Mama said.

"No, ma'am," Rannee said.

"The one restin on my kitchen taber? The one what disappear?"

"*That* ole box? That box *empty*. Weren't nothin *at all* in that box."

"I knows that. But that box were *there*. An purty soon that box *not* there any more. Somebody took that box an somebody didn't say nothin about it. Other words, somebody *stealed* an somebody *lied*."

"Yes, ma'am," Rannee said, bending her head lower into that empty shoe box.

Mama picked up her plate and went out to the porch.

"You wanna cry, Shoo," Daddy said. "You jes go ahead an cry. Right into that empty box. That box needin fillin up somehow."

Rannee cried into Daddy's shirt instead. "How she know?" Rannee said. "How she always know?"

"Like I said," Daddy said. "That there candy box magic." But it was Mama, Rannee thought, who was magic.

The family didn't go to church that day because it wasn't Sunday. They just sat around in the kitchen eating salt pork and cornbread and syrup as usual, except Mama who sat alone, huddled into her coat on the back porch, as usual. But this time when she wanted anything, Rannee let one of the other children get it. No one mentioned Jesus on Christmas Day. Birthdays were never celebrated in Simms Quarter.

After supper, Mama went into the front room and brought back a paper bag. "Here, Sister," Mama said, holding it out.

"Thank you, ma'am," Rannee said, but she didn't really mean it. She found the apple and the orange and the candy cane and the nigger toe, everything but the little naked doll.

47

Usually she made her presents last for weeks, eating them very slowly, one tiny piece at a time. But tonight, she ate them all right away, stuffing them in. Later, when no one was looking, she took the paper dress out of her pocket, tore it into tiny pieces, and threw it into the stove.

Lying in bed that night, she felt a pain, as if all those presents were stuck in a great lump in her chest. She folded her arms over it, as she used to fold them over the little naked doll. But she could not sleep.

Finally, when everyone was in bed, she put on her coat and shoes and ran up to Uncle Floyd's. But the cabin was dark and the two chairs on his porch were still firmly on their rockers. She knew that Uncle Floyd never went to Montgomery on Christmas. He went to Uncle Doc's. But Uncle Doc's cabin, like everyone else's, was dark. She remembered Mama calling Uncle Floyd wild. She remembered that scar on his lip and his cussing. She felt very scared.

Winter kept coming, a mean time when the days were all worn out before supper and the real food was all eaten up. Sometimes, toward the end, there was nothing but flour gravy and rice, or melted sugar and bread. Rannee thought of that woman up North who had nothing to eat at all and made her children sit down to an empty table. She wondered why they didn't have flour gravy and bread up North. She would have to ask Uncle Floyd, if she could find him.

Mama was sterner than ever in winter, as if her lips were frozen. She hardly ever seemed to move them except to say, "Sweep that porch," "Scrub that taber," "Fetch that switch."

Rannee was scrubbing the table one evening when Mama was standing at the stove, fixing Daddy's supper. All the other children had gone to bed, but Daddy was still up in the woods. Rannee went on scrubbing and Mama went on stirring, standing at the stove very straight, very stiff, as if she were nailed together. She didn't say anything, she didn't even hum; she just went on standing straight and still at the stove with her back to

48

Rannee. Pretending she's all alone, Rannee thought, pretending I don't exist—except for some hands and feet. It made Rannee feel very lonely.

She finished scrubbing the table and left the kitchen very quietly and went to sit on the floor in the back room, in the dark, listening to the sound of deep breathing right beside her. She went on feeling lonely, in spite of all the other children asleep in the double bed. For God hadn't paid any attention to her prayers. There were five of them in the back room now. But Beet, the next one up, was always over at the cousins' doing something to her hair and Bay, her favorite, the next one down, was too young. He didn't know any answers. He didn't even know any questions. The others were only different-sized babies for her to feed and bathe and mind. She longed for someone to talk to. She wondered if Mama and Daddy ever really talked to each other when Daddy wasn't working at the mill or in the fields, when Mama wasn't cooking or scrubbing or tending to the children. Maybe at night, she thought, in that big double bed, when the last baby had been moved out and the next baby had not yet arrived.

Finally she heard Daddy coming home. She jumped up and ran to the kitchen. At the doorway, she stopped. Daddy was walking slowly and talking funny and she knew he had been at the still with the uncles. Usually he didn't say anything, just went on to take his bath, and Mama didn't say anything either. She just went on getting his supper. But tonight, Mama said, "Why you stay out so long, Reed? I waitin an waitin for you to come back and you went up to those woods and stayed."

"Sorry, Miss Lucine, ma'am," Daddy said, pulling off his hat and bowing and smiling. "I most terrbul and partikkular sorry." But Mama kept her back turned. Rannee could tell, just looking at Mama's feet, that she was frowning.

Daddy went around and tried to kiss Mama on one cheek, but she turned her head. Then he went around and tried to kiss her on the other cheek, but she turned her head again.

"Wassa matta, woman?" Daddy said, letting his voice go up very high. "You wantin me to kiss yo *ass?*"

Rannee, crouched behind the door, stared at her parents. She wondered why Daddy had stopped being polite and why Mama wouldn't let him kiss her. She felt lonelier than ever.

Later, after Mama and Daddy were asleep, she ran up to Uncle Floyd's. His cabin was dark again, and the two chairs had not yet been settled for the night. She walked slowly around the cabin, humming "Only Believe" very softly. But no light came and no sound, except the chairs on the porch, rocking gently in the wind.

Mama was waiting at the door when she got home. "Where you been, Sister?" she said.

"Out to the back house, ma'am," Rannee said.

Mama stared hard. "You lyin, Sister," she said. "I 'member this. I lay it on the shelf."

"Yes, ma'am," Rannee said. She knew it would be a hard whipping this time. But she didn't care. She was much too worried about Uncle Floyd. Where was he? But she dared not ask.

# 4

Everyone wore something new and looked different at Easter, except Daddy. He wore the same old hat and the same old smile and passed out the same little bows to the aunts and cousins and all the ladies from all the other Quarters around Chawnee. Uncle Floyd wore his black suit, all ready to read the Lesson. He gave Rannee a wink and a big grin that stretched out his scar like a string.

"Where you been, Uncle Floyd?" she whispered. "I been to see you las night an you not there. Where you been?"

"Not there?" he said. "*Musta* been there. Where else *would* I be?" For a moment the scar settled down to an ugly bump underlining his nose. But suddenly he smiled again. "Don't you worry," he said. "Ain't nothin to worry about."

"Yes, sir, Uncle Floyd," she said. But she *was* worried. It was the first time he had not answered her question.

After the service, everyone sat down beside a table in one corner of the church where there was a nest full of colored eggs with a big plastic rabbit in the middle looking very pleased, as if he had just laid those eggs himself. The grown-ups sat very still on little folding chairs with their big black stern Sunday shoes

51

sticking out in front of them, and listened to the children. Each child recited something he had chosen from the Bible himself. Odette Peters, who was very good at arithmetic, always picked something very long with lots of numbers: "'. . . two cubits and a half shall be the length thereof, and a cubit and a half the breath thereof, and a cubit and a half the height thereof.'" Daddy moved his hat round and round in his hands and Mama picked at her Sunday smile like a piece of basting she had to undo. Rannee always chose something very short from Proverbs: "'The legs of the lame are not equal,'" she said weakly, and sat down.

Grandma and Grandpa and Aunt Billie came home for dinner after church. Grandma Sukey was a tall, skinny black woman in a long dress with a long apron and a man's narrow-brimmed felt hat. She wore huge, lopsided glasses with enormous earpieces—to help her hear better, Rannee decided. She knew all about children because she had eight of her own, all sons, all grown now and still living right there in Simms Quarter. And they all looked just like her, as if they didn't dare grow away, even in appearance. It seemed strange to Rannee because, though the uncles didn't look much like each other, they all looked like Grandma Sukey, except Uncle Doc, who was the oldest and the biggest and had a bit of Grandpa Vernon trapped in one eye. Grandma Sukey was a fierce, possessive woman, given to long, drawn-out labors of terrible intensity. Pulling a baby out of Grandma Sukey, Miss Martha Jane said, was like trying to pull the core out of an apple.

Rannee was afraid of Grandma, but she was even more scared of Grandpa, who was small and stiff and always carried a stick in case he saw someone who needed a whipping. He was a hard man, set in the ways he had learned as a boy, working fifteen hours a day for Earl Henchman, first as a farm hand and then as a sharecropper. The Henchmans were known to be the meanest whites in the state and Earl Henchman was the meanest of the lot. He had long black hair to his shoulders and he always wore boots and spurs, even—people said—to his own christening, and rode with a gun across his lap. If he saw any niggers on the road, he would stop his horse and start cussing. If they didn't get out of the way fast enough, he began to shoot.

"Didn't matter if he hit you or not," Grandpa said. "Got his fun jes watchin you jump."

His wife was mean too, small and mean. She rode around in a silver buggy and cleared the niggers off the roads with a horsewhip.

Grandpa's daddy was Isaiah Simms, a big, strong, cheerful man who had worked hard and prospered and sometimes felt the hand of the Lord on his thigh. One night, when Grandpa was still a boy, his daddy was walking home from church all alone. It was a calm night with a big pale watery moon floating around in the sky and splashing moonlight all over the pavement. Grandpa's daddy was walking softly and stepping over the puddles. He had been to choir rehearsal and had stayed behind to help the deacon sweep the church. He liked to go to church, to visit the Lord in His house and sit down in His Presence with His breath like a mist on the panes. And walking home, he would hear again the promise the Lord had spoken to that earlier Isaiah long ago: "And my people shall dwell in a peaceable habitation, and in sure dwellings, and in quiet resting places." And he knew it was the hand of God that had measured out those fields and given them over to him, Isaiah Simms, that he might live and prosper and give thanks to the Lord. So Isaiah gave thanks whenever he could, in church and at table and from beneath his bent back in the field. He was giving thanks that night, walking softly on his way home down the dark streets with the lights pale beneath the moon and the shops all shut up.

He heard a buggy behind him. "Hey you, boy!" a voice shouted. "You breakin the curfew." It was a high, shrill, sharp voice, like barbed wire. Isaiah knew, without turning, that it was Mrs. Earl Henchman in her silver buggy. But he was giving thanks to the Lord. He kept on walking.

"Hey, you damn nigger. You stop an listen when a white lady talks to you."

But Isaiah Simms kept walking, whistling softly, "What a friend I have in Jesus."

"You'll need a lot more than that when I'm done with you," Mrs. Henchman screamed. But Isaiah turned the corner and was gone.

Later that night, word was out that Mrs. Earl Henchman had been raped by Isaiah Simms right in her own buggy, right in the middle of Main Street. Isaiah took the night train out of Montgomery, leaving his wife and his sons and his lands. His wife died two months later, run over by a silver buggy. She got—some people said—what her husband deserved. Earl Henchman got everything else: Simms's land and Simms's sons to work it.

So Grandpa and his brothers went to work for Earl Henchman, saving every penny they could while Mr. Henchman got drunk and rode around shooting stray niggers. After a few years, Grandpa's brothers managed to run away. But Grandpa wouldn't be chased off his land any more than his father would be chased off the street. Grandpa went on working, saving penny by sweaty penny, and put his sons to work as soon as they could walk between the rows. And in the end, miraculously, Grandpa won. Mr. Henchman drank more and more and worked less, mortgaging off most of his land. One night when he was very drunk and chasing one of his own black servants through the house with a machete, he fell down the stairs and split his own skull. After the funeral, Mrs. Henchman rode out every day on his horse with his gun across her lap. In the end, she went completely crazy, shooting at whites as well as blacks and had to be put away.

Grandpa continued to prosper. In ten years, he had bought back his daddy's farm and Earl Henchman's as well. But it left him a rigid, angry old man who walked very straight. He didn't bend one way or the other, not to smile or laugh or even to look down at the shoes he had mended to see if they fit. He mended all the shoes in the Quarter and made brooms too, now that he was too old to work. Rannee hated those high-topped shoes. She thought that Grandpa sewed them on lopsided on purpose so they would hurt. She took them off whenever she could and planned to wear sneakers as soon as she was grown-up. Most of the time, Grandpa sat on his porch with his eyes sunk like pockets and spied on his grandchildren.

Rannee, sitting next to him at Easter dinner, could feel him spying on her now. She felt scared, too scared to eat. She handed him her chicken leg. He took it with both hands. Grandpa Vernon didn't trust anyone. Rannee bent her head and began to pile beans on her biscuit. Aunt Billie, sitting opposite in her green hat and skinny beads, was shaking her head. "Never woulda done it like that in Birmingham," she said. "Never 'lowed it at all in Birmingham."

"'Lowed what?" Rannee said, scraping up gravy with her knife. Aunt Billie pinched her lips and Rannee knew she would be punished for sassing a grown-up.

"Weren't no fit Easter service neither," Aunt Billie went on. "Not like they got in Birmingham. Hardly nothin at all 'bout Jesus. Look like they forgot all about Him." She clasped her hands on her breast. "But I 'members Him," she said, raising her eyes. "I 'members that po' sweet Jesus. I 'members Him lashed with lashes and scourged with scourges." She closed her eyes and began to rock back and forth. "I 'members Him hangin on that cross, oh Lord," she moaned softly, "an sufferin for the wicked o this world, oh Lord, with the nails through His hans an feet, oh Lord, an nowhere to rest His head." All the other grown-ups said, yes, they remembered too, and went on eating.

After dinner, Rannee helped Mama wash the dishes and sweep the floor and scrub the table. Then Daddy hitched up the wagon and took everybody to the fair in Madisonville. Everybody but Rannee, who had sassed Aunt Billie. "You stay home an study your manners," Mama said.

Rannee sat on the back porch and stared at her fat, shiny

Sunday shoes lolling on the stairs beside her. They were point-ing straight ahead, all ready to walk down those steps and on down the road and right out of Simms Quarter. But she didn't know anywhere to go except Chawnee and that was full of white people. She couldn't even go to Uncle Floyd's. He had gone with Preacher Brown to read the Lesson in Pine Hill.

Suddenly, she saw Bay running down the road toward the house. He was a skinny little boy with great man-sized eyes staring out of his skinny face and great man-sized knees staring out of his skinny legs. He was grinning and shouting at her. "Hey, Tink! Lookit, Tink. Look what I got!" He was holding out two large teacakes. He hadn't gone to the fair at all, but only as far as Grandma Sukey's where he saw a plate of tea-cakes sitting in her kitchen window. He had jumped off the wagon when no one was looking. "For you an me," he shouted.

She stared at him in admiration. She had never had more than *half* a teacake at one time in her whole life. "You stole *two whole* teacakes?" she said. "You gonna git a mighty big lashin."

He grinned and shook his head. "Won't nobody know," he said. He had moved the other cakes around on the plate. "Won't nobody *ever* know." He grinned again. "Two *whole* tea-cakes," he said, "just for us."

The children carried the cakes to the woods and ate them behind an enormous oak. "I gonna tell my wife to make me teacakes every single day when I growed," Bay said.

Rannee grinned. "I be over for dinner every single day," she said.

"No you won't," Bay said. "They be *my* teacakes. You stay home an make your own."

But Rannee said she wasn't going to stay around any Simms Quarter making any teacakes when she was grown.

"What you gonna do then?" Bay said.

"Dunno yet." She had never told anyone her dream of going to live in Montgomery with Uncle Floyd. "Be a candy man mebbee," she said. "Ride around in that big shiny car all day eatin chocklits and drinkin Cokes."

"Oh, no you won't," Bay said. "You can't. Ain't no *girl* can be a candy man. Beside, *I* gonna be the candy man."

"Can't." Rannee said.

"Can too."

"No you can't. You *colored*. Ain't no colored can be a candy man neither."

She saw his sharp little face jerk and his eyes blink. He got up and ran down the long bolt of hill toward home. She stood looking after him, feeling stunned. Then she went slowly back into the woods and lay down under the sweet gum tree with her arms spread wide and her ankles crossed, like Jesus. She thought of Him whipped with whips and lashed with lashes and scourged with scourges. She tried to imagine Him hanging all alone on that cross with the nails through His hands and feet and nowhere to rest His head. But He had the thin black face and pleated lips of Cousin Travers.

When she got home, everyone was back. Mama took a tiny silver thimble out of her apron pocket. "Won it over to the fair," she said shyly, handing it to Rannee. "Tellin how many beans layin in the jar." She picked up her plate and carried it out to the back porch.

"Thank you, ma'am," Rannee said, slipping it on her little finger. She stood in the doorway watching Mama, wishing she could hurry and grow up to be like Mama, strong and tall with her head high above the mess of Simms Quarter, escaping to the peace and quiet of the back porch, calmly pouring sugar all over her food. But Rannee was still short with a straight, solid up-and-down body like the new pump, and a round, putty-colored face; not like Beet, already so tall she had a whole slice of the double bed to herself. Mama's hair was beautiful too, thick and crinkly and soft, buttoned down by the little round bun. Rannee hated her own hair, so tightly braided it felt stitched on, showing her bare scalp like little seams all over her skull. Once Beet made her comb it out to see how she would look. "Teerbul," Beet said. "Like a piece a ole knittin. Knit one, purl one, all over your head." But Mama's hair looked beautiful and comfortable too.

Mama was holding her empty plate and rocking back and forth. She was never completely still, Rannee thought. Some part of her was always moving. Even in her sleep, Mama was probably busy smoothing the quilt or patting the back of the newest baby sleeping beside her. There were two double beds in the back room now.

"That you, Sister?" Mama said.

"Yes, ma'am," Rannee said.

Mama turned her head and smiled.

Rannee stared in wonder. Mama's smile, like Mama's tune, was secret, private, kept for herself alone. But now it was turned on Rannee; a soft, silky smile slipped over her like a new dress, making her feel beautiful. Rannee longed to wear it forever. But the next minute, Mama had turned away again, an aging woman holding an empty plate and staring at the chinaberry tree as if it were still another child to be fed and whipped. She held out her plate. "Fetch me a little more a that fried bread with a little more syrup on top," she said.

"Yes, ma'am," Rannee said. Suddenly she felt very sorry for Mama.

# 5

Daddy put his spoon in the sugar can and took it out again. "Where the sugar at, Lucine?" he said.

"Ain't no more," Mama said. "Not less you got stamps. On accounta rationin for this here war."

Rannee, eating watermelon jelly and biscuits, heard three words she had never heard before: "rationin" and "stamps" and "war."

People began to talk more and more about the war, blaming it for the rain and the drought and the children turning sassy. But Rannee couldn't really see that the war made much difference. The candy man didn't come as often and Grandma Sukey's jelly tasted sour and Mr. Junius refused to sell Cokes to niggers. But nothing else changed. Rannee still went to school and came home and did her lessons and bathed the little ones and cleaned for Mama and worked in the fields for Daddy and got whipped as usual. She even managed to sneak up to Uncle Floyd's once in a while. He was always there in the early morning with his whistle wandering down the path to meet her. But at night his cabin was often dark.

Later, after the war had been on for a while, all the uncles went for a "physical," one by one, taking the train all the way to Montgomery. Even Daddy went in his good Sunday pants with a new ribbon tacked to his hat, and the whole place looked different. The yard seemed bigger and emptier, as if the chinaberry tree had backed away and left a lot more dirt around the house. Daddy's hat wasn't bobbing in the kitchen at five in the morning anymore or wandering along the edge of the sky in the evening.

Two days later, he was back, sitting at the kitchen table with his old smile strutting all over his face and Mama right across from him, smiling too. She looked different sitting down opposite Daddy with Daddy's smile all over *her* face, as if it had jumped the table and landed on her when she wasn't looking. Rannee sat on the back porch and listened to Daddy tell how the white men didn't want him in their war because he had flat feet.

"Flat feets!" Mama said. "Course you got flat feets. Them white peoples over to Montgomery got humped-up feets?"

All the other uncles came back too, except Uncle Link. Rannee wondered if it was Grandpa's high-topped shoes that had flattened out his sons' feet. But Uncle Link must have had humped-up feet because they took him into their army and kept him there.

He was the youngest of the brothers and the smallest, the only one who hadn't waited nine and three-quarters months to be born, as if Grandma Sukey, weaker then, had compromised at last, willing to take less if she could have it sooner. Born small, he never quite caught up. But in spite of his size, he was well-made from the start. His head rode his shoulders and his skin rode his bones and he rode the ground around Simms Quarter like a man not only well favored but well pleased. His wife, Lovey, was small too, and he had two small twin sons, soft and round like a pair of bedroom slippers. Everything about Uncle Link was different, so it wasn't surprising that his feet were different too.

But he must have gotten them flattened out somehow because after a while he came home too. Everyone went up to his cabin to eat and drink and celebrate and hear him tell about the war. The other children all played outside, but Rannee hid behind the kitchen door and listened.

Uncle Link told how they shaved off all his hair and sent him to a place called Florida where there wasn't any war at all. They made him dress up like a soldier anyway, though they kept him in the kitchen most of the time, washing dishes and scrubbing pots. Sometimes he had to clean the buildings, called "barracks," and the white officers' beach, called "mosquito project," picking up the white officers' cigarettes and the white women's Kleenex and the white children's candy wrappers.

"Weren't no war at all," Uncle Link said. He hated it. He hated being in the kitchen all the time like a woman, or cleaning up the grounds like one of his own children. And whatever he did, there was always a great crowd of strange people doing it with him, sleeping and eating and pissing, pushing and shoving and shouting. And wherever you looked there were white people—on the post or off—white people watching. Uncle Link couldn't stand the noise and the crowding and the white people watching.

One night he was lying on his bunk all alone in the barracks, thinking about his wife who always slept stuck up against him like a postage stamp and his sons growing up with no daddy to teach them to hoe or drop corn or chop or plow, and his field lying flat and empty as the palm of his hand with nothing in it but dirt. He missed the sound of the tree toads and the smell of wood burning in the stove and the squirrel stewing in the pot. He missed sitting beside Lovey on the porch after supper, watching the sun send waves of color across the sky like the waves from the officers' boats on the lake. He was afraid the war would go on forever. Lovey would be an old woman and his sons grown-up, ignorant as poor white trash, before he ever got home.

After a while, he heard the men coming, big, beef-fed, white

61

men, shouting and cursing and laughing. They crowded around him. He could smell the whiskey on them.

"This here one's real perlite," one man said. "I seen him in the kitchen, bowin his ass to the dishwater and salutin them pots real nice."

"How you know this the same one?" a big man shaped like a duffel bag said. "Can't tell one from the other in the daytime when you stone sober. How you know now? You gotta prove it."

"You a perlite little nigger, George?" the first man said, sticking his face down into Uncle Link's.

"Yes, sir," Uncle Link said.

"Then how come you don't stand up when you see a white man? How come you still lyin in that bunk like you a ignorint, stuck-up, no-good, mother-fuckin nigger like the resta them?"

Uncle Link got up and stood beside his bed.

"Ain't enough," the big man said. "Hell, any fuckin nigger'll do that."

"He's right," the others shouted. "He gotta do more'n *that*."

"What else can you do, nigger?"

"Don't know, sir."

"Ain't much else a nigger *can* do, is there? 'Cept lie in the sun an eat watermelon. That right, George?"

"How 'bout sof-shoe?" someone said. "All nice perlite lil niggers can do sof-shoe."

"That's right," the others shouted. "Sof-shoe. Do us a nice snappy sof-shoe, boy."

Uncle Link looked around that circle of men, men with pushed-in faces and eyes like plug nickels and thick bodies, surrounding him like posts in a fence. "Don't know no sof-shoe, sir," he said. He had never even heard the word before.

"Don't know no sof-shoe? Sweet Jesus! You all hear that? Poor lil ole George. We all gonna take pity on this dumb sonuvabitch lil nigger an teach him a few things?"

"Yeah, that's right. We oughtta teach him *somethin* 'fore he gits outta this man's army. We oughtta teach him a lil sof-shoe."

"But he can't do no sof-shoe in no army uniform. Agin regulations. He gotta strip first. Can't have no nigger doin no sof-shoe in no army fatigues."

They made him take off all his clothes and fold each piece carefully and lay it on the end of his bed. Then they made him stand at attention in the middle of the barracks, stark naked, surrounded by thick-bellied, drunken men covered in khaki.

"OK," someone said. "You all ready for that famous sho-nuff nigger dance. The sof-shoe. You go on an give us a real nice rendition, boy."

When he did not move, they began to poke him, prodding him with their hands and feet and guns, picking up his legs and his arms and his penis. "Higher boy," they shouted. "You gotta git it up higher. That there ain't no sof-shoe, boy. You gotta git it *all* up higher, much higher." In the end, they had him down on the floor. They weren't teaching him any soft shoe any more.

The next day, Uncle Link went out into the fields behind the barracks all alone, and two weeks later he was home. He had managed to have flat feet at last, by shooting off both his big toes.

Rannee thought about Uncle Link a lot after that, when she was working in the house or the fields or just watching the clouds nudge each other across the sky. She thought about those white men always watching and the mean ones in the barracks and she wondered if she really did want to grow up and leave Simms Quarter after all.

She was thinking about it walking to school one morning with Beet and the cousins, carrying her shoes and her syrup can. "Where you all goin when you all growed up?" she asked Marbelle.

Marbelle grinned. "That depen, don't it?"

"On what?"

"Who I fixin to marry, dumbbell. But I ain't decided yet. Could be Silo Johnson. An then agin, could be JoJo Burns."

"You mean when you all growed up you gonna leave Simms Quarter an go live in the Johnson Quarter or Burns Hill?"

"You knows somewhere else to go?" Marbelle said.

Rannee stared at her. "What you gonna do there?" she said. "In them other Quarters? You gonna cook an clean an work in the field an have babies like your mama?"

"You knows somethin else to do?" Marbelle said, staring back.

She was right. There was nothing else she *could* do—except work in some *white* man's field or clean some *white* woman's house. Rannee had never heard of a colored woman doing anything else. Certainly not singing on the radio. Not around Chawnee. And now she was terribly afraid of that other world full of white men.

She sat down on a log, squeezed her feet back into her shoes, and walked on, slowly, toward the school, to squeeze herself onto a bench and into Miss French's notion of a Wednesday. It was Rannee's turn to light the stove, a job she hated. Her whole life, she thought, was full of jobs she hated, one after another, like stairs. She saw herself climbing those long steep steps: today, tomorrow, next week, next year. She looked up but she couldn't see any end. She would just go on and on, one foot after the other, but she would never get off those stairs.

"Who lit that stove?" Miss French said.

"Me, ma'am," Rannee said.

"How come you can't do better'n that? A big girl like you. Look like Satan hisself couldn't teach you nothin."

Rannee thought that Satan probably lived in the back of that big, black stove, right behind Miss French's desk, helping her to see both sides of the room at once and into children's pockets.

When the dinner bell rang, Rannee waited till the others left to eat on the steps of the school or on logs in the yard. Then she took her syrup can and went, all alone, to a special place she had found in the graveyard and sat down with her back against a tombstone. It was a very special stone with a finger pointing right at her and the name JAMES W. BUMPUS carved on it. There was even a little grave right beside it for James W.

64

Bumpus's left leg. It was shaded by a large tree and it was always very quiet there. She liked to think of all the dead people lying so close together, a little like the double beds in the back room at home, except that the graves were warm and dry with all the "beloveds"—husbands and wives and fathers and mothers—all resting. Some were resting "in peace" and some "in Jesus." She imagined Him with His arms full of people, like Daddy in the night with his arms full of children whenever Miss Martha Jane brought Mama a new baby.

She sat down and opened her syrup can, trying not to notice that the syrup had spilled all over the greens and the biscuits were swollen up like fists. Suddenly, she heard a sound behind her. She turned and saw Uncle Floyd leaning against a tree. He was wearing his black Sunday suit. The sleeves were torn and his tie hung down like two tails and he was leaning against that tree as if he couldn't stand up by himself. As she watched, she saw him slide down the trunk and collapse on the ground. She jumped up and ran over to him. He was lying very still with his eyes closed.

"Uncle Floyd!"

He opened his eyes and smiled up at her. "Don't be worryin yoself," he said. "I jes weak."

"You hungry?"

He nodded.

She gave him her syrup can and watched him eat. His shoes and trousers were covered with mud and his hands and face were dirty with the dirt stitched way down into the cracks of his skin. When he was finished, she filled the empty can with water from the pump behind the church. "Thanks," he said and grinned up at her. "That better. Much, much better." He sat up with his back against the tree. "Ain't had nothin to eat for two days."

"What happen, Uncle Floyd? You cuss out a white man again?"

He laughed and said he never cussed anything anymore but his toes on the rail at home. "They after me," he said. "But not for cussin. You tell your Daddy when he git home tonight. Tell him come git me with the wagon. I be waitin right here. But tell him be very very carefer." They had killed one man already, he said, a *white* man, all the way from New York City. They had shot him down outside the union meeting. Uncle Floyd had been hiding in the woods for two days.

"A *white* man?" Rannee said. "Who kill a *white* man?"

"Other white mens," Uncle Floyd said. "Call theyselves the Klan."

"Who that?" Rannee said. But once again, Uncle Floyd didn't answer.

"You jes tell your Daddy be very very carefer," he said. "Be sure you tell him, the Klan."

"I 'member," Rannee said.

"Don't tell nobody else," Uncle Floyd said.

The school bell rang. "You better be gittin on back," Uncle Floyd said. "I be waitin right here."

She nodded and picked up the syrup can. "Bye, Uncle Floyd," she whispered. At the schoolyard, she turned and looked back. But all she could see were the tombstones.

That evening, she walked round and round the chinaberry tree waiting for Daddy. When she told him, he took off his hat and rubbed his head. "He say to tell you be very very carefer," she whispered.

He nodded.

"They kill a white man, Daddy," she whispered.

He nodded again. "He say who all is chasin him?"

"White mens," she said. "Name of Klan."

Later that night, watching behind the kitchen door, she saw Mama wrapping up biscuits and salt pork and Daddy emptying the jam jar. Then Mama sat down at the kitchen table with her chin in her hand and said, very quietly, without turning, "Sister?"

"Ma'am?"

"You ain't *seen* nothin an you ain't *heerd* nothin. An you never set eyes on Uncle Floyd since he read the Lesson in church last Sunday. Now you go on an git back in that bed."

66

"Yes, ma'am," Rannee said. But later, looking out of the window, she saw Daddy and Uncle Doc hitching up the mule. As soon as they were gone, Mama turned out the lamp. But Rannee knew she was sitting in the dark, listening.

Rannee remembered two or three other times when someone had to leave town fast. Word would go round the settlements that "They" were out looking for Todd or Schuyler or Watson or Huck, and she knew that if they were found they would be killed. So Todd and Schuyler and Watson and Huck got away as fast as they could. They never came back and their names were never mentioned in the settlements around Chawnee again. She wondered what had happened to them and she wondered what would happen to Uncle Floyd.

The next morning, she walked up to his cabin. It looked exactly the same with the two rockers—his and hers—side by side on the porch and bits of wood shavings on the floor. She climbed the steps slowly and sat down in her chair and put her feet on the rail. It was very quiet. She could hear the wind fingering the door. It was terribly lonely sitting next to Uncle Floyd's empty chair with the little pile of shavings blowing around her feet. Finally, she got up and swept them off the porch. She was about to leave when she heard the two chairs rocking, in unison, in the wind. She went back and leaned them very carefully, heads down, against the rail.

# 6

The only person Rannee ever knew to drop out of high school was her own sister, Beet, who left to marry a preacher with a huge new refrigerator and what he called a king-sized bed. Rannee couldn't blame her for wanting dry sheets and a little hip room, though Reverend Sugar was much older and getting fat all over. Mama and Daddy were very sad about Beet's not finishing school. Mama cried and said it was wicked and Daddy shook his head and said it was foolishness. "*I* sorry now, Beet," he said. "But *you* be sorry later." He told Rannee to be sure and finish her high schooling. He even wanted her to go to college so she could sit in an office, clean and cool and quiet, and write things down and drink coffee from a cup, like Miss Kettle at the mill. Miss Kettle had told him all about that Negro college in Jeffersonville. If Rannee studied real hard and learned real well, she wouldn't have to pay at all. She could go to college *free*.

"Four more years a school," Beet said. "Soun teerbul to me."

It sounded terrible to Rannee too. She didn't want to go to another colored school and she didn't want to sit in an office all day writing things down and go home to Simms Quarter every night. She wanted to go up North and find Uncle Floyd and keep house for him and sing duets with him, in the choir or in the kitchen or maybe even on the radio.

One Saturday afternoon, Mama and Daddy took Beet over to Pine Hill where the Reverend Sugar lived. Two hours later, they came home alone, and Rannee knew that Beet was married.

Beet's husband called her Bethulla, which made her sound like some place in the Bible, and gave her a son named Nicodemus to match. Rannee didn't see much of Beet once she was married. When she did, Beet always looked angry, like Grandma Sukey and Mama and all the other ladies in Simms Quarter. Or maybe, Rannee thought, she just looked married.

Beet would shove her baby at Rannee and say, "Take him. I sick to death a the smell a him. Look jes like his daddy. All swelled up like he ready to be stuck. Like a pig. Only it's *me* gittin stuck. By that fat ole man whenever he feeling the hand a God on him. Is a layin on a hans every night in that house. I gotta git away 'fore there's another lump a Sugar stewin in the pot. You think Mama would keep this here baby for me? So's I kin go up to Birmingham an git me a job an buy me a dress."

"What kinda job you think you gonna git with no high school diploma?" Bay said. Rannee looked at him in surprise. He was right, she thought. He was growing up smooth and smart, with his bony knees covered up and his big eyes settling down.

"Don' matta, jes so's I git away," Beet said. "This ole man give me nothin. Nothin but this here ugly baby an a mess a dirty clothes every day."

"An a king-size frigerator, don' forgit," Bay said.

"I stuffed and starvin and crowded an lonesome all at the same time," Beet said.

Me too, Rannee thought, and vowed there would be no Reverend Sugar for her. She'd better go to that college in Jeffersonville after all, she thought. She might learn something. Like how to find Uncle Floyd and how to read the Lesson, loud and smooth, with no mistakes.

Reverend Sugar was away a good deal, comforting the sick with his pocket watch in his palm, and burying the dead, and preaching all over the county. When he was gone, he kept his money in his back pocket and his wife locked up. "I'd be crazy not to," he said.

Eighteen months after she was married, Beet strapped her baby to the kitchen table and ran off with the iceman. "Thought that there frigerator made ice all by isself," Bay said.

Everyone else stayed in school right down to the last day of the twelfth grade. It was the only way out—away from the fields and the settlements and the seasons locking them in. There were hardly any Negroes over eighteen left in Morgan County. Even Marbelle decided she would rather go stay with her cousin in Cleveland, who scrubbed the colored latrine in the bus station, than marry a Johnson or a Burns and live in a Quarter. And no one wanted to get away more than Rannee, with a crowd of children pushing up behind her. She did not want to be like Mama, who had escaped no farther than to the back porch.

At first, she tried very hard in high school. But the teachers were all old and colored with cracked voices and wrinkled faces as if all the learning had been squeezed out of them long ago. Books were scarce, available mainly from white students at jacked-up prices. Rannee tried reading in the school library but there was almost nothing in it but old newspapers and old magazines and a tattered copy of *The Book of Knowledge,* volumes R and S and U.

One day, reading through the Rs during recess, she found a section called RACE which told all about white people who weren't Americans at all but something called "Caucasians." That day she was late to class and was sent to Mr. Huckaby, the principal. He was a big, moist man—moist eyes, moist lips, and big wet teeth. He always carried a cane, walking down the halls or sitting at his desk or visiting a class, leaning on it, stroking it, balancing it on his palm. He did all the whipping in the school personally. None of the teachers were allowed to beat the children. They sent them to Mr. Huckaby to do it. As principal, Rannee decided, he could choose the line of work he preferred.

He was waiting in his office with Mrs. Huckaby sitting at a little desk outside. She merely nodded at Rannee, but Mr. Huckaby sprayed his damp smile all over her and reached into the umbrella stand behind his desk. It was full of canes. "This one, I think," he said softly. "For first offenders. Is a sweet, gentle little fellow."

"Is not!" Rannee told Odette later. She was sore for days.

She was whipped often at school: for being late and for being early and for sitting down at her desk instead of waiting in the hall. She was whipped for knowing and for not knowing, for forgetting the boundaries of Morgan County and for calling white people Caucasians. She learned not to volunteer information just as she had learned, long ago, not to ask questions. Whenever she got whipped at school, she got beaten again at home. Sometimes—far worse—she was kept from a dance or a game or a visit to the traveling fair. If she begged for a whipping instead, she got both. She learned not to interfere, even in her own life. Squeezed into the overcrowded colored school bus, she watched the white bus pass by, going in the same direction. It was always half empty.

One day, riding home, she saw two wrecked cars on the side of the road with several white men standing around them. There were two jackets stretched on the ground with two pairs of legs sticking out, one in tan trousers and one in a flowered dress. One of the men held up his hand and the bus stopped. Two men picked up the flowered dress and put it on the floor of the bus with a pair of high-heeled shoes beside it. The children crowded back against the seats. Rannee could see that it was a white woman with long yellow hair like broken egg yolks spilling down all over her head. She had her eyes shut but she was moaning, a low steady sound. Rannee had never seen white skin so close up before. It wasn't really white at all, except for the legs, which were much paler, as if they were kept wrapped

71

up for special occasions. Gradually, a trickle of blood crept out of one corner of her mouth. The moaning stopped.

At the hospital, two men in white carried her out on a pallet with her shoes beside her. There was a big empty space where she had been. No one moved to fill it.

Riding home, Rannee wondered if that white lady had died in the bus. Had Rannee been staring into the face of a dead person? She remembered Cousin Travers lying in his coffin with Uncle Doc's shoes tied around his ankles. Nobody in Simms Quarter ever went anywhere without shoes, including the grave. But that white woman had been carried away in her bare feet. Rannee sat listening to the hum of the tires, like the sound of that hurt woman, all the way home.

That night, ironing in Grandma Sukey's kitchen, Rannee went on thinking about that white woman. Her face had been full of little bumps and holes like a buttermilk biscuit and her hair was black at the part, and that trickle of blood had hung from her mouth like a piece of string.

Suddenly, Bay appeared at the back door. He was panting and his long skinny face swayed like something at the end of a hook. He came in quietly and sat down at the kitchen table. "Reckon that there hurt white man dead by now," he said softly. "All stretched out on the road like he was."

Rannee nodded. "Wonder how come we didn't take him along too," she said.

"Wouldn't come," Bay said.

"How you know that?" Rannee said.

"I heerd him," Bay said. He always sat up front. "Say he waitin on the next bus, the *white* bus. Say he not taking what might be his last ride in a bus fulla niggers. He rather die right there."

Rannee put down the iron and went to sit beside Bay. She saw her hands lying on the kitchen table, sticking out of her long cotton sleeves. She had never really looked at them before, big and dark with the pink oozing over the edges. She stretched out her arms so the hands would be as far away as possible at the end of the long sleeves, just an odd pair of hands left lying about, waiting to be used. She longed to get up and walk away and leave them there. But she went on sitting, staring at those hands, *her* hands, waiting for the rest of her to join them.

She grew into a withdrawn, silent girl, with small matching features inside a soft, round face. She learned to keep still, like Mama, hardly ever smiling, with no cracks showing so no one could look in. It was a pretty face but people looking at it felt uncomfortable. "Like a empty plate," Grandma Sukey said. "Ain't nothin in it. Like she was always holdin somethin back." Perhaps that was why she was beaten so much. "No one like sittin down to a empty plate," Grandma Sukey said.

Rannee kept trying at school but most of it seemed so stupid, like learning the boundaries of Morgan County and the names of the governors in chronological order, nothing that would be of any use to Uncle Floyd up North. What wasn't stupid was difficult. No one ever explained what she did not understand. If she made a mistake, she was told she was wrong, but not why. If she asked a question, she was scolded. If she persisted, she was whipped. For a long time she kept going back to the school library whenever she could. She liked to read, liked to see the words all neat and tidy on the page like stepping stones leading her on. She liked to read in the library, which was always quiet and empty and where she could choose the books herself. For the first time, she wondered why the words in the books looked so different from the words she spoke and heard. "Papa" instead of "Popper," and "mouth" for "mouf" and *be*cause and *re*member. For the first time she wondered if they should be *said* that way. But there was no one to ask.

After a while, she realized that the books were either too simple or too difficult. She tried looking up the words she did not know in the dictionary, but most of the Cs and Ds and Ss were missing, and all of the Bs. She kept reading *The Book of Knowledge* but only the easy parts, the myths and legends and the "Book of Golden Deeds." She was fascinated by Richard the Lionhearted and Robin Hood and the strange story of

Romulus and Remus, found by a she-wolf under a tree. She was fascinated but confused and had no idea how to separate fact from fiction.

The only person who really taught her anything in high school, Rannee decided, was Charlene Stubbs, who was a year older and had grown up in Montgomery and had had four fathers going on five. Rannee met her in the Girls' Room one morning. Rannee was standing with her legs crossed trying to keep her insides from leaking out. Soon she would be bleeding all over the floor.

The first time it happened, she had been home, walking in the creek behind the woods, carrying her shoes and holding up her dress with her feet so heavy she could hardly lift them. It was like walking through jelly. She felt terrible, as if her insides were all knotted up and being pulled out between her legs: the hand of God reaching down and yanking the living daylights out of Rannee Simms. She kept her knees together, shuffling slowly, hardly lifting her feet.

Around the bend in the creek, she saw Mama and Grandma Sukey fishing. From the distance, they looked exactly alike, two big women in dark dresses and big hats, and poles sticking up in front of them like scolding fingers. They loved to fish. Everyone in Simms Quarter loved to fish. It was the easiest thing anyone could do except sleep, even easier than rocking on the back porch, tipping the world this way and that, being careful, always, not to let it go too far one way or the other. But on the bank of the creek, Mama and Grandma were still as bushes.

Suddenly, they began to scream and hack at her, shouting and pointing. "You, Sister, you get outta that water, hear? You wanna catch the pneumonia? Get outta there quick, you crazy girl. You wanna die?" They went on pointing and screaming at her.

Rannee looked down and saw blood in the water where she was standing. Her insides really *were* coming out, like the hogs that the uncles slaughtered every fall. Her liver and kidneys and heart would probably plop out too. Suddenly, she remembered that Grandma Sukey had been asking her for months now, every time she went to the back house, "You see anythin? You notice anythin?" She even insisted on examining Rannee's underpants. But Grandma Sukey never said why.

Mama took Rannee home and made her drink her terrible "tea." "You drinks that every mornin for ten days," Mama said. "An you be extra carefer now. That bleedin mean you a growed lady now."

"That bleedin mean you all fixed up to have a baby now," Beet told her later. "Got all the necessary equipment now. Yessir. You is all ready."

Rannee was terrified. "Don't tell Miss Marfa Jane, will you?" she had said.

"Whatsa matta?" Charlene Stubbs said now. "You got your Granmommy?"

Rannee stared at her.

"You know what I talkin about?" Charlene said. "You unerstan my vocaberlery?"

Rannee shook her head.

"How come you so ignorint? You from Flat Rock?"

"Chawnee," Rannee said.

"Where *that* at?"

"Near Pine Hill."

"Pine Hill? That ain't nothin but a squiggle with a fillin station in the middle. I see I gonna have to give you some instructions. Don't nobody know nothin roun here. You is the third girl in this here school I has instructed. Them two give me nice things cause they not able to pay cash. I got a real nice ashtray say 'Schlitz,' an a matchbook say 'Camel.' What all you gonna give me?"

"Nothin."

"Nothin? Then you stays ignorint. How come you so mean 'long with bein so dumb?"

"Got nothin *to* give."

"They sure make em poor *an* dumb in Chawnee." But she decided to teach Rannee anyway, saying the poor and the dumb needed her instruction worse than anybody. She gave Rannee a Kotex from her book bag and taught her where babies came from and how they got there. She was a thin, restless girl with long straight hair that looked as if it had been pressed out daily with a flat iron. She wore very thin dresses, even in winter, and carried a supply of sanitary pads and a copy of *True Confessions* in her book bag. One day she showed Rannee a diaphragm she had stolen from her mother. "You sticks it over your belly button," she explained. "That way, no babies." But it was only for married women. Till then, she said, only the men could do it. That's why she went with older men. They knew how.

She played hookey a lot. Often, she invited Rannee along on a "date," which meant sitting in the back of a colored café with some strange man while Charlene went off in a car with his friend. The man was always quite old, like Mr. Huckaby, and wore a black suit and called her "Purty Lil Girl," patting her arm and smiling. He would buy her a root beer and sit smiling and watching while she drank it, feeling up her arm as if looking for a muscle. Sometimes, he suggested a "lil" walk or a "lil" rum in her root beer, but she always said, no thank you, it was too hot and, besides, she had to get back, the school bus was waiting. She clutched the bottle and felt the sweat behind her knees and cursed Charlene for leaving her all alone with an old man. "They's safer," Charlene said. "Young men is just plain dumb. An selfish. I don't want no more selfish peoples in my life." But the old men frightened Rannee. They smiled and smiled and didn't seem to care that she never smiled back. After a while, she refused to go along on Charlene's dates. But she continued to admire Charlene, who lived in Flat Rock and was free of the school bus and knew so much about men.

Rannee preferred high school boys: Rock and Fletcher and Cyril and Washington. But she could never see them except in crowds at school functions, with Simms Quarter looking on. Whenever she went anywhere—to a game or a fair or a dance or anything away from home—a grown-up from Simms

Quarter always went with her. Right through high school. If she tried to sneak away without telling, there was always someone in the crowd who knew her. There was no way to escape Simms Quarter. And there was no way around the tyranny of the school bus waiting to take her home.

No boy was ever allowed to visit her except Allister Burns whose mother was a friend of Aunt Effie's. He was planning to be a preacher, Aunt Effie said, and was waiting for the call. On Sundays, he waited in Grandma Sukey's parlor in a white suit and white shoes, staring at the clocks on his ankles. Rannee stared at the clock on the wall. He sat at one end of the room and Rannee sat at the other, with Grandma Sukey in the doorway between them, quilting and dipping snuff. He was given one glass of lemonade and two tea cakes.

"You receive that call yet?" Grandma Sukey said one Sunday, after they had been sitting for about fifteen minutes.

"No, ma'am. I still waitin."

Grandma Sukey waited another fifteen minutes. "You spectin it soon?" she said.

"Yes, ma'am. I expectin that call real soon." He sipped some lemonade. Rannee went on studying the clock on the wall.

"An your poor mama spectin *you*," Grandma Sukey said fifteen minutes later.

"No, ma'am," Allister said. "She ain't expectin me. She at a Revival meetin over to Fleetwood. She ain't waitin on me at all."

"A boy's mama is always waitin on him," Grandma Sukey said, standing up.

It was not until senior year that Rannee met Ward Peters. He was twenty, all grown-up and farming with his daddy. He drove his sister, Odette, to the bus stop every day in a beat-up old pickup truck. No matter when Rannee arrived, he was always there first. He wore faded overalls that were much too big and an enormous straw hat that covered most of his face except for a jerky little smile that wandered around his mouth whenever he looked at Rannee. He was very thin and shy and

77

walked way over on the edge of the road and sat way over in the corner of his truck.

One day, he poked Odette. "This here my brother, Ward," she said, poking him back. "OK, Bro Ward. Talk."

But Ward just smiled and said, "Mornin," and went on walking way over on the edge of the road. But Rannee had the feeling that he was making room for her.

After that, he got braver and pretty soon he was walking up and down the road beside her, waiting for the bus. But he never did much talking.

One day, he asked her to meet him in the café near the school during lunch. He bought her a huckleberry pie and a sarsparilla and sat looking at her while she ate. Soon she was meeting him almost every day. It was much nicer than math or science or even lunch in the cafeteria. He did not scare her like Charlene's old men and he was much more exciting than the boys her own age. He was quiet and slow but he knew how to arrange things. She liked sitting beside him in the pickup truck with the wind on her cheek, watching his hands on the wheel. She liked sitting opposite him in the café, watching him order, watching his lips smiling at her, listening to him tell her, so softly, how pretty she was, how sweet she was, sweeter than sarsparilla through a straw. No one had ever talked to her like that.

One day, he kissed her good-bye, right on the mouth. No one had ever kissed her like that either. Walking back to class, she could feel that kiss still lingering way down inside her as if she'd tucked it into a deep pocket.

After that, he kissed her regularly, hello and good-bye and in-between, sitting in the truck with his arm around her. Sometimes she was late getting back and had to go to the office where Mr. Huckaby waited, wiping his lips, rubbing his cane, and showing his big teeth full of stains, as if his skin had run. She held out her hand, stared at the spots on his teeth, and thought about Ward and kissing and huckleberry pie.

She began to think about Ward all the time, in school and

out. She stopped going to the library to try to read. She went out with Ward instead. She stopped trying to learn in class. She sat thinking of Ward instead, waiting for the time when he would put his arms around her and kiss her, kisses that slid all the way down to her knees and melted all over her insides. They made her forget everything—school and Mr. Huckaby and Mama's new baby coming soon.

One day, he drove her out to an orchard where the peaches hung big and heavy and ready to burst. He got up and spread a blanket beneath the trees for her. Then he filled his hat with peaches and poured them into her lap. She smiled and began to eat one. The juice ran down her chin.

He knelt in front of her. "I wipe it off for you," he said. He licked her chin and kissed her lips and sucked the peach juice from her mouth. Soon they were lying side by side on the blanket. She smelled sawdust and sweat and ripe peaches. He began to stroke her and kiss her. She closed her eyes and felt him all over her, on top of her and even inside her, in her mouth and between her legs. She felt herself melting, dissolving, flowing away beneath him. "What about babies?" she said suddenly, opening her eyes.

"Ain't nothin to worry about," he murmured. "I takes care a it."

She lay back and closed her eyes and he began to pump away inside her, slowly at first, then faster and faster, raising her higher and higher, filling her fuller and fuller till she burst—and found herself weeping into his neck. She had not cried since that Christmas morning long ago when she had wept into an empty box.

"You love me, Peachers?" he asked one afternoon just before graduation. It was raining and she was lying in the truck. It smelled of kerosene and burlap. She felt safe and warm and dry with Ward for a covering. Behind her was Simms Quarter. Ahead was . . . ? College, as Daddy had said? She knew she could never go to college. She had learned nothing in high school. She hated high school, in spite of Charlene and Ward

79

and the outings in the pickup truck. College would be much worse, a strange place full of strange people: a *colored* college with more tired old colored teachers and another mean old Negro principal and no books in the library. She would learn nothing in college either, and no one would ever give her a job in an office. She would have to work in white people's fields and white people's houses, or stay home and work for Mama and Daddy and Grandma Sukey and make room for another new baby. She would never find Uncle Floyd. He had disappeared completely. She could hardly remember his face and even his house wasn't his any more. One of Uncle Lester's sons was living in it. It was called Cousin Simon's house now. She thought of that tree in the woods that had fallen down, blocking her path, fencing her in. There was no Uncle Floyd, now, to take her hand and help her over it. She would be shut up in Simms Quarter forever.

In August, after the picking and the canning and Mama's new baby, she married Ward.

# 7

Rannee moved into Ward's room in the Peters's house. It was a nice, empty house, for all the other children had left, including Odette, who had gone to live with an aunt up North. Even the cousins and the uncles and the aunts were gone, as if Ward's mother, Miz Zophara, had scared them all away.

Ward went out with his father very early in the morning to work in the field, leaving Rannee alone in that strange, empty house with nobody but Miz Zophara and nothing to do but clean that one room and cook Ward's dinner. He came home at night with his head collapsed between his shoulders, too tired to talk. He sat on the porch with his father after supper, watching the sun burn up the sky and the light drop, like cinders, through the trees. When it was dark, he went inside and took Rannee to bed without a word, sliding into her like a slipper. She was grateful for his arms around her and his tongue in her mouth and his body plugged into hers.

Miz Zophara never let Rannee help with the housework. "You jus res yourself," she said. "There be exceedin much for you to do by'n'by." She swept through the house with her mop and broom, a big, black hitching post of a woman with huge silver loops in her ears and a "crazy" left eye that went its own way through the week. "That there a 'hag eye,'" Miz Zophara said. "That eye bequeath." It had been handed down from daughter to daughter for generations. "Mama give me hers 'fore she pass," Miz Zophara said, "a great glorification." It could hypnotize bugs and see through pie crusts and observe the souls of dead folk squatting around the table. When Miz Zophara was still a girl, she had seen old Cousin Emmaeus sitting at breakfast with the rope still tied around his neck and his head bowed as if he were saying grace. He was sitting in her daddy's chair, and she knew that her daddy would never sit there again. He died that night. But Miz Zophara, who loved her daddy, didn't cry. She never cried. She couldn't. Not with that crazy eye. She never laughed much either but kept her head very straight so as not to jiggle her bequeathed eye.

She kept very quiet too, as if the sound of her voice might spill the water she had laid out in saucers in front of the doors and windows. The whole family was quiet, even during meals. Rannee could hear those dead souls swallowing all around her. She longed to carry her plate to the back porch and eat all by herself, like Mama.

There were never any empty chairs at Miz Zophara's table. If someone didn't come to a meal, she moved his chair out on the back porch and sprinkled water on the doorstep. "Dead folk don' never presume to go cross water," she said. She made everyone drink hot lemon juice every night. "Keep yo souls all nice and clean and squeezed down," she would say. "We don't want no puffed-up, snickety souls roun here." Rannee longed for a place of her own.

"Yo very first daughter gonna get this here hag eye," Miz Zophara told Rannee. "But you betta hurry. Otherwise it liable to go to my niece Satine's child, which is entirely too sassy and prune-lipped. So you hurry and fascinate that baby along." But Rannee didn't want any child of hers wearing that crazy eye. She didn't want any child at all.

The only time she saw Pa Peters was when he chewed silently

beside Miz Zophara at meals or sat on the porch in his old army coat, left over from World War I, with Ward, and dipped snuff like Grandma Sukey. Only Grandma was always doing something else too. But Pa Peters just dipped and rocked and moved his hands in and out of his coat pockets. He had been found crawling around near the front with a dead soldier handcuffed to his wrist. No one, not even Miz Zophara, ever knew what had happened.

"You keep outa that war, hear?" he told Ward.

"Ain't no war on, Pa."

"There will be, son. There will be."

Every Saturday, Ward and his father went to town to buy supplies. Ward wanted Rannee to come too, but Miz Zophara didn't want the mother of her grandchild breathing the air in the general store, full of tobacco and whiskey and the cussing of white folks.

"Like me to bring you somethin?" Ward said. "Coke or Orange Crush or some peanut-butter crackers?"

"White man food," Miz Zophara said. "Shrivel up that baby fore she even begins."

One afternoon Rannee found an old newspaper Pa Peters had brought home because of the picture of the prize bull on the front page. She didn't care about the bull, but she knew there would be lots of other stories to read. She picked it up and carried it to her room where Miz Zophara wouldn't see her reading it. "Wearin out yo eyes on white man's lies," she would say. "That baby gonna be born blin."

After that, Ward always brought a newspaper back from town for her. She read it from cover to cover and back again. She wished she had *The Book of Knowledge,* Volume R or S instead, but it was better than nothing. She could recite all the weather reports and radio programs for an entire week. She read about white people getting engaged and married and buried and finishing high school. Once in a while, she found stories about colored people. They never seemed to get engaged or married or finish high school. They robbed and raped and got "executed" or "lynched."

She had never seen those words before. There was no one to ask what they meant. She worked them out for herself.

She kept the old newspapers under her bed—like that candy box long ago—and read them until they were tattered. Then she burned them in the woods—like the uncles burning the feathers of that Thanksgiving turkey. There was, it seemed, always something to hide.

One afternoon, after she had read the last newspaper seven times—the account of a country-club dance, ten weddings, and the "suicide" of a young colored man in the county jail—and when she felt she could no longer bear the silence and the loneliness and the boredom, she walked the long road back to Simms Quarter. It was many slow, hot miles. When she got there she realized that she could not face the mess of children in Mama's house or the stern silence at Grandma Sukey's. She made a wide detour around the cabins and went on up the hill, beyond the patches and the border of woods to the field. It was empty. Daddy was still at the mill and the older children were still in school. Only the silence and the heat were there. She stood staring at it. It was just a field now, she realized. It was no longer a room in her life. The sun bubbled in the sky, giving off clouds like puffs of steam. She turned and walked back. The red clay stretched between her old home and her new like a road of fire.

Six weeks after the wedding, she was pregnant. "How come I broke a leg?" she asked Ward.

He grinned and put his arms around her. "You mean it? Oh, Peachers, honey, ain't that sump'n? Ain't that really sump'n?"

She pushed him away. "How come, I wanna know?" she said. "How come? I tole you, no babies. An you promised. You promised to be carefer. 'I be very very carefer,' you said. 'Always. Very very carefer.' So how come you stop being carefer?"

"I very carefer, Peachers," he said. "But I think maybe that baby ready. You can't keep a baby from being born *forever*. This one been waitin a long time. You a married woman now, you wanna let that poor lil baby go ahead and get born."

"No!" Rannee said. "I don't. Not to *me* I don't." She left him and walked up to the trees that stopped in a semicircle behind the house. They may as well go on growing, she thought, making a *full* circle, locking her in. She was stuck worse than ever now, with a "crazy-eyed" woman and this thing inside her, pushing its way through her flesh, pushing her bones and her organs aside. She was nothing now but a box for that baby.

She was nauseous in the morning and, in the afternoon, when she felt better, she would sit in the woods, staring at a sky that looked like curdled cream, waiting for the baby to come. It would be someone to talk to, she thought. And someday it would even talk back. This baby would be a real talker, like her Daddy. He might even be a preacher and live in a nice red-brick house beside the church like Reverend Sugar. Only it would be in some faraway place up North, like Detroit, where the streets were all paved and there were lots of buses going everywhere all the time. No one, Odette had written, ever *walked* in Detroit. There were times when Rannee could hardly wait for her son to be born and start growing. But there were other times when she remembered that there were at least twenty years to go—twenty years of Peters Quarter and Miz Zophara's left eye glaring at her, making her pregnant. She would end up like Mama after all, with a baby coming every year. Walking home to Simms Quarter one afternoon, she saw the huge vines again, covering up the trees. But this time, she realized that they were growing in *two* directions: up the road to Simms Quarter and down the road to the Peters's.

She was sitting on the Peters's back porch when she saw Pa Peters drive up in the pickup truck all alone at two in the afternoon. It frightened her. She watched while he got out and came slowly up to the house, all bent over with his nose almost scraping the steps. "What happen?" she said. But Pa Peters just kept coming, climbing those stairs one at a time, his right foot waiting for his left, and said nothing.

"Where Ward at?" she said. "Whatsa matter you don' talk? Where Ward at?"

"In the backa the truck," Pa Peters said at last and buckled into a chair. She looked and saw a couple of lumpy feed sacks stretched out in the back. She got up and began to walk toward them.

"You stay here," Pa Peters said. "Don't you go near there. You stay away from there. Go call Miz Zophara. Tell her to come quick."

"What happen?" Rannee said without moving.

"It Ward."

"What happen to Ward?"

"He dead."

She reached for a wall that wasn't there. "How come he dead?"

"He shot."

"Ward *shot?* Somebody shot *Ward?*

"In the wood," Pa Peters said. His voice was cracking and splitting and his face was laced up so tightly he could hardly talk.

"What wood?" Rannee said.

"That old wood. Backa the ole Sutcliffe place. One minute Ward standin there. Next minute I hear a noise and he layin down with the blood comin outa his pocket. 'Trespassin,' the man said."

"What man?"

"Man with a gun. Big white man. Shoutin somethin. Ward scared. He run."

"You shootin wile turkeys?" Rannee said.

"You crazy? We just cuttin down that old dead oak for firewood like we always do." He put his head in his hands and cried.

Rannee felt sick, stuffed, nauseated. It was the wild turkey, she thought. Uncle Doc had killed it and she had eaten it and Ward had died for it.

That night, in bed, she reached out for him for the first time, patting and stroking the empty space beside her, grabbing fistfuls of air to stuff in her mouth. At the funeral, she sat dry-eyed in the front pew, absolutely still. But inside she was screaming in anger and outrage and grief, screaming at that big, strong white God who was everywhere and knew every-thing and watched white men shoot colored men dead and did nothing at all. Why, she wanted to know. Why? Why? Why? But there was no one she could ask. The others sat around with their heads bowed like people caught in the rain who know there is nothing they can do but submit. Uncle Floyd had probably been shot dead by now, too, by some white man who didn't like the way he swung his arms when he walked. Uncle Floyd always had a wild walk. Inside her, she felt her grief turning and kicking like her baby, fretting for his dead father.

Three weeks later, Daddy came and took her home in the wagon to the extra room he had built just for her. Pa Peters and Miz Zophara stood in the yard to see her off. Pa Peters had his old army coat over his arm and Miz Zophara had a patch over her left eye. "I practicin," she said. "Gettin ready to bequeath." She took a small box out of her apron pocket. It had nothing in it but a wad of cotton. "In case," Miz Zophara said.

"In case what?" Rannee said.

"In case I pass 'fore she born."

Pa Peters held out the army coat. "You take it," he said to Rannee. "I ain't never gonna need it no more. You take it. Keep it for that there grandson."

He not gonna need it neither, Rannee thought. But she thanked him and kissed him. She would wear it for him.

She was back in Simms Quarter again, with an extra weight inside her now, anchoring her down for good. She had a room and a bed all to herself, but not for long. She had wanted a husband without a child. Instead, she would have a child with-out a husband.

The rest of the family left her alone. She was a married

woman now, a Peters, not a Simms, a guest in the house. Even Mama didn't tell her what to do. Mama didn't even tell her about babies. All Rannee knew was what she learned at the clinic in Flat Rock that had a white doctor and a special day, once a month, for the colored.

Sometimes Daddy took her in the wagon and sometimes she caught the mail truck at six in the morning, though the clinic didn't open till nine. Sometimes she had to wait all day to see the doctor. She didn't mind. She liked to read the magazines in the waiting room with the pictures of baby clothes and baby equipment—for *white* babies. But most interesting of all was a book with a picture of a white baby on the cover. It was by a *man* and it told white mothers how to treat their own babies. It was a fat book. It told them *everything:* how to nurse their babies and feed them and dress them and talk to them and play with them; it told when to pick them up and when to put them down. White babies ate meat every day and vegetables and fruit and cereal and bread, and slept in a bassinet. They had something called "natural childbirth," but white mothers had to have a "special obstetrician" to do it. White mothers had to worry about all kinds of accidents to their babies from cars and carriages and refrigerators and had to be very careful about toilet training, which seemed to be both difficult and dangerous. The book told white mothers how to punish their children and when, and what to say about it. Rannee thought of Mama saying, "Fetch that switch," and Grandma Sukey saying, "Is so." She couldn't imagine the women of Simms Quarter letting any strange man—black or white—tell them how to treat their own babies.

The doctor in the clinic didn't tell her anything—except to read the pamphlet in the waiting room. It explained about the vagina and the uterus and the fallopian tubes. It might have been describing the engine of a pickup truck. She read *What to Name the New Baby* instead.

She wore Pa Peters's old army coat buttoned up to her chin whenever she went to the clinic, right through April and May and June. Except for that trip, she stayed home. She was ashamed of being pregnant. Daddy brought her a used newspaper from the mill in Chawnee whenever he could. The rest of the time she sat waiting with clenched fists.

All the colored babies around Chawnee were born at home. Her child would begin as she had. She sat rocking like Mama. She was not allowed to eat anything wild—no rabbits or squirrels or possum or coons—just like Mama. "Why?" she said. She could, she realized, ask all the questions she liked now.

"Is so," Grandma Sukey said.

Rannee rocked hard to get through the days and the weeks and the months. "You stop that," Grandma Sukey said. "You churnin up that baby somethin awful. He gonna come out lumpy an yalla like peanut butter." Rannee went on rocking just the same. Sometimes Mama came and sat with her. She looked smaller now, and weaker, not like the big, strong woman who had guarded them all so vigorously with her switch and her "tea." If only, Rannee thought, Mama could shake the baby out of her as she had that chinaberry long ago.

"You gone again?" Rannee said.

Mama shook her head. "I vacant now," she said. "Completely unoccupied." She grinned. "I think maybe I ain't got no more babies lef inside me. I think they all out now, praise be the Lord."

"Amen," Rannee said. Lucky Mama. She had Rannee to take her place.

The pain came, trying to saw its way out. Instead of the doctor, Miss Martha Jane and Grandma Sukey and the aunts came, sitting around her silently, watching. "Is a nice lil boy chile," Rannee heard Miss Martha Jane say after two days of labor. Rannee was lying in a pool of blood and mess with a little naked baby against her hip, screaming and shaking, his tiny fists sticking up like horns. She had gone through her pregnancy with clenched hands and her son had come out fighting. She felt nothing at all, just tired. She would stay tired for the rest of her life. Mama had gone through this eleven times, she thought before falling asleep.

They made her go right on taking Mama's place, keeping her in bed and then in the house, just like Mama. They would not let her bathe or wash her hair which had gone all heavy and kinky with the straightening all grown out. It itched and smelled.

"No water on your hair for six months," Grandma Sukey said.

"Why?"

"Is so." Rannee had to use cleaning fluid instead.

But she refused to nurse her baby, remembering the women in church with bits of cotton over their naked breasts, remembering Mama's babies stuck to her like clamps. She fed him out of a vinegar bottle.

Miz Zophara came to see the baby, bringing two silver-hooped earrings for Rannee. "Like mine," she said. "From my Great-great-aunt Steller. Those hoops offa a slave chain."

Offa a loose-leaf note book, Rannee thought, thanking her.

Miz Zophara was looking at Rannee with her right eye and the baby with her left. He began to cry.

"Look just like my brother Rodney," Miz Zophara said. "Gone to New Orleans. He a big man, Rodney. A big shrimp man. Very big. Biggest shrimp man in the whole Delta. No one mess with Rodney. You gonna call that baby Rodney?"

"Name's Lance," Rannee said. It was a name she had found in the book in the clinic.

"Lance?" Miz Zophara said. "Who he?"

"My great-great-great-uncle," Rannee said. "From Natchez. Big crocodile man. Very big. Biggest crocodile man up and down the whole Mississippi."

The days settled heavily in her lap. There was nothing she had to do, not go to the field or scrub pots or do chores. She didn't have to do anything but take care of her baby. Sometimes she chaperoned her younger brothers and sisters when they went to a game. Mama was much softer with them now and Grandma Sukey never bothered with them at all. Rannee knew she had been born too soon. Watching them, she felt old, like Mama. Sitting alone on the porch in Mama's rocking chair, she saw what Mama saw: the dirt yard and the chinaberry tree and the woods, the scrubby, scruffy woods, circling the house like a worn fringe. Up above was Grandma Sukey's house and down below was Aunt Effie's, both with their rockers on their porches. In the middle was Mama, bolted down to that piece of wood. Rannee could feel the screws turning beneath her. One night she told Mama and Daddy that she wanted to go to Montgomery.

They were out on the back porch, Mama in her rocker, Daddy sitting on the steps, and Rannee leaning against the post. She looked down at them. They seemed smaller, thinner, paler, as if their flesh, their strength, even their color, had run out into all those children.

"What you wanna do in Montgomery, Shoo?" Daddy said.

Find Uncle Floyd, she thought. "Fine me a job," she said. "You lend me the fare?"

Daddy looked up at her. She wondered if he was thinking about that college in Jeffersonville. She might have been sitting in an office by now, wearing low-cut store shoes with a big blotter and a picture calendar on her desk, like Miss Kettle at the mill. But Daddy just nodded. "All right, Shoo," he said. "You wait till next month when I git the cotton in?"

"I wait," Rannee said.

"Where you gonna stay?" Mama said.

"You think Aunt Vee and Aunt Berthadell would take me?" They were Mama's sisters who wrote every Christmas.

"I think so," Mama said. She stopped rocking. "What about Lance?" she said. She was looking at Rannee the way she looked at the chinaberry tree in the pause between cleaning and cooking. She would have to go on looking at that tree a little longer, Rannee thought.

"You keep him for me, Mama?" she said.

Mama's chair did a little dip. "I keep him," she said.

# THE
# TOWN

# 8

She was in Montgomery at last, but not as she had planned, not with Uncle Floyd. He had passed through very quickly, Aunt Vee said, on his way north. And Rannee knew that he would never dare set foot in Montgomery again, not with the streets all tangled up and the white people everywhere, watching. They watched from car windows and bus windows and big shiny store windows. They even watched from special little booths set out on the sidewalk.

Aunt Vee and Aunt Berthadell lived in a house that was really just one big room divided by a partition. Aunt Berthadell had a husband but Aunt Vee just had a couch that turned into an extra cot at night, so Rannee slept with her. The kitchen and stove and dining table were all in Berthadell's half. There was an inside toilet and hot and cold running water and pleasant smiles all around.

Aunt Vee was a thin woman with very light skin and silver spectacles pushed up against her face. She put her arms around Rannee and said she was glad to see her. Aunt Berthadell was nice too, but much older, with thicker glasses and a peppermint smell which, Rannee learned, came from the Doublemint gum

95

she kept permanently lodged behind her back teeth. Her husband, Uncle Clyde, worked in an aluminum plant and always looked very clean and neat with shiny teeth and a tube of Pepsodent in his lunchbox every day.

Aunt Berthadell and Aunt Vee both worked at the Cloverleaf Café, Berthadell during the day and Vee at night. They had, Rannee realized, only one of everything—one room, one husband, one job, and, she suspected, one uniform—between them. They both worked in the kitchen. Night or day, only white people were allowed out front.

Rannee often went to the restaurant with Aunt Vee at night to help wash the glasses and the dishes and scour the pots. There was nothing else for her to do and no one to do it with. She knew she had cousins somewhere in town, near the railroad, but she didn't know exactly where or how to get there. She was afraid of the city.

The stores, with the white people watching, terrified her. She would walk down one side of the counter and there would be a white saleslady walking down the other, right opposite, staring at her. She remembered what Uncle Link had said about those white people in the army, watching, watching, watching. Once, admiring a display of ribbons, she had stroked one gently with a timid finger. Suddenly, a white woman was shouting at her. She was a big woman in a pink dress and shaped like a squashed berry. Her red hair was done up in metal curlers that looked like rolled-up sardine cans. "You wan that?" she had shouted. "You wan it? You mess with it like that, you gotta buy it." Rannee paid for it and left it on the counter.

She never touched anything in the stores again. Even when she was ready to buy, she merely pointed and said, "I'll have that one, please, ma'am." Often she had to wait while the shopkeeper served all the white people who had come in long after she did. She had learned to wait for white people in Mr. Junius's General Store back home, silently, patiently, for hours. But she hardly ever went to the stores. She had no money and she was still afraid of them, except for the candy store on the corner that had newspapers and magazines and a few paper-back books stacked up outside.

One morning, walking by when no one was around, she stopped and read the headline: MAYOR AXES TOP AIDE. She was horrified. She wondered if *he* would be executed or lynched or even sent to jail. She tried to read more but noticed the owner staring at her through the doorway. In another minute, Rannee thought, she would come rushing out shouting: "You wan it? You can't jus stan aroun like that readin it for free. You read it, you gotta buy it." Rannee fled.

She walked back and forth between the house and the Cloverleaf Café, listening to the music sifting through the screens, seeing the figures arranged in lighted windows or crouched in silhouettes on the porches, always in groups of two or three. She felt her loneliness beside her, thick enough to punch. At home she would lie on her bed with her shoes off and stare at the thin wiggly cracks in the ceiling, paint cracks, not like the ones back home, not deep enough to let the stars in.

She stared at the ceiling and thought of Simms Quarter and Lance, whom she had torn off like a loose button. He had Ward's big eyes and Ward's scared look, as if he knew what was waiting for him at the end of that dirt road. That was how she thought of Ward, in overalls and a big hat, walking away from her down a dusty road; not as she had last seen him, dressed in a black suit with a pointed handkerchief in his breast pocket and his hands, looking huge and helpless, flattened out against his thighs. She had leaned over and touched the tip of that white handkerchief briefly, not looking at his face. When she thought of him, he was still in his overalls with his big hat covering his eyes.

After two weeks, she got a job in the county hospital, working from seven to seven. She walked three miles, there and back, wearing a dark blue uniform and a worried look. She scrubbed toilets and made beds and carried trays and mopped floors. Sometimes, in the nurses' lounge or the white ladies' room, she found a magazine or a newspaper. Instead of throwing it away, she took it home and read it on the back porch or in bed or wherever she pleased. She didn't have to read in secret anymore. But there wasn't much to read in the magazines which were mostly just pictures of white women lying around—on beaches or beside pools or on long, low chairs—doing nothing except smoking or drinking or smiling or waiting for their skin to turn brown.

Once, she found a book called *A Tree Grows in Brooklyn*. She had no idea where Brooklyn was, though it seemed to be a big city up North. It was supposed to be about a poor family, but they didn't seem poor to her. They lived in a big building and wore store clothes and bought store food and slept in separate beds. She enjoyed reading about the little girl who didn't have to chop cotton or work the patches or clean the house or mind the little children. She could play in the street and listen to the bands; she had music and drawing in school and a desk all to herself; she could go to the library, a library with lots and lots of books, whenever she wanted; and she even had a lady who came to her house and gave her piano lessons! She got wonderful Christmas presents including *ten* real new pennies! Maybe, Rannee thought, they were poor for white people.

The hospital was full of poor old colored women crammed into beds along the walls and in the corridors and even on the staircase landing, right under the EXIT sign. They were all either very fat or very thin with various parts missing. But old age had settled like dust on them all, obscuring the differences. They were all called "Granny."

The white nurses sat at one end of the ward, drinking coffee and keeping their uniforms clean. Dr. Sargent came occasionally, in the morning, a tall white man in a white coat, his cheeks glistening with lotion. He walked with his head forward, spying out the sick, a man marching through enemy territory. The head nurse stayed beside him, taking down the "orders," while the students formed a bodyguard behind him. He stopped at the foot of each bed and read the chart aloud in a stern, accusing voice. "Louisa Wilmington Warfield, aged eighty-two, carcinoma of the lower intestine, fifth day postoperative."

"Guilty as charged," a student whispered.

"How you feelin this mornin, Granny?" Dr. Sargent said.

Mrs. Louisa Wilmington Warfield opened her eyes. "Turble, doctor." She was a huge mound of a woman with skin so dry Rannee thought she could hear the tears dropping on her cheeks. She was delirious most of the time, screaming for them to take her baby quickly. She had had twelve children with the pain like a jackknife opening inside her but this time was the worst. "You take it now, please, doctor," she said. "The pain crawlin an shovin an squeezin me somethin fierce." She paused to moan and Rannee saw the sweat on her face. "Whoever in there wantin to git out somethin wicked. You take it now, quick please, yes, doctor?"

"You doin jes fine, Granny," Dr. Sargent said.

"Then you give me some pills for the pain, yes, please doctor? Some pills for the pain, please doctor."

"Let's have a quick look at that incision," Dr. Sargent said. He moved to the side of the bed and pulled back the covers, yanking up the hospital gown and exposing Mrs. Louisa War-field, a dusty pile except for the white bandage across her middle where, as Dr. Sargent put it, he had "gone in." Standing well away, he stretched out an arm like a man unscrewing a radiator cap and pulled off the bandage. "As you can see," he told the students, "we had to go in here so as to avoid what might possibly have been an even nastier . . ." He was peering into the wound with raised eyebrows. "Mmmm," he said, nodding at his handiwork. "Coming along nicely, very nicely. Notice how the edges are beginning to . . ."

"Beautiful, doctor," the nurse said. "Such a small, clean, *dainty* incision."

The students murmured.

"It's tricky, of course," Dr. Sargent said. "Takes years of practice. Even now, I need to do at least three or four a week. To keep my hand in, so to speak." He smiled, a small puckered-up smile like an old scar. "And, of course, the important thing in a case like this," he turned to the students, "is to be sure . . ."

"Doctor," Mrs. Warfield's voice came feebly from the other side of the mound. "You give me a pill. For the pain. Yes please, doctor?"

"You doin jes fine, Granny," the doctor said again. "And you're in excellent hands. Remember that. You leave everything to Miss Skinner and me." He smiled at the nurse and turned to the students. "Terminal case," he told them. "Notice the texture of the skin . . . the respiration, the discoloration . . . the dilation. . . . In advanced cases like this, of course . . . ," he turned and began to walk away, followed by Miss Skinner and the students, with Mrs. Warfield's voice far behind. She lay with her hospital gown around her neck and her remaining parts exposed, including that huge hole where Dr. Sargent had gone in and come out, not bothering to cover it up. Rannee pulled the blankets up around Mrs. Warfield's hips but dared not cover Dr. Sargent's handiwork. She wondered if he had ever looked at Mrs. Warfield above or below that spot.

Later that day, Mrs. Warfield began a steady scream that kept up all afternoon, begging the doctor to take this, her thirteenth child, hacking its way out with a skewer. She was still screaming when Rannee went home.

The next morning she was told to scrub down Granny's bed. Mrs. Warfield was no longer in it. But that afternoon, the empty bed was filled by another musty old colored woman called Granny who crackled when she moved: another patient of Dr. Sargent's getting ready to be sent upstairs. As if, Rannee thought, they had a special place where they kept old colored women to be dried out before they brought them to be cut open by Dr. Sargent, a tidy man who liked to keep his hand in.

Rannee had been in Montgomery for two months when she met Jarvis Lyle. He was a city man, tall and slim with a square little mustache stuck neatly up under his nose. He wore a plaid suit and a white hat and shoes that looked almost red under their high polish. He worked with Uncle Clyde in a big aluminum plant where they made important things like pipes and gutters to be shipped all over the world. He came to the house several times to see Uncle Clyde but Rannee was always out. "He really come to see you, Niece," Uncle Clyde said. There was no phone in the house so Jarvis kept coming.

Once, turning the corner on her way home, Rannee saw him leave. He was hurrying down the street toward her, glancing at an enormous gold watch in his palm. There seemed to be little glints of gold coming from all over him: his shirt, his lapel, his wrist, his fingers. He even had a long gold chain hanging out of his pants pocket. She blinked.

"Who that just lef here?" she asked Aunt Vee.

"That Jarvis."

"*That* Jarvis?"

"Uh huh. Come lookin for you again, I spoze, an missin you again."

But Rannee was sure that someday he would come when she was home. Sooner or later, that enormous watch would tell him the right time.

When they finally met, she was ready. Aunt Vee gave her a dab of cologne to pat behind her ears and Aunt Berthadell gave her a stick of Doublemint gum to tuck behind her teeth. She sat on the porch in her new nylons trying to remember not to cross her legs for fear of ripping them. Ward, she thought, had never seen her in nylons.

Jarvis was both a talker and a doer. She had never met anyone like him before. He could talk high and he could talk low and he knew his way all over town: which bus went where and when. He took her to little downtown cafés full of colored people, with colored lights and music and smoke. He bought her things to drink and showed her how to dance a new way that made her legs turn to treacle right out in public. He took her to the movies for the first time in her life, movies where colored people were allowed to go. It was a small, smelly wooden building way downtown, stuffed in between two garages with urine marks all over the outside and huge pictures peeling off the walls. Inside, it was hot and crowded and smelled like Daddy's work shoes. But she forgot everything when the lights went out and huge people began to move across the wall, talking and singing and dancing and kissing. She was hardly aware of Jarvis's arm around her, slipping lower and lower off her shoulder. Sometimes they just walked—all over town, holding hands, stopping now and then to buy ice cream or sodas or pausing at fish fries. They would stroll along eating fish sandwiches and end up holding hands again, their palms glued together with grease. Sometimes they sat in the park on the grass, soft and thick like one of Mama's quilts doubled over; or on the swings, and he would point out the moon as if he had just switched it on, just for her. It did look special, hanging between the buildings, fat as Jarvis's pocket watch.

She liked being with him, but she was glad he had no car and no place to take her where they could be alone. He lived with his parents and she lived with her aunts so they had to remain vertical. For a while, he went on just holding her hand and kissing her and, occasionally, in the park or at the movies, checked her over as if to make sure her parts were all there and all in the right place. "You a mighty sweet dish, Doll," he said.

That was more than enough for Rannee. "I got one chile on my head already," she told him, showing him Lance's picture. It was a tiny snapshot which she kept on the corner of Aunt Vee's bureau, a little piece of Simms Quarter sneaked into Montgomery. Only Lance's head showed, with his enormous eyes and his scared little mouth and his tiny ears pressed flat against his head as if he'd rather not hear what went on around him. After the first week, she turned it to the wall. One look at it, she realized, could send her halfway to the bus station before she knew it. She had been home several times, but it took all day and all her money.

"That's a real sweet chile, Doll," Jarvis said, holding the tiny picture in his huge palm.

"Yes," Rannee said. "An *only* chile. He like it that way. He ain't plannin to have no brothers or sisters."

"You make a real sweet baby, Doll," Jarvis said, still staring at the picture.

"Maybe so," Rannee said. "But I ain't makin no more." She was sending almost all her wages home to Mama for food and clothes for Lance. "You place your orders somewhere else," she said. "Cause I retired. Permanently."

"That's a real, downright, honest-to-God shame," Jarvis said, handing back the picture. He smiled, showing the glint in his teeth.

She was glad he wasn't angry. It was wonderful to have someone to go out with at last. Without him, there would be no one. The other colored employees at the hospital were all old women with sore gums and sore feet. She was grateful for Jarvis. He even took her to church, smelling good and dressed in checks and stripes, bright and shiny as oilcloth.

One Sunday, after church, he took her home for dinner to a small, immaculate house full of furniture and paper flowers. Papa Lyle was a short man with an enormous paper poppy in his buttonhole. He ran a small trucking business and whenever Jarvis's voice rose excitedly, he would pump an imaginary footbrake and murmur, "Slow down, son. Slow down." His wife, Florrie, was a respectable, ladylike person with fragile ankles that turned in slightly, and was so kind that the flies in her house grew fat. Jarvis towered above them. They seemed slightly in awe of him, as if they were still not quite used to his size, like something they had acquired knocked-down and had only just finished putting together. Jarvis's head hit the light fixtures and his legs, stretched out under the table, went halfway through the door. "I too big for that ole house," he told Rannee later. "That there a *boy's* house. I needin a *man's* house. With my own woman in it. Now. Away from here. I ready to move out tomorrow."

He began to talk of getting married more and more. He talked marriage up and down the avenues and in and out of side streets and across squares and circles until Rannee felt it coming at her from all directions, scaring her, as if she were forever crossing against the lights. She tried not to listen. She knew she did not love Jarvis any more than she had loved Ward. But walking at night, holding Jarvis's hand, she remembered the nights when she had been all alone, so lonely she had held her own hands for company.

"You like him?" Mama said on one of Rannee's trips home. They were sitting at the kitchen table, on the benches with no backs. Mama was much thinner, a shrunken little old lady. It was hard to believe that eleven people had come out of her.

"Is a very pleasant man," Rannee said. "Very patient and considerate and polite."

"He want to marry you?"

"Yes."

"An you?"

Rannee looked at Mama and then around her. She could hear the children in the yard and on the porch and in the back room. On the floor beside her, Rosaleen, Mama's last baby, was filling the pot. Rannee felt Lance under the table, pulling her shoe laces. "No," she said. "Don't wanna marry no one. Never again." She heaved Lance into her lap.

"No more babies?"

"Specially no more babies." Mama, she thought, had provided enough for three generations. Rannee could sit the next one out. Lance was standing on her lap, sticking his fingers into her nose and eyes and mouth. When she left to go home, he was down on the floor again, hugging her ankles.

She sat in the park with Jarvis, near the playground, where the swings hung like shadows and a brand-new moon was ready to take off from the Montgomery Savings and Loan. Jarvis put his arms around her. Tonight, she realized, he was tired of merely checking her over. Tonight he was looking for a way in. She got up and sat on a swing.

He laughed good-naturedly. "Wan a push, Doll?" he said. He stood behind her and began to push, very gently, then harder and harder, swinging her away from him and back again, higher and higher, out and back. She felt his huge warm hands on her shoulders and waist and back and rump, moving up and down, leaving his mark all over her. She stopped pumping. He stopped pushing. They sat in the dark under a clump of trees with their fingers intertwined, resting on Jarvis's leg. She stared at the moon, curved like a rocker, while Jarvis moved her hand slowly up and down the inside of his thigh. Finally, he stood up and, with their hands still locked, led her back into the trees. She went, feeling that she could no more stop this than she could have stopped Mama's raised switch or that swing once Jarvis began to push. She lay perfectly still while Jarvis's big sure hands stroked her and petted her and arranged her to suit his needs.

They were married at the county seat with Aunt Vee and a maintenance man as witnesses. The maintenance man was hard of hearing and made them say everything twice. After the ceremony, Jarvis took Rannee and Aunt Vee to the Chicken Shack for supper. Then Aunt Vee went back to the night shift at the Cloverleaf Café and Rannee and Jarvis went to their new home on the other side of town, a one-room attic apartment right above his parents. The next day Rannee went back to Simms Quarter and got Lance.

# 9

Her second child was born on an examining table in the emergency room of the county hospital while Jarvis and Aunt Vee wandered up and down the halls looking for a doctor. Rannee was there for five hours. By the time someone came, the baby had arrived. She named him Jarvis but called him Flash because, she said, he would not wait, even to be born. They took him away and left her on that hard examining table covered with blood and sweat. After a while, she got up and dressed herself. The nurse came back with the baby wrapped in a towel. Jarvis drove them all home in Papa Lyle's dump truck.

Home was still only one room and now there were three other people in it. There was no stove and she had to go downstairs to her mother-in-law's to cook. But it was the first time in her life she had ever had her own front door. It had a nice yard out front and a big fenced-in porch right outside her kitchen window. She could hang her wash out there and put Flash out there in his "baskinette," a laundry basket lined with quilts. Lance played close to her legs and the baby waved his fat feet and the sun splashed all over the floor. Jarvis kissed her very carefully when he left in the morning and his voice rose two flights to meet her in the evening. "You all right, Doll?" he would shout from the bottom of the stairs. "You still right there in my house where you belongs, huh, Doll?"

"I right here, Jarvis," she would tell him. "Right where I belongs."

"That's good, Doll. That's real good. That's the way it's gotta be always, see? You right here in my house. Always." He bent low over his new son and swung Lance to his shoulders and kissed seven-eighths of his wife's exposed surface.

She planted morning glories in the window boxes and laid linoleum under the kitchen table and smiled at Jarvis's pants filled by the wind and kicking like an odd pair of legs on the line.

She began to sing while she worked. At Simms Quarter, she had sung softly to herself, unless she was with Uncle Floyd. At the Peters's, with Miz Zophara around, she had, like Mama, kept the tunes closed up inside her mouth. But now she sang often when she was alone, loud and strong, up and down and around corners. She sang hymns—"Only Believe" and "Lead Me to the Rock" and "Watchman, How Long?"—and "My Country Tears of Thee," but she didn't know many words to that.

Sometimes Jarvis's mother, Florrie, came to visit, bringing a pie or a freshly knitted sweater for the baby and a toy for Lance. All her other children, she said, had left long ago to work for the public: a sanitation engineer in Atlanta, a bus driver in Milwaukee, and a restroom attendant in New York. Only Jarvis was still home, working for himself.

"For that aluminum company," Rannee said.

Which was funny, Florrie went on, because Jarvis wasn't really her child at all. She had found him one Sunday morning outside her front door with one foot on the curb and the other in the gutter. He followed her to church—on the opposite side of the street—and waited in the graveyard till she came out. Then he followed her home again, matching her footsteps from across the street, the hot, sunny side.

At home, he stood in front of her house with one foot in the gutter and the sweat pouring off his face and his eyes big and soft as gum drops.

"You hungry?" she had said.

He nodded.

She opened the door and took him in.

"Musta been 'most twelve by then," she said, "but his head hardly reach halfway up the ketchup bottle and his fork drown-in in syrup, eating hoecakes by the barrel. A real sweet chile. Always was a real sweet chile. I use to tie the house key roun his neck in the mornin and when I come home at night—I workin regular at Mrs. Starbury's then—there he'd be, not out in the streets like the others, but sittin quietly by hisself in that locked-up house in the dark. Said he didn't want no one to know he was home. Wasn't even scared of the dark."

"Seem like maybe he scared of somethin else," Rannee said.

"Didn't never complain," Florrie went on. "Jes set there on that bottom step in the dark with his finger stuck through the keyhole." She smiled and reached up to pat Rannee's cheek. "You should be real happy, chile," she said. "You got yourself a real sweet man."

"I knows that," Rannee said. "An I is. I is."

One Sunday they all piled into Papa Lyle's dump truck and went to visit Uncle Clyde and Aunt Berthadell and Aunt Vee. But when they got there, there was just Uncle Clyde and Aunt Vee sitting on the porch, drinking Dr. Peppers. Aunt Vee jumped up when she saw them, waving her soda bottle, and ran to meet them in her house slippers. She kissed them all, spilling Dr. Pepper all over them, and praised the baby who, she said, looked just like his Uncle Clyde around the gums. Everyone laughed and Uncle Clyde flashed his big white teeth and grinned.

"Where Berthadell at?" Rannee said.

"You all didn't git my letter?" Aunt Vee said.

"What letter?"

"That letter, 'bout Berthadell."

"We never got no letter," Rannee said.

"*That's* why you never come to see her fore she pass. Or the funeral. A real nice funeral. Everybody there. All the peoples from the church and all the peoples from the Cloverleaf Café— both shifts." She began to cry. "Reverend say Berthadell cookin for the angels now. Which, praise God, she be. Amen. Amen." She wiped her eyes with two fingers and took a swig of Dr. Pepper.

"That letter never reach," Rannee said.

"You all come on in now," Aunt Vee said, taking Rannee's hand. Rannee saw the wedding ring on Aunt Vee's finger. "Congratulations," she said, pressing Aunt Vee's hand.

But riding home, Rannee felt sorry for Aunt Vee, who had never had anything of her own. Even her husband had been shared. She imagined Uncle Clyde slipping the ring off Berthadell's dead finger and giving it to Aunt Vee.

One day, Jarvis came home in the middle of the afternoon. He rushed up the stairs and into the apartment with his mustache jumping around under his nose and shouted to her to get out on the porch.

"What for?"

"Jes do like I say, Doll. Please. Git out on that porch."

"What I wanna git out there for? With all that wet laundry hangin down."

"Police comin, dammit," Jarvis said. "Tha's why. Now *git*."

She grabbed the baby and Lance and ran. By then she could hear feet pounding up the stairs. A policeman came out on the porch and looked around. He never saw them. They were down behind the sheets. But they found Jarvis and took him away.

Later, Uncle Clyde came and told her what had happened.

Hewett, the new foreman at the aluminum plant, was the new manager's brother-in-law. He was a tight-faced white man with sharp little eyes set for trouble. "Watchin us all the time," Uncle Clyde said. "Keep comin through the shop all the time, with those lil eyes watchin. Even in the lunch break. Lookin to see are we cleanin up the crumbs and back at work when the whistle blow. Resta the time, he settin in his office, watchin us through that winder."

Jarvis hated him. "Seem like everytime Hewett comin through," Uncle Clyde said, "Jarvis doin somethin else: going to the latrine or comin from the latrine, or blowin his nose. 'You ever do any work, boy?' Hewett say."

One day, when Hewett appeared, Jarvis had turned off his machine and was standing beside it, examining the parts. "Machine not workin right, sir," Jarvis said before Hewett could open his mouth.

"Then fix it, boy," Hewett said. "An fix it quick."

The next time Jarvis heard Hewett coming, he stopped his machine, turned off the power, and bent to tie his shoelace.

Hewett looked at him and looked at the machine. "You fix that machine like I tole you?" he said.

"I fix it, Mr. Hewett, sir," Jarvis said.

"Then how come you ain't runnin it."

"Jes stop it for a minute while I . . ."

Hewett pulled the lever but nothing happened. "Then how come it don't work?" he said.

Jarvis stood up slowly. "Got to throw the power switch first, Mr. Hewett, sir," he said.

The men snickered.

The next day, during lunch break, Hewett stopped in front of Jarvis. "What that there thing you got pasted up under your nose, boy?" he said.

"A mustache, Mr. Hewett. Sir."

"What you wanna wear it up there for?" Hewett said. The men watched and listened.

"Keep the bad smells out, Mr. Hewett. Sir," Jarvis said and went on chewing. Someone laughed.

Hewett went red in the face. "Zat so? Then how come I never seen none on no nigger before?" he said. "How come I only seen them on white men?"

"I dunno, Mr. Hewett," Jarvis said. "Maybe they needin it more. Bein roun white men all the time."

There was a long silence.

Hewett folded his arms across his chest and stared at Jarvis. "That's funny," he said slowly. "That's mighty funny. Only it ain't the real reason. I know cause I been studyin it real good ever since I seen you. Cause when I observe a nigger sashayin around with sump'n I know to be sclusively for white men, I get curious. I wanna know how come. An you know what I found out? I found out that when a nigger goes around with one of them there fancy hairpieces up under his nose like a white man, it mean only one thing. It mean he's some white man's fuckin bastard. Yessir. That's exactly what it mean. Long as you paradin around with that there thing on your face, you just advertisin that fact to the whole world. Bet your wife know that. Bet she's doin just like your mammy right now." He smiled.

Jarvis got to his feet. He was panting and rocking slightly with his fists clenched.

"So, I gonna do you a favor," Hewett went on. "Snotty uppity sonuvabitch nigger that you is. I gonna do you a favor anyway. A real act a mercy. I gonna take that there lil tell-tale thing right offa your face for you. Right now." He pulled a razor out of his pocket. But Jarvis grabbed his arm and bent it back behind him. By the time the men got to him, Hewett's arm was broken.

They sent Jarvis to jail for six months. Rannee was five months pregnant.

She left the children with Florrie and took a job cleaning house for a white lady named Mrs. Lauramae Starbury. Jarvis's mother had cleaned for Mrs. Starbury's mother. The Starburys were an old family. They had inherited almost everything.

Mrs. Starbury lived in a big white house with a long strip of driveway curling around it and big white pillars outside. There were lots of pictures of Mrs. Starbury inside and lots of mirrors in all shapes and sizes with Mrs. Starbury's face sliding around the edges. Mrs. Starbury gave Rannee instructions and advice and thirty-five cents an hour. She was a short woman under a whirl of blond hair who had terminated her only pregnancy by douching herself with vinegar and driving her car up a dry creek bed. "I'm too delicate," she told Rannee. "I knew it before I ever started. I told Malcolm. You want babies, honey, I said, you shoulda married Ella Jean Maytag. She just *made* for carryin babies. Shaped like a laundry bag. But Malcolm's *so* stubborn. An so *sweet*. Always givin me presents like this lil ole jade lavaliere with my picture inside to cheer me up. Though nothin in this whole world could ever console me for bein a barren woman an carryin this empty womb around all my life."

Rannee thought how lucky Mrs. Starbury was.

Mrs. Starbury didn't seem to do much with her time besides talk on the phone and admire her empty womb in a big three-way mirror. Rannee did everything else. She scrubbed the floors and the windows and the walls and the front and back steps and the front and back walk. Mrs. Starbury believed firmly in *manual* labor. "That means hands, not mops," she said. Rannee did the laundry and the cooking and washed the dishes and tended the garden. Every other week she had to include extra jobs: polishing the silver, cleaning the basement, scrubbing the cupboards, shining the shoes, mending rips, and washing combs and brushes. She was grateful that Mrs. Starbury was so barren. Sometimes Mrs. Starbury was grateful too—or just feeling good because of a new stole or an invitation in the mail. Then she might give Rannee a little something special: a cracked decanter or an extra thirty-five cents. Once, she gave her a peach satin maternity gown. "You'll get lots of wear out of it," she said. "A big healthy girl like you." She sighed. "I never got to wear it at all."

"Thank you, ma'am," Rannee said and sent it back to Mama to be cut up for quilts. She never told Jarvis she was working.

One morning, hurrying to work, she noticed the FOR RENT sign on the house across the street. It was one-half of a two-family house, the half nobody wanted. It had been empty for a long time. The porch leaned over toward the empty lot next door and the steps tumbled down into the yard.

That evening, she went to have a look at it. The rooms were

full of dust and cobwebs and the paint lay in huge chunks on the floor, as if the former occupants had been yanked out bodily and had clung, in desperation, to the walls. The rent was twenty-five dollars a month, but she could, she was told, clean it up for nothing.

"Long as you're improving the property," Mr. Butts, the landlord, said, "you can work on it absolutely free." He was a bulky white man with flecks of powder on his cheeks and very wide hips. People said it was from all the money in his pockets which he carried in two wallets, one on each side, for balance, like a mule. He owned most of the real estate in the colored part of town. He lived in a trailer, people said, and made his wife drive around all night, while he kept an eye on his property. "I won't charge you rent till you're all moved in," he said.

Rannee worked days cleaning for Mrs. Starbury and nights cleaning for Mr. Butts. Her arms and back ached and the skin peeled off her hands and knees and bending over so much made her nauseous. She was turning a useless dump into an attractive apartment for Mr. Butts for nothing, so attractive he could even raise the rent.

The house had two bedrooms and a little fenced-in yard. Papa Lyle came on Sundays to help put up the doors and lay down the floors and paint the ceilings. Mr. Hickey, the junk man from the next block, came, a small white man with dusty hair and a dusty black suit, as if he'd been stored with his merchandise. "I can fill your whole house for fifty dollars. Guaranteed. And buy it all back whenever you're ready to dispose." He smiled benevolently at Rannee. The furniture was broken and unpainted and missing parts. "Sounds more like charity than business, don't it? You think I'm a little crazy, huh? Well, maybe you're right. But the way I look at it, that *is* my business. Taking the stuff off of hands that don't want it and getting it into hands that do. *That's* my business. Nice and friendly and cozy. Course there isn't much profit in it. But I don't mind. Long as it's cozy."

"Thank you, Mr. Hickey," Rannee said, looking at the three-legged table and the broken springs in the armchair. "You a real natural-born Robin Hood."

"White or colored," Mr. Hickey went on. "Don't make no difference to me. We're all cut to the same basic pattern, disrespectful of color. That's what I always say and that's what I tell the competition. We all got the same basic equipment and we all need the same basic furnishings. You ever hear different, let me know."

"I will, Mr. Hickey," Rannee said, counting out the bills. They smelled of coffee from being in that old Maxwell House can so long. "I certainly will."

She got some dishes and pots from Florrie and an old stained sheet and two torn blankets from Mrs. Starbury. "My, my," Mrs. Starbury said, observing Rannee's bulge and her own full-length profile in the mirror. "Aren't you the lucky one? Another lil colored stranger in your house. And so soon!" She turned to view her stomach from the left.

The couple in the other half of Rannee's house, 126B, were young. Rannee thought of them as a couple, though the man was there only on weekends. The rest of the time, the woman was alone. She kept the shades of her house down all the time, but occasionally Rannee saw her in the backyard in very short shorts and a halter, drinking Southern Comfort from a cup and doing her toenails or her fingernails or plucking her eyebrows or straightening her hair. She was always doing something to herself. Sometimes, Rannee heard loud music coming from her living room and often, on weekends, she saw the man in shorts and nothing on top at all, smoking and drinking in the yard. After a while, she realized that it wasn't the same man but many different men. But none of them seemed to interest the woman as much as her little fingernail or her left eyebrow.

Rannee's third child was born in a hospital delivery room and arrived before the doctor. The baby lay against her ribs, a tiny bit of flesh like an odd thumb wrapped up in a blanket. His lower lip stuck out as if he were always about to cry. She named him Reed, after her father, and tried to imagine him in a jaunty little hat, saying, "Beg your pardner," and smiling and bowing. She rubbed the baby's lip with her finger but the pout remained.

When he was a month old, she left the other children with Florrie and took the baby to see Jarvis on the other side of the state. She sat with the baby in her arms and stared out the window at the world she had given him: at the broken-down towns that looked as if they had collapsed all of a sudden on their way to becoming big cities, strewing odd parts around the landscape; at the dust and the clay and the fields and the small slack-jawed cabins with little colored children spilling out into the dirt. The whole state, she thought, was full of Simms Quarters.

The prison was an ugly square building harnessed up to an enormous quarry where black men with chained ankles swayed under their picks and shovels while white men with guns stood and watched them. Inside, everything was gray too, walls and furniture and men, as if it had all been dunked in gravel. Even Jarvis didn't glitter any more. They had shaved off his mustache and clipped his hair and taken away his ring and his watch and his tie pin. Even his teeth didn't glitter, as if they'd taken away his fillings too. Or was it simply that he didn't smile any more?

"What you got in that bundle, Doll?"

"A present for you, Jarvis."

He leaned over and lifted the blanket and stared into his son's face. "My, my," he said. "Is a real sweet chile. I always said you made a real sweet chile, Doll."

"*We* made him, Jarvis," she said.

"You see *me* there, Doll?"

"I see you, Jarvis."

"Where? Where you see me, Doll? Ain't hardly nothin there but some hair and a blanket. You think he resemble me, Doll?"

"He resemble you, Jarvis. He resemble you in that great big lip." She began to laugh. "He got the biggest lip I ever seen on a baby. I think he fixin to grow a mustache like his daddy."

Jarvis put his arms around her and the baby and kissed her very gently, a long melancholy restrained kiss as if he were being especially careful not to take too much.

"How you, Doll?"

"I fine, Jarvis. How you?"

"You miss me, Doll?"

"I miss you, Jarvis."

"I be home soon, Doll." He smiled and she saw the glitter in his mouth again. But what she mostly remembered was the dust, like gray, in his hair.

# 10

A week before Jarvis got out of jail, Rannee moved into the new house. The day before he came home, she told Mrs. Starbury she was leaving.

"What do you mean, *leavin?*" Mrs. Starbury said. "Nobody *leaves* here. You damn well wait till you're fired like everyone else."

"Then go ahead an fire me," Rannee said. "Cause I leavin. My husbin don't want me workin no more."

"Your *husband?* What in the world has *he* got to do with it?"

"He my husbin."

"How much he payin you to stay home and work for him?"

"Like I said, Mrs. Starbury. He my husbin."

Mrs. Starbury glared and breathed and strode out of the kitchen. Rannee could hear her phoning in the living room, calling the Busy Bee Employment Agency to get Rannee blacklisted forever. "Completely unreliable," Mrs. Starbury said. "I thought you ought to know. God knows what she's stolen. I don't keep inventory. But you can take my word for it, you keep sending her out on jobs, I promise you, you'll never get another customer, not in *this* state. I've warned all my friends already."

She paused. "Course I don't know her *last* name. I don't even know if she's got one. With a first name like hers, she doesn't need one."

Rannee went home and tried not to think bout money. Jarvis would be back tomorrow and Jarvis wanted her home. "You be there when I gits home," he had written. "I wants you *there*, right *there*, waitin on me." He always did. He never wanted to come back to an empty house again.

He came back to a house full of family, *his* family, and, for the first time in his life, to a place that was really his. For the first time, they did not have to share a kitchen or a bathroom, carrying a dish or a piece of soap down the hall. When Jarvis saw his new home, his mouth wobbled. "You do this, Doll?" he said. "How you do it? How?" He grinned and opened his arms as if he wanted to put them around his house. "Is beautiful, Doll," he said, putting them around her instead. "Beautiful. Like you."

He had trouble finding a job. The old firm refused to take him back and it seemed as if no other place would hire him either. He came home walking slowly, awkwardly, as if his ankles were chained together again.

One night, he rushed into the kitchen, swung her off her feet, and gave her a kiss that seemed to go right through her and on out into the middle of the next block.

"What happen?" she said when he finally put her down.

"*It* happen."

"You got a job?"

"I got a job. And, baby, what a job!" He was working in a bottling plant, nice and clean and easy.

He began to grin and gleam again. Even his mustache, she noticed, was growing back. For a moment, all she wanted to do was smile too. "How come you got that job?" she said finally. "They know you been in jail?"

"No, Doll. This time I didn't tell." He kissed her and grinned again. But she did not smile back.

Ten days later he was fired.

118

"They foun out?" she said.

"They foun out."

"How come they foun out?"

"I dunno," Jarvis said. "I jes don' know."

He went out early every morning as before and came home late every evening, moving like the men in the quarry. She should go to work again, she thought, though she knew Jarvis would never allow it. And then she remembered Mrs. Starbury and the Busy Bee Employment Agency. She would never be able to get a job in this town either. They should move, she thought, looking at the freshly painted walls and the shiny floors and the curtains she had made, inch by inch, on Mrs. Starbury's old sewing machine in the odd moments when Mrs. Starbury wasn't there. She had smuggled them in, piece by piece, in a family-sized Kotex box and out in a huge old Gladstone bag. Old clothes, she told Mrs. Starbury, for her brother-in-law who was being dried out in the county hospital. Mrs. Starbury, she knew, loved to hear about shiftless, no-good niggers.

"So many?" Mrs. Starbury said, staring at the enormous, bulging bag.

"He in for life," Rannee said.

The curtains hung gracefully, stiffened by lies, and Rannee knew she could never go through all that again. Besides, she would never find a place they could afford as nice as this, with Florrie right across the street. So she said nothing and prayed that Jarvis would find something soon.

But he came home night after night with his walk reduced to a shuffle. He ate in silence, his head close to his plate, wolfing his food as if a bell might ring at any minute to march him back to his cell. After supper, he sat with his chin on his chest and stared at an empty wall socket.

"Ain't never gonna find a job in this town," he said one night. "I seen Clyde today. He say Hewett braggin all over the plant. Say he fix it so I never gonna work in this town agin. Fuckin bastard. I shoulda broke *both* his arms."

Rannee stared. She had never heard him talk like that before. "What we gonna do?" she said.

"You never mine," he said. "You jes leaves it all to me. You jes leaves everythin to me."

"What *you* gonna do?"

"Ain't no one ever tole you not to be askin so many questions? I tire answerin all them questions." Rannee felt she was back in Simms Quarter again.

The next night, after supper, he announced that he was going out. He had never done that before. Rannee looked up but said nothing. Later, she realized that she should have done something about that night, should have nailed it to the wall to keep it from spreading. For after that, Jarvis went out almost every night. He would sit in the armchair after supper, jerking his knees and snapping his fingers and wiggling his mustache as if he had to keep moving somehow. In the end, he almost always got up and went out.

He began to change, quickly, drastically, as if he'd been spun around in one of those revolving doors and had come out headed in the wrong direction. She never knew where he went or what he did. He still got up early and left the house early as if he still had a job to go to. But when he came home, he was angry. The smiles and the kisses disappeared. Even his appearance changed. His neat, well-behaved little mustache seemed to have shifted to one side from his constant shouting. She sniffed for the liquor on his breath but all she could smell was rage. She began to dread his step in the hall.

"You call this mash potater?" he said one night, holding up a forkful. "Taste jes like boil cotton. You never hear of no salt or pepper?"

"There plenty a salt an pepper in there," Rannee said. "An bacon fat. Jes like always."

"You shut your mouf," he yelled. "Ain't nothin but lies comin outa your mouf." She stared at him. His face looked all stiff, as if he were afraid the features would fall off. Maybe he needed some of Mama's "tea." Maybe he had caught something in town, some sickness from some mean person.

But the sickness got worse. He shouted that the rice was burned and the bread stale and the gravy thin. Rannee stared at her knuckles and the babies cried and Lance covered both ears with his fists. One night, Jarvis took his plate and dumped it out of the window. Rannee saw salt pork and beans lying in the bushes the next morning. He got worse and worse. Soon there was cooked food in the yard almost every day. He went out earlier and stayed out later.

One night, he came racing into the kitchen with his tie and his mustache dangling and a great big grin way over on one side of his face, and stuck a handful of bills down her dress.

"What happen?"

"Been celebratin."

"Look like it. Celebratin what?"

"Now, Doll, what would I be celebratin?"

"You got a job?"

He lifted her up and swung her around and kissed her in five different places. "Yes, ma'am," he said, laughing and slapping his thighs. "I got me a job."

"What kinda job?"

"A junior assistant deputy foreman, Doll. Yessir. That's me. A junior assistant deputy foreman."

"What you do?"

"I assists, Doll. I assists."

"*Who* you assists?"

"I *tole* you. I the junior assistant deputy foreman. I assists the assistant deputy foreman. Whatsa matta with you, Doll? You dumb or sump'n?"

But the next night he was restless again and went out without finishing his supper.

"What this here deputy foreman?" Rannee asked him one night. "What you do exactly?"

He groaned. "My God, woman, bad enough I gotta *do* it all day. I ain't gonna talk about it too. Besides, it'd take till Tuesday to esplain. You got sump'n for this here junior assistant deputy foreman to eat?"

He became very strange about money. Some nights he

stuffed it in fistfuls down her bosom. Some nights he gave her very little. One night he handed her five dollars.

"That all?" she said.

"Tha's all."

"For the whole week?"

"For the whole entire week. An tha's borrowed."

"How I gonna buy food for five peoples for a whole entire week with that?"

"Tha's your problem. Ain't no more so shut your face." He threw himself down on the bed. "Jes you stop your hackin and shut your face."

"What ailin Jarvis?" Florrie said. "I hear him shoutin an fussin all the way over to my house."

"I dunno," Rannee said. "He angry an wroth all the time now. Seems like I can't do nothin right."

"Used to be such a mighty sweet chile," Florrie said, shaking her head. "He drinkin?"

"I don't think so. Never smells of nothin but that underarm stuff he spray on his hair."

"On his *hair?* He sweatin up *there?*"

She nodded. "He say from all that figurin he gotta do for the deputy foreman. Beside, he like the smell." She paused. "I think maybe he gamblin."

"Gamblin?"

"He very funny bout money. Very stingy. Give me five dollars this week like I spozed to buy the whole state a Montgomery for five dollars."

"Don't he never win?"

"Mostly never." Though once in a while he would act as if he had gone out and come back in through the old door again with his neat little mustache back up under the middle of his nose and the old Jarvis hitched up behind his smile. "Hiya, Doll," he would say, throwing his arms around her. "Lookee here what I got for my Doll," sliding the bills down her dress, making sure they were safely stowed. Then he would kiss her hungrily as if this time he found the seasoning just right.

But there were many weeks when Florrie bought the groceries for both families. She would carry them into the house herself when Jarvis wasn't there and put them away carefully behind Rannee's back, as if they had been there for days.

Jarvis began to sleep badly, tossing and moaning and even, occasionally, talking in his sleep. "Can't do it, Doll," he shouted one night in a completely strange voice. "It don't fit, I tellin you. It don't fit. I can't do it, Doll. I can't."

What can't he do, she wondered. What won't fit? She looked at his face in the dirty morning light. It was a face she knew well but it was *all* she knew, except that he still liked lots of vinegar on his greens. Everything else had changed, as if a stranger had slipped down behind that face, a stranger who, as a child, had sat in the dark for hours with his finger in the keyhole. What, she wondered, was he trying to keep out.

But worst of all, Jarvis was very mean to Lance, screaming and yelling at him the minute he was through the door. "Hey you, Lance! Bring me that newspaper." "Go git me a beer." "Bring me my slippers."

"He only a baby," Rannee said. "Why you screamin an givin orders like he a whole grown-up regimin?"

Jarvis turned and shouted at her for ten minutes by the kitchen clock.

"It don't do no good," she told Florrie, "to talk back to Jarvis."

One day when Lance was playing in the yard, Jarvis took off his shoes and threw them out the window, almost hitting Lance on the head. "Hey you, boy," Jarvis shouted. "You bring me those shoes. Quick. Both of them. Mighty damn quick."

Lance's eyes grew bigger and his ears seemed to shrink into his skull. He stayed closer than ever to Rannee. She could almost feel him taking root in her thigh. One night she dreamed that Jarvis was wearing Lance's head, instead of his watch, at the end of his long, gold chain.

But Jarvis never mistreated Flash who grew big and fat and

smiled his bubbly smile constantly. Jarvis bought him lollipops and chocolate bars and rubber balls.

"Where's Lance's?" Rannee said.

"Shut your mouf," Jarvis said. He paid no attention at all to baby Reed who had been born while Jarvis was in jail.

One night when Jarvis came home, Rannee was holding Reed on her lap. Lance was playing on the floor close to her knees.

"Here, you lil ole man," Jarvis shouted at Lance. "Time you was doin somethin roun here. You ole enough. You take care a that baby for a bit. So your mama can cook my supper."

"Your supper's cooked," Rannee said.

"Maybe I got other things for you to do," Jarvis said. He took the baby out of Rannee's arms and dumped him into Lance's tiny lap. Lance began to cry and the baby screamed.

"You, Lance, you stop that blubberin, hear?" Jarvis shouted. "You hear me? I can't stand no blubberin. You make that boy stop blubberin, woman. Now!"

Florrie appeared in the doorway. "An you stop that shoutin," she said quietly, standing in front of Jarvis, breathing into his shirt front. "They listenin to you across the street and all the way down to City Hall. Shoutin like that. At that poor lil chile." She picked up Lance and carried him home.

She came quite often after that, to take Lance away before Jarvis got back. Sometimes she took Lance to the store and bought him a toy. He would come home happy, with a smile just beginning to sprout. But he remained a quiet child. Whenever Jarvis kissed Flash or brought him presents, Lance sat alone and watched. He stayed as close to Rannee as he dared, playing endlessly by himself with pots and spoons and bottle tops. His eyes got bigger and bigger but his ears stayed small and close to his head. He hardly seemed to grow at all.

"Is a mystery," Florrie said one day when she came to get Lance. "That sweet, perlite, agreeable Jarvis chile. Folded his napkin like a restaurant and carried out the garbage every Friday and spoke so soft you had to put your ear to his mouf, almost, to make out what he was sayin. Like he always scared someone was listenin. So how come he turn so mean alluva sudden? I askin you. How come he turn so mean?"

But Rannee shook her head. She had known lots of mean people in her life: Grandpa and the Misses French and Mr. Huckaby. Not to mention Mr. Hewett at the plant and a whole county of Henchmans and Sutcliffes all the way back to Mr. Kincaid. No one ever asked, "How come?" about them. "He jes one more mean man," she said.

One night he was lying on the bed, fully dressed before going out. "Is cole in here," he shouted. "That there fire gone out. It needin more wood."

She looked at him.

"I said it needin more wood."

"I heerd you. Wood on the porch."

"I know that. I tellin you to git it."

She turned toward the bureau and began to undress. "Git it yourself," she said. She heard him jump up.

"What you say?" he shouted.

In the mirror, she saw Lance standing in the hall with his fists over his ears. She hurried out.

"Where you goin?" Jarvis shouted.

"To git that wood."

In the hall, she picked Lance up in her arms. "What you doin out here?" she said.

He put his arms around her neck and his head in her shoulder and breathed heavily. She carried him slowly back to bed. "You go to sleep now, hear? An don't be worryin. Everythin gonna be all right." He stared up at her. She smiled down at him, but he did not smile back. Just stared at her with those enormous eyes, fixed as stones. Turning off the light, she remembered the dream she had had as a child in Simms Quarter after a slaughtering. She dreamed she was forced to walk barefoot down a long road paved with the eyes of butchered animals. She bent swiftly in the dark and kissed him. She had not done that, she realized, since he was a baby. Then she went to get the wood.

"Please, Jarvis," she said one night when he had come with some money in his fist and a great big wagon for Flash. "How come you never bring nothin for Lance? Never. Not once. He only a chile too."

"He not *my* chile, that's why. He your lil bastard chile. So jes shut your mouf and don't be tellin me what to do. He your lil bastard chile, ain't he? You think I don't know all about you an your fancy man an your fancy ass sashayin all over Chawnee?" He jumped up and began to shake her. He was becoming more and more violent. Sometimes he threw things.

"Jes a simple question," Rannee told Florrie, "git you a whole week's conversation plus a lotta loose hardware in your face."

"Sound like he gone plumb crazy," Florrie said.

But Rannee refused to believe that. He was the father of two of her children. Having him just plain mean was bad enough. "Maybe they done somethin awful to him when he was very small. 'Fore he got to you," she said. "Somethin makin him all twisted and ugly."

"He all nice an smooth when he livin with me," Florrie said. "Must be sump'n he breathed in down to that luminum plant."

"Or that prison," Rannee said.

"Why you act so mean all the time now?" Rannee asked him once. "Like you wish we all dead an gone. You wan us to go, jes say so. We glad to go."

"You try it," Jarvis said. "You jes go ahead an try it. An two days after you be gone, you be dead." It frightened her, but in some strange way, it made her feel sorry for him too.

After supper, he lay on the bed with his clothes and shoes on, resting before going out. He made Rannee sit in the chair beside him. "You set right there where I can see you, hear?" he would say. "An stay there." She would sit tense and silent, staring at the wall while he stared at her. If she moved, he snarled. "You set!"

Like I'm a dog, she thought.

Sometimes he made her bring him a cigar or a shot of whiskey or a glass of water. He made her light the cigar and drink some of the whiskey and the water. He began to make her taste all the food she served him too. Often, he made her come to bed with him. He wanted sex after supper, an appetizer to his night out. When he came home later, he was too tired. "Come on," he would shout. "I want you over here." Her mouth and her legs clamped shut. But he was strong. He could split her like a bun.

"Baby cryin," she said one evening, sitting in the chair beside the bed.

"Don't hear no baby." He never did. "What baby?" he would say.

*My* baby, she thought. She remembered how Reed had looked in the hospital with his tiny face permanently set to cry. "*Your* baby," she said.

"My baby? That ain't no baby a mine. That baby born when I in prison. That ain't never *my* baby."

"That baby born when you in prison *five* months. Take *nine* months to make a baby."

"That there weren't no nine-months baby. That there was a mighty small baby right from the start. More like a *five*-months baby. An how come you call him Reed?"

"For my Daddy."

"For *his* Daddy, you mean."

She stared at him. "You is completely crazy," she said. "You must be."

The baby was screaming with fury now.

"Go shut that bastard up," Jarvis said. "An come right back here."

By the time Rannee got to him, the baby was soaked in perspiration and urine and rigid with rage. She picked him up and his arms closed tightly around her neck. She settled him against her shoulder, a damp, convulsive lump, and walked up and down, stroking his back and crooning until the crying and, finally, the shuddering stopped completely. Then she changed him, whispering to him, smiling at him while he kicked his legs with delight and smiled back. She held him until he was fast asleep. But when she put him back to bed, his lip, she noticed, was sticking out again, ready to be outraged once more.

One night at supper, Jarvis sat silently, staring at Lance who was eating Jell-O with his head down, carefully picking out the tiny pieces of fruit. Rannee stood leaning against the stove.

"Hey you, Lance," Jarvis shouted. "Where your daddy at?"

Lance jerked and stopped eating but kept his head down.

"You, Lance. You hear me?" Jarvis shouted.

Lance nodded, still staring at the Jell-O.

"You looks at me when I talkin to you, hear?" Jarvis said.

Lance raised his head.

"I akst you, where your daddy at?"

Lance stared and slid both thumbs into his mouth. Just like Bay long ago, Rannee thought.

"Why you don't go home to your daddy?" Jarvis said. "Why you always hangin around here, hornin in on *other people's* daddy? You hear me, boy? Why you don't go on home to your own daddy?"

Lance was crying silently now, letting the tears run down into his fists.

Rannee went to the table and picked him up. He wrapped his arms and legs around her. "Never mind, Lance," she whispered. "You jes never mind that foolishness." Without a glance at Jarvis, she carried Lance out of the house and across the street to Florrie's.

When she came back, Jarvis was stretched out on the bed. Resting up after all that meanness, she thought. The younger children, still strapped into their chairs, were crying and spreading food all over the floor. She bathed them and put them to bed and cleaned up the kitchen, doing the dishes slowly, very slowly, letting the water run long after she was finished, banging clean pots around aimlessly. But, at last, she heard Jarvis call. She turned the water on harder.

"You hear me callin you, woman?" Jarvis shouted.

"I hears you."

"Then come on."

"No!"

"You say no to your husbin?"

"You no proper husbin to me."

"An you no proper wife say no to her husbin. Look like I gonna have to teach you. You come when I calls, hear?"

"No."

He jumped up, grabbed her, and threw her on the bed. Suddenly, he had one arm around her neck and was holding a small pocket knife to her throat.

He left the knife open on the bureau after that and made her lie down with him every night as soon as she had finished the dishes. She lay rigid while he jabbed into her, nailing her to the mattress. She lived with a permanent wound between her legs.

# 11

Her fourth child began to arrive one night while Jarvis was out. Florrie stayed with the children and Papa Lyle drove her to the hospital in the dump truck. She was still in labor when Jarvis rushed in, dropped down beside her bed, and threw his arms around her. "Why you not home when I get there, Doll?" he said. "Weren't no one there but Florrie and those boys and no Doll at all. I thought you gone an lef me, Doll." He put his head on her breast and cried. "I tole you, don't never go off and leave me, Doll. Don't never go off like that again." Two orderlies had to drag him away. Between contractions, she pitied him.

She named the baby Carter after her brother, Bay, whom no one had ever called by his right name. She would call her baby nothing but Carter—in Bay's honor. That would give her a reason for bringing another little Lyle into the world. She had produced four babies in virtually four years. Like an old sack, she thought, forever being filled and emptied.

When she got home, she realized that she was living in crowded quarters again. The new baby cried most of the day and all night. Jarvis refused to have him in their room so she sat in the living room with little Carter in her arms to keep him from waking the other children. She rocked him through the night, bearing down on the darkness till the new day burst with a scream all over the sky. But when she put the baby down, he began to cry.

"Chrissake," Jarvis yelled. "Make your bastard chile shut up."

"He *your* chile too," Rannee said.

"He no chile a mine. Not with a head like that. Look like a toilet bowl. An runnin all the time."

"He colicky," she said. It was a word she had heard in the hospital. But when she picked the baby up, he was quiet. He would lie in her arms and stare up at her, wide-eyed and peaceful. And she knew he was not colicky, just scared. Scared of Jarvis. The whole place smelled of Jarvis. The baby just wanted his mother's arms around him when he breathed. She smiled down at him and held him tighter. She realized that she had almost never heard a baby cry in Simms Quarter.

But the crying had its advantages. Jarvis began to stay away more and more. "Can't stand the racket here," he said. Sometimes she did not see him for days. When he came home, he was meaner than ever—or nicer. The pendulum was swinging wider and wider. Soon it would go through the wall—on one side or the other. Sometimes he came home with his arms full of presents again, fancier than ever: pralines and pecans and nougats, a baseball suit for Flash, and a fancy nightgown for her. He would open his arms, letting the packages fall, and close them around her. "Hiya, Doll. Where you been? I miss you, Doll. I miss you somethin awful." He would stuff handfuls of bills down her dress, smoothing them carefully, and kiss her from east to west and north to south. But most of the time he came home empty-handed and mean.

One night he lay snarling on the bed, ordering her to come and lie down beside him.

"No," she said from the kitchen, holding on to the sink with both hands.

"How you mean, no?"

"Doctor's orders."

"What you mean, doctor's orders?"

"I all smashed up inside."

"How, smashed up? What you talkin about?"

"That's what he say. I no good to you no more."

"Since when a fuckin white doctor know what's good for me?"

"Other words," she said slowly, "*you* no good for *me*. I not havin no more."

"What?"

"An *you* not havin no more. Not here. You want it, you git it somewhere else."

He jumped up. "You shut up that shit an come here."

She turned and ran out of the house. Florrie's apartment was dark, so she kept running, on to Aunt Vee's and Uncle Clyde's way on the other side of town. She had not seen them since Jarvis turned so mean. She was too ashamed. She thought of the unknown cousins who lived near the railroad station. But where?

Jarvis caught her on the corner and dragged her back. He pushed her into the bedroom and closed the door. "I tole you, don't never leave me, Doll," he said. And then, for the first time, he beat her. She saw the blood running down her leg. In Simms Quarter, no one but the slaughtered animals ever bled. Jarvis took a shower, put on his plaid suit and his white hat, kissed her good-bye, and left.

She sat in the chair beside the bed with a blanket over her legs and rocked back and forth, back to her past with Mama in Simms Quarter, crowded with children, and forward to Montgomery and Jarvis and the babies coming every year. She had never left Simms Quarter at all. She had been carrying it around with her all the time and she knew now that she always would. She would just set it down wherever she was and go on living inside it, with the rest of the world locked out. Only now it was worse than ever. Now she had let Jarvis in with her. She was more isolated in the middle of town than she had ever been in Simms Quarter. She went on rocking, staring at Jarvis's side of the bed which looked permanently dented, as if he slept with rocks in his pockets, pressing her down, flattening her out, leaving her with a mouthful of grit.

After that, he beat her more often. To pass the time, she thought.

She never told anyone about the beatings—not even Florrie. She kept her arms and legs covered up. Sometimes she thought of running next door for help. But she never did. If Miss 126B ever heard the sound of shouting and beating on the other half of the house, she never said so. She had her nails and her Southern Comfort.

"Mama," Lance whispered one night. "Tell Daddy to go way. We don't want him here. Too many peoples in this house. Tell him to go way, please, Mama."

She stared down at him. He had nightmares about Jarvis. Last night he woke screaming that Jarvis was hiding in the bureau. He was coming to get Lance. Lance saw him, a huge man with enormous black shoes, climbing, feet first, out of the bottom drawer.

"We could go way, Mama," Lance said. "Way way far away. So he couldn't never find us."

Where, she wondered. Back to Simms Quarter with four children? Mama was still raising most of her own. There was no room and no money in Simms Quarter, and no work for her except in the field, work she could no longer do. Besides, she could not run away from her husband. No one in Simms Quarter ever ran away—except from the white man—any more than they ever asked questions or talked back. They took what came: the heat and the hunger and the work and the whippings. That was what was beaten into them every day of their lives. "Is so," Grandma Sukey always said. "He my husbin," Rannee said at last. She had stopped singing and stopped dreaming about Uncle Floyd.

There was almost no money most of the time now. Rannee saved whatever Jarvis gave her for rent and Florrie bought most of the food and the children's clothes. Rannee still wore the same three dresses she had brought with her from Simms Quarter, including the dress she had worn at both weddings. She no longer bothered to alter the hems.

"Listen, honey," Florrie said one afternoon. "I got a surprise for you." She was carrying three large bundles.

"What kinda surprise?" Rannee said. "I ain't gonna let you buy me nothin, hear?"

"Oh, chile, don't be so snickety. Easter comin. Everybody needin somethin new an purty for Easter. Even you." She opened the boxes and presented Rannee with a dress, a hat, and a pocket book.

Rannee thanked her and said it wasn't right. But Florrie said the only thing that wasn't right was Jarvis.

After she had gone, Rannee tried on her new clothes. The dress was white with purple flowers growing all over it and made her look like somebody's back fence. The pocket book was very stylish and very big but Rannee had nothing to put in it. The hat was tiny and square and much too small. She might have been wearing a postage stamp. She put her face in her pillow and cried.

She could hear the children playing quietly in the living room. They were always quiet now. Even little Carter, after the first few months, had settled down into a docile, undemanding child. They were never sick, never cranky, and they never fought. They were as well-behaved as the children in Simms Quarter, though she had never raised a hand to any of them. Even Jarvis never beat the children. He preferred to beat her. But Rannee rarely kissed them either, like Mama and the other parents of Simms Quarter: a legacy from slavery, perhaps, when families were torn apart constantly. It didn't pay to get too used to someone who could be snatched away. Only Daddy allowed himself to hug and kiss his children, as if he'd picked that up from the white man too, along with his hat and his "dainty" speech. White people never had to worry. They could hug and kiss their children as much as they pleased.

134

She got up and walked heavily into the living room. The children were scattered around the floor. In one corner, Lance was playing house with a saucepan, using the salt and pepper shakers for people. He might have been back in Simms Quarter, like his mama, she thought, playing under the "scaffer." Flash was pushing a cigar box vigorously around and under the furniture, saying softly every now and then, "Slow down, there, son. Slow down." In the far corner, the two little ones sat opposite each other with their legs spread, solemnly rolling an empty bourbon bottle back and forth between them. Drops of liquor were spilling out onto the floor. Soon the whole room would smell of bourbon. She sat down in her rocker and watched. She sat there for a long time. But no one turned to her, no one noticed her, as if, little as they were, they had learned to manage without her already. It was what she wanted for them, it was how she had trained them, but it hurt too. Or was it merely that, seeing her for once in new clothes, even her own children could not recognize her?

"I gotta fine a job," she told Florrie on the way home from church the next day. "But I can't go to no employment agency. You know anyone needin housework?"

"I inquire," Florrie said.

"Gotta be near a bus," Rannee said. "I can't spend no time walkin."

"I investigate," Florrie said.

"Gotta be after he leave in the mornin an 'fore he gits back at night. So he won't never know."

"I fix it," Florrie said. She knew everyone in the neighborhood: the junk man and the grocery man and the garbage men who collected deep inside white territory.

One day she came to Rannee with a name and an address. "Mrs. Leona Fetterman, 2 Ashtabula Avenue," she said. "She spectin you this mornin."

Mrs. Fetterman was a tall woman with a skinny body taped up in a house dress and a loose gray bun sliding around on top of her head. She had just moved down from New York, she told

Rannee, which was probably why she talked so funny. "Such a climate," she said, wiping her neck. "For orchids, not people." She was very polite, the first person who ever called Rannee "Mrs."

"You have children, Mrs. Lyle?" she said. "So go home, be with your children, they shouldn't be abandoned."

"They with their Grandma," Rannee said, touched that Mrs. Fetterman should worry about her children.

"So, good," Mrs. Fetterman said, "we will commence in the den." She put an old stocking over her hair, handed Rannee a broom, and picked up a mop. Rannee had never heard of a den in a house before.

It was a small room, stuffed with furniture and dirty ashtrays full of cigar butts, and pictures of babies and old men in big hats, and a card table covered with checkers. There was a bookcase along one wall, full of books, all kinds of books: big and small, fat and thin, hard and soft, dark and bright. Rannee had never seen so many books, not even in the library of the Chawnee High School for Negroes. She longed to take them down and look at them and see what they said. She had not read anything in a long time. She never met Realtor Fetterman in all the time she worked for his wife, but after seeing all those books and the Fettermans' enormous double bed, she decided that he was a wise and generous man, and considerate to his wife.

Mrs. Fetterman gave Rannee five dollars a day and strange, sharp-smelling food in jars. "So be well," Mrs. Fetterman always said when Rannee left.

Rannee thanked her and gave the food to Florrie to take to her church suppers. Rannee wished Mrs. Fetterman would give her one of those books instead.

Rannee hurried home after work, stopping at Delchamps on the way to buy bread and milk and eggs and whatever could be cooked quickly. She fed the children, washed their hands and faces, and cleaned up the kitchen. When Jarvis came home everything was spotless and they were all sitting down at the table as if waiting for supper.

"Why you not cookin?" he said.

"Got nothin to cook."

"Why you not buy sump'n?"

"Got nothin to buy it with."

"Then git it from Florrie, for Chrissake. Whatsa matta with you, woman?"

"You go. I tireda spongin offa that woman. She *your* mama. *You* go."

Sometimes, they had supper twice. The children said nothing. They were used to saying nothing when Jarvis was around.

He came home angrier and angrier. Everything she did provoked him. "Jes me breathin make him boil over," she told Florrie. One night he found the empty bourbon bottle behind the sofa. "What the hell," he said, picking it up and sniffing around the room. "Who spillin my whiskey all over this house? You an your fuckin friends? Or maybe your fuckin lil bastards." He started toward the children's room. Rannee ran ahead of him, clutching a wire hanger. Near the door, he grabbed it from her. Then he beat her with it. When he was finished, he fell on the bed and went to sleep. She called the police.

She saw the patrol car drive up and two white cops get out, one young, one oldish. They stood on the sidewalk for a moment, looking at the house and laughing. Rannee rushed out.

"You lock him up," she said.

"Yeah?" the old cop said. "What's your reason? You gotta have a reason. We can't go round lockin folks up. Not even niggers. Not without we got a reason."

"I got a reason," Rannee said. "He beatin me regular and I fed up. I ain't takin no more."

"Who?" the young cop said. "Him?" He pointed at Jarvis standing in the doorway.

"Yeah, him," she said. "Jarvis P. Lyle. My husbin."

"She your wife?"

"Yes, sir," Jarvis said, smooth as corn syrup. "She my wife.

137

But she excited, confused. You know? I never lay a finger on her."

"That there's one big fat puffed-up lie," Rannee said.

"Well," the young cop said. "What we gonna do? You say he beat you, he say he don't. Ain't no blood on you. Ain't nothin broken."

"Wanna see?" Rannee said.

"So, maybe he pushed you around a little," the young cop went on.

"He didn't push me roun a little. He *beat* me. An it not the first time. More like the fiftieth time."

"How come you never called us before?"

"Cause I didn't want no arguments. Like this."

"Then how come you called us this time?"

"Cause this time he done it with a wire hanger. This time I cover with blood worse than ever. This time I fed up. Wanna see?" She pushed her sleeves up but no one bothered to look.

"So you want us to lock him up, huh?"

"Yeah. Lock him up good."

"We lock him up, we gotta lock you up too."

"*Me?* What *I* do?"

The older policeman sighed. "Look, we ain't got time for this kinda shit. You wanna sleep separate, go to a motel. Why bother us?"

"Look," the young one said. "Why don't you two gwan back in there and talk things over."

"Ain't nothin *to* talk over," she said. But the policemen were getting back into their car. Walking to the house, she noticed the neighbors standing silently on their porches and their door-steps—watching. She would never call the police again.

The next day, her body throbbed and shook and perspired all the way to work, as if with fever—or shame. She was glad the bus was empty.

"My God," Mrs. Fetterman said when she saw her. "You're dripping and shaking both. What's the matter, you're not well? In the kitchen, please." She made Rannee sit down and gave her a towel to wipe herself with and poured out two glasses of iced tea. "Now," she said, sitting down opposite her, "take off that sweater, you'll feel more comfortable."

"No, thank you, ma'am, I cooler now."

"At least roll up the sleeves."

"No, thank you, ma'am. I fine now."

Mrs. Fetterman leaned across the table and began to push up Rannee's sleeve. It was like pulling off skin. It *was* skin. Pieces of it were coming away with the material.

"My God," Mrs. Fetterman said.

"I fell down," Rannee said.

"*That's* from falling down? No. From falling down you don't look like that. You scrubbed yourself with broken glass maybe?"

"I be all right," Rannee said.

Mrs. Fetterman leaned across the table. "You fall down like this often?"

Rannee did not answer.

"At least go home," Mrs. Fetterman said. "Rest. You can't work like that."

"I be all right," Rannee said. "I work fine."

"No," Mrs. Fetterman said. "That I couldn't allow. Positively not. Here, I pay you anyhow. You make it up some other time."

"Please, ma'am," Rannee said. "I can't make it up no other time. I only able to work weekdays, nine to three. How I gonna make it up?"

"So don't make it up. It's all right. Only go home. Ach, it looks terrible." She shook her head and put her hands over her eyes. "Ach, *die Schwarze*," she murmured.

And Rannee knew that it was not only pity and horror that had upset Mrs. Fetterman. It was disgust as well.

She insisted on staying so Mrs. Fetterman gave her sitting-down jobs to do: polishing the silver and the keys of the piano and Mr. Fetterman's size 13 shoes. Walking to the bus stop, with her sleeves rolled down again, she felt the flames of her humiliation higher than ever. No one had ever beaten his wife in Simms Quarter. She remembered the beatings she had had as a child. They were different. They never broke the skin. The pain always stayed *outside*. "Be well," Mrs. Fetterman had called before closing the door. Rannee had exposed her shame at last—to a white woman.

At the bus stop, a large colored woman shouted at her from across the street. "Don't you be waitin for no bus tonight, Sister. Tonight you walks."

"Where's the bus at?" Rannee said.

"Ain't none. Not today. Not for colored folk."

"Why not?"

"Strike! Ain't you heard?"

But Rannee had heard nothing. She might never have left Simms Quarter. She was no longer living in a city with movies and parks and cafés and fish fries. She was living in Jarvis's back pocket. She looked up and noticed a leaflet tacked to the telephone pole:

> Don't ride the bus to work, to town, to school, or to any place on Monday, December 5.
> Another woman has been arrested and put in jail because she refused to give up her seat.

Rannee remembered the empty bus that morning, and felt ashamed that she had been in it, the only person in the colored section.

She saw several colored women coming out of the white houses on Asthabula Avenue, carrying their house shoes in paper bags and their heads high. They all walked right on past the bus stop. Rannee began to walk too. She walked slowly, for she was still very sore, as if she had spent her life not in the *back* of a bus but *under* it. She walked on, out of the white section and on downtown where more and more people were walking: colored people who had walked miles already that day, people from factories and hospitals and restaurants and hotels. They walked slowly, painfully, as if their feet were screwed on back-

140

ward. But they smiled and laughed and said, "Hi!" Rannee smiled too. She no longer felt tired and sore and alone. It was like a Homecoming at church in Chawnee, she thought, with the streets full of smiling faces. Some people were jammed into old cars, some rode wagons, some mules. But mostly they walked. A bus rattled by. A few white people were sitting up front. The back of the bus was empty. The colored people were walking. All over the town, colored people were walking. And Rannee was walking with them.

Near home, she became worried. She was very, very late. What would Jarvis do if he got home and she wasn't there? "He here an gone," Florrie said, buttoning up Reed's pajamas. "I had to tell him you at work. He very very wroth."

"Where he gone?" Rannee said.

"To the devil, I hope," Florrie said. "Want me to wait up with you?"

"No, thanks," Rannee said. "That'd just put it off."

"Put what off?"

"Whatever he got planned for me."

Jarvis came home very late and very drunk. She had never seen him like that before. He lurched through the kitchen and fell into bed without supper and stayed there fully dressed except for his belt on the bed beside him. He made Rannee sit in the chair next to him, except when she had to care for the children or pour him another drink. When he was awake he shouted abuses at her. "I hear you workin agin," he said. "I hear you waggin your tail all over town, agin." She sat stiffly in the rocking chair, but she did not rock. When he fell asleep for the night, she got up and went into the living room. But she did not sleep. She sat bolt upright for six hours, steadily, without moving, a stone for the darkness to beat against. The next day, sitting beside Jarvis, she was rigid as the wood of her chair. She could hear the children playing quietly: Lance playing house and Flash playing speed demon and the little ones rolling a milk bottle.

Every now and then Jarvis opened his eyes, looked at her,

and reached for his belt. Her very stillness seemed to madden him.

"Gimme another lil drink," he said once. The children were all in bed and the house was deadly quiet.

She got up and began to pour.

"I said *lil*."

"Why you don't finish the bottle?" she said. "That way maybe you passes out for good. Or be filthy drunk, then there'd be a reason why you so mean rotten ugly."

"Don't need no reason other than you hackin at me all the time. I gittin tireda it, hear? Nothin ever comin outa your mouf but the same ole shit. I tireda it, I tellin you. I sick to death a it." He grabbed the belt and jumped up. She ran out of the room but there was no place to hide. He had long since taken the locks off all the inside doors. She ran into the kitchen and picked up the skillet. It slipped and fell on his foot. He howled and began to beat her fiercely, picking up anything he could find—a flashlight, an umbrella, a chair—shouting and cursing till the chair fell apart. She broke away and ran sobbing out of the house. Her clothes were torn and there was blood all over her. She saw Miss 126B in the yard, brushing her hair. For a moment Rannee hesitated. The woman stared. Then she raised the brush.

Rannee ran across the street, but the dump truck was gone and she knew that the Lyles were out. She ran on, stumbling and sobbing through the crowds and the traffic, ignoring the lights and the pedestrians, all the way to Aunt Vee's.

Uncle Clyde opened the door. He stood in the hall, staring at her. She rushed past him into the kitchen.

"Your Aunt Vee ain't home," he said. "How come you all messed up like that?"

"You gotta help me, Uncle Clyde. You gotta."

"What I gotta do?"

"I dunno. Only somebody gotta do somethin. Someday he gonna kill me. An I got all those chirren."

"*Who* gonna kill you?"

"Jarvis."

There was a long pause. Uncle Clyde put his hands in his pockets and rubbed his crotch. "I dunno as I kin do that," he said. "Jarvis your husbin. I ain't got no right to interfere 'tween a man an his wife. I ain't even kinfolk. I just your aunt's husbin. Ain't no real kin at all."

"Don't matta what you is. Please, Uncle Clyde. You gotta help me."

The doorbell rang. She could hear Jarvis shouting and hanging on the door.

"Don't let him in, Uncle Clyde. *Please.* Look at me. He done that. He do worse if he could."

"What *you* done?" Uncle Clyde said.

"Me? Nothin. Ain't done *nothin*. 'Cept breathe."

The bell was ringing harder now and Jarvis was shouting louder. "C'mon, Clyde. I know that bitch in there. You lemme in. Tha's my wife you got in there. I got a right to come in."

Uncle Clyde looked at Rannee and looked at the door and rubbed his crotch. "He right," he said at last. "He your husbin. I don't want no trouble. I never interferes 'tween a husbin an wife." He turned and opened the door.

Jarvis rushed in, grabbed Rannee by the arm, and dragged her out. She looked back at Uncle Clyde but he had already shut the door.

Jarvis beat and pushed and dragged her home. People standing in front of their houses or walking the streets or sitting in their cars all stopped what they were doing and watched. It was like a parade passing by. No one said anything, no one did anything, except Rannee, sobbing and moaning while the cement peeled the skin off her arms and legs. But no one made a move, no one said a word. They just watched as if she were a free show they were enjoying on a Monday night.

At home, Jarvis dropped her inside the front door like a loaded sack and went to bed. She lay there moaning for a long time. Finally, she got up and walked heavily to the bedroom. Jarvis was asleep on his back. She sat down in the chair beside him and stared at his face, the meanest, ugliest face in the country and the state and the whole world, she thought, now that Hitler was dead. She tried to remember how Jarvis looked way back, before they were married, when, as Aunt Vee used to say, he was "the sweetest, honeyest, most sugar-natured man in town." Now all Rannee felt was hate, filling her up and spilling out all over the room, providing another whole world for her to live in. She could walk right in and shut herself up in that hate. But she had something else to do first.

She went on sitting there, staring into his face, waiting for him to snore. When he snored, she knew he was dead to the world. She could get up and dance on the blankets when he snored, or cut out his liver with his pocket knife. She would never be able to find his heart.

The moment he began to snore, she got up quietly and left the house. She left her children asleep in their beds and her pride all rumpled up in that rocking chair, and ran. She was still wearing her torn clothes, and her arms and legs and face were dirty and covered with blood and bruises. She went as she was, half running, half sobbing, all the way across town to the police station, zigzagging through the back streets, taking a long, roundabout route in case Jarvis should wake up and follow her. This time she didn't bother to phone. This time she took her blood and her wounds to them.

"Lock him up," she said, standing in the station house with one sleeve gone and the skin on her arms and legs in shreds. "Lock him up or I'll kill him. Lock up his butt real good so no one can git him out or I stayin right here. You kin go ahead an lock me up too, if you wants. For safety. Cause I promise you, you make me go back there with him, I kill him. I kill him dead. I wants him locked up good an tight. Otherwise, you hear me sayin it, I gonna kill him."

Two policemen took her home in a patrol car. She sat in the back crying and moaning, telling two completely strange white men the story of her miserable marriage, with the car radio turned up high the whole time.

At home, Jarvis was still asleep. "You git him outa here an into that jail," she said. "An you lock him up so he stay locked up. I don't wan nobody be able to git him out. No lawyer, no judge, no bail, *nobody*. Not till I gone. You jes keep him locked up tight till I git outa town. Tha's all I ask. Cause I gonna take my chirren and leave. I goin an I ain't never comin back. I promise you."

Finally, they shook Jarvis awake. He went quietly with his wrists handcuffed behind his back and his eyes on her. "Why, Doll?" he said. "Why you wanna do a thing like this? What I do, Doll?"

When they were out of sight, she went back inside the house and locked the door and began to pack. She stuffed as much as she could into an old duffle and her old Gladstone bag and a laundry basket and several paper sacks and grocery cartons. When they were all full, she hurried around to Mr. Hickey, the junk man, and told him to come and take his stuff back. "Like you promise," she said. He gave her fifteen dollars for the lot, including an almost new crib. "A drug on the market," he said. "Population stopped exploding." She put the fifteen dollars in her shoe and took the children over to Florrie's.

Back home again, she piled as much as she could into Flash's wagon: dishes and pots and pans and bowls and brushes and washtub. When it was crammed full, she took it outside and locked the door behind her. Then she began to walk, pulling the loaded wagon all the way through the town, to the unknown cousins she had never seen who lived somewhere down near the railroad station. She left the wagon on the porch of a small house beside the tracks.

Back home, she made a huge fire in the yard. Then she ran through the house, pulling down curtains, yanking up sheets and blankets and pillows and mattresses and threw them all in the fire. The neighbors gathered silently outside the yard and watched. She could see their faces through the flames. They made her cheeks burn. They deserved nothing, she told herself. She kept working feverishly, throwing on quilts and rugs and whatever Jarvis had given her, and the dress she had worn to their wedding. She had worn it often since then, but she would never wear it again. Whatever was left that she couldn't pack went into the fire. It was all hers, after all. She had paid for it all—in time and muscle and money, including the house itself. At the end, she threw in her wedding ring.

By morning, the house was completely empty except for a few bags and bundles. She took them all over to Florrie's. "This here Jarvis's stuff," she said, handing Florrie two pillow cases crammed with clothes. Then she went back and walked slowly through the empty rooms. There was absolutely nothing in them now, not even a cobweb. It was emptier than when she first saw it. She went out, leaving both doors wide open. Anyone could look in the front door and see right out through the back door. There was nothing left in that house but empty space. The last thing she did was to remove the outside lock.

She was back in Simms Quarter again, with four children this time. Three of her children slept in the back room with Mama's. Beet and Bay had gone, but the others were still there, crowding her, stifling her. She felt her eyes and ears and nostrils and pores close up against them. At night, when everyone else was in bed, she sat on the porch in Mama's chair and rocked, like Mama and Grandma Sukey and all the other ladies of Simms Quarter. She was one of them now, screwed down for good, with no escape except to the back porch like Mama, pouring sugar over everything, the only way she had of sweetening her life.

One night, she dreamed that Jarvis was crashing through the house, carrying a load of extra arms and legs and heads stuffed into a pillow case. "These yours, Doll?" he said over and over. "Please, Doll. Jes lemme see is any a these yours.

She heard about him in letters from Florrie. He had gotten religion, she said, and had gone to stay with his Aunt Ruby who ran a boarding house in Chicago. She got him a job in the post office. He delivered the letters but took the magazines to the city dump, explaining that he refused to spread such filth. "Lies and deceptions and temptations of the flesh," he said. When the post office threw him out, he took up palmistry, but saw nothing but sin and retribution in the hands of Aunt Ruby's boarders. When she threw him out, he went across town and became a preacher. They would have short prayers and long collections, Rannee thought.

"He say it all *your* fault," Florrie wrote. He claimed that Rannee had saved him the night she stripped him of all worldly possessions and left him with nothing but his naked soul. "He figure he better save *that*," Florrie reported. Rannee imagined him standing in the pulpit with his back teeth aglow, pouring out God's words like whiskey from a bottle. She pictured him in his plaid suit and white tie and the carefully balanced little mustache, the Jarvis she had known long ago, talking the sweet talk she had heard long ago. Maybe that was something he could still do.

One day, coming home from the field, she heard his voice on the back porch. She turned right around and went right back. At suppertime she stayed up in the field but sent a message back with Daddy. "Tell Jarvis I ain't comin till he gone. He wanna see the chirren, OK. But tell him he be sure an leave them right there. *All* a them. An tell him, don't bother to come back. Tell him don't *never* come back."

He was very polite, Mama reported. Very kind and considerate and polite. He talked about his new religion and his new soul which Rannee had saved for him. He had given the children ten dollars and left with a sad smile for them all and his new soul shining through the lining of his jacket.

"How you know that his soul?" Rannee asked.

"What else *could* it be?" Mama said.

But soul or no soul, Jarvis knew where Rannee was and she no longer felt safe at Simms Quarter. She would join Beet and Bay up North. Daddy would have to lend her some money again. He moved his hat back and forth on his head. "I 'range it for you, Shoo," he said.

147

"You keep my chirren for me, Mama?" Rannee asked. They were sitting on the back porch one afternoon. Rannee, staring at Mama, noticed there wasn't much lap to Mama anymore. Now that she was empty all the time, Rannee could see what a small vessel Mama really was. She wondered why the Lord had sent so many to lodge there.

Mama smoothed the dress on her bony knees and turned toward Rannee. Mama was looking right at her, Rannee thought, not across the yard or sideways over the washtub or the stove or the baby in her arms. She was looking at Rannee. The smooth flat face, Rannee realized, had tiny scratches all over it now. Someone had been gouging away at it for years. Rannee blinked and looked away. "I take the baby," she said. "You keep the others? Jes for a bit? Till I settle?"

Mama was looking out across the yard again. "I keep them," she said.

# THE
# GHETTO

# 12

Beet met her at the bus station in a yellow fur coat and pointed shoes with tall skinny heels and a brown wig piled up in a peak. She looked like a steeple on stilts. Her face was all colored in— blue lids and red cheeks and purple lips—with the cheeks puffed up like muffins from all the bleaches she used. "That you, Beet?" Rannee said.

"Well, well, well," Beet said. "If it ain't my lil sister with another lil choklit drop in her arms. You sure got a sweet tooth, sugar. How many that make now?" Her eyebrows wandered up into her forehead and her lashes stuck out straight and stiff. She hugged Rannee and pushed her into a taxi. It was a cold, windy day with a sky like an unmade bed; torn posters of Ike hung off the walls, his smile split in two. The city was full of stone buildings and sharp corners and white people rushing around. Rannee, staring out the window, found herself looking for a small, thin, black man in blue overalls, whistling "Only Believe."

"How Bay?" she said.

"OK, 'cept for that stuck-up bitch he marry. That there Merleene. She from 'Lantic City and she spend so much time

151

paradin up an down that boardwalk, she think she Miss Universe."

"He still workin for that phone company?"

"Yeah. Got a real good job. Only that bitch spendin it all on bathin suits."

Beet took her home to live with her and Spencer Bibbs, her latest husband, and four little girls. They lived on the second floor of a small two-family frame house on the edge of the ghetto. Beet unlocked the door. The little girls were home alone, two were still babies in diapers. They seemed to have emptied all the drawers and closets and trash baskets on the floor. Beet picked her way through the litter. "This here your Aunt Tink," she said. "An your Cousin Carter. They be stayin here for a while so you be quiet an keep that trash count down." She gave Rannee a tiny room in the back of the house with a little yard just below, and left her alone. Rannee saw the little girls standing silently in a semicircle outside her door. She tried to talk to them but they refused to answer. They just stood and stared, four pairs of big black eyes examining her, searching out her secrets to be dumped with the rest of the trash when her back was turned. Finally, she got up and closed the door. Then she sat down with the baby in her arms and looked through the dirty window at the scruffy yard below.

Spencer was a big pleasant colored man with a low voice and his head hanging low on his neck. He worked for the army and made good money which Beet seemed to be throwing away by the fistful. She had charge accounts all over town. Huge packages arrived at the house constantly, and the door-to-door salesmen knew her by sight. But Beet herself was hardly ever at home, except to change her clothes and her wigs: a yellow wig with her yellow pants and a silver wig for her silver pants. Often she was out all night and came home after Spencer left for work. She would sleep for a few hours and then go out again, but never with Spencer, never to the base. "I not 'sociatin with no stuffed shirts in no khaki uniform," she said. She never cooked or cleaned or washed clothes. Spencer ate at the base and did his laundry at the base and went to dances, alone, at the base. Rannee fed the children and bought the groceries and cleaned up the mess. The next day it was back again.

At night, when Carter was asleep, she sat near the window with the light out and looked into the dirty backyard. No matter how far she traveled, she thought, she always seemed to be sitting alone in the dark, staring at the same view. Only this yard was smaller than ever.

One night, she heard Spencer's voice raised in the kitchen. "Where you been for three whole days?" he shouted. "How come you go off an leave your children like that?" The next morning all his clothes lay in a heap outside the front door. He never raised his voice to Beet again.

On Sunday, Bay came in a shiny new Mercury to take Rannee out. She had not seen him since she left Simms Quarter for Montgomery four years ago. He had been in the army since then. The army had stretched him out and smoothed him down and poked his eyes back into his face. He was wearing a light blue suit and jerking his knees like a city nigger. But his smile, when he saw her, threatened to turn the corners of his face. "Well, if it ain't my favorite sister with an extra lil bonus in her arms." He gave her an enormous kiss and took the baby. "Looka here, Merleene," he said. "Ain't that a bag a somethin?" He kissed Carter and handed him to his wife.

"Mmmm. Sweet," Merleene whispered with her lips against Carter's cheek.

Like a lollipop, Rannee thought. Merleene kept Carter in her arms for the rest of the afternoon.

"She plannin on givin him back?" Rannee asked Bay in the car. Merleene was sitting in the back with Carter who was fast asleep. "Like he don't even know which is his mama," Rannee murmured.

"She very fond a babies," Bay said. "Lost hers two months ago. Miscarriage. Doctor said to wait a while. But she got all those baby clothes sittin there like that baby comin home tomorrow, ready to put on them booties and one a them long

153

dresses an climb into that buggy hisself. How 'bout you let us keep that chile for a while? Just till you stablish. That Beet house no fit place for a baby."

Rannee turned and saw Merleene dozing with her chin on Carter's head. She was a pretty girl, meant to sit in a nice blue car with a handsome husband like Bay and a sweet baby like Carter in her arms.

"He *mine*," Rannee said. "He stayin with *me*."

"Sure, sure," Bay said. "Nobody arguin that. But just till you settle, with a job an a place'n all. How you gonna git a job with that baby in your arms? We just keep him till you fixed up. You come see him any time."

"All right," Rannee said. "Jes till I settle. But I comin to see him *all* the time."

She got a job in the Acme Laundry Company, right behind the town's oldest, fanciest cemetery. On windy days, you could smell the damp heat blowing above the graves. Sometimes, on nice days, she walked there during her lunch break, but she dared not sit on the plots with their huge monuments, like little houses, with the owners' names carved over the doorways: Trowbridge and Townsend and Coolidge. She could lodge her whole family in one of those houses.

The rest of the time she pulled sheets off a conveyer and folded them for eighty-five cents an hour. She stood in a column of sweat all day while the sheets lurched at her. If she didn't grab them in time, they got all tangled up. Sometimes, they whipped themselves around her and threatened to squeeze her to death. The other workers were mostly women, colored and Puerto Ricans. "On accounta Mr. Acme," one woman told her. "He favor the colored. He say they able to stan the heat better. Counta their black skin."

"Not *this* black skin," Rannee said as a sheet caught her around the neck. She had trouble breathing in that damp heat and the smell of the steamed sheets—releasing urine? sweat? semen?—made her sick. "It probably the asman," one woman said. After two weeks, Rannee quit.

She went to work downtown in an old shirt factory. It was a long, low room, crowded with tables and white women. Rannee felt strange walking past all those white women. If anyone spoke to her, she said, "Yes, ma'am," and, "No, ma'am," and hurried to the back of the shop to old Shubah, the only other colored woman and the only other machine operator. The two women sat side by side all day. They ate their lunch together at their machines and took the bus home together at night. They sewed buttons on shirts. Rannee wondered if Mr. Piscotti, the owner, had given her that job because it was easy or because he liked to keep the colored women together in the back, away from the others. He was a small, thin man with a worried, hairy face, as if he couldn't decide whether to grow a beard or not.

"He Eyetalian," Shubah told her the first day.

Rannee didn't know what Eyetalian was, any more than she had known what Puerto Rican was. In the South there had been only two kinds of people, colored and white. She thought Eyetalians were probably white people who talked funny, just as Puerto Ricans were colored people who talked funny.

The other women were mostly short with thick arms and legs and thick black hair stuck up in balls on the side of their heads. They laughed a lot and shouted a lot in high voices. "Where's the fuckin thread?" one woman yelled. "Jesus, May, you got me all bawled up again. What the hell I gonna tell Piscotti? This here looks like a piece a shit." Rannee felt the words crawl over her skin. Mama would have made her suck sacking soaked in vinegar for talking like that, and poor Uncle Floyd had been marked for life for saying "damn" when a white man dropped a shovel on his foot. But here, dirty words dropped like inchworms all around her. Sometimes, she had trouble breathing. "It my asman," she said and kept close to Shubah.

Shubah was small and old and skinny. She had had three husbands but, one way or another, they had all disappeared. One was killed by accident during the war, by his own troops. One was killed by accident in jail, waiting to be tried. The third was killed deliberately by someone in a hurry for his wallet.

Shubah's children were all gone too. They wrote to her from Chicago and Cleveland and San Diego and Lexington Avenue, urging her to come. Shubah thanked them but stayed where she was, sewing buttons on shirts, eyeing turtlenecks with alarm. Rannee admired Shubah, who kept a pair of earmuffs beside her, even in summer, and put them on as soon as the swearing began.

Rannee worked from eight to four-thirty six days a week with half an hour for lunch and two ten-minute breaks. She sent Mama as much money as she possibly could for clothes and food for the children. But it was not enough. She had promised Mama she would send for them as soon as she was settled, but she still had no place and not enough money to keep them. Even Carter was still at Bay's.

"Me an Merleene, we wants to 'dopt him," Bay told her one Sunday. Carter was smiling at Rannee but kept his arms around Merleene's neck.

"No!" Rannee said. "He *mine.*"

"C'mon, Tink," Bay said. "Why you wanna be so selfish?"

He had changed, Rannee thought. His house looked as if he'd spent the past ten years shopping for it. It was stuffed. The walls, the floor, the shelves, the tabletops were all covered. Even the fish in the bowl looked crowded. Merleene was beginning to look like something he had brought home to fill that empty spot on the couch. Rannee wondered what empty space they wanted Carter to fill.

"C'mon Tink," Bay said. "You won't hardly ever miss him."

"You got all those others," Merleene said.

"I want this one too," Rannee said.

After a while she got a job in the post office to increase her income. She worked at the factory from eight till four-thirty, went home, rested, ate, and worked at the post office from eight till twelve. She liked the post office, where she could work by herself, mopping and dusting and tidying. She liked to think that she was working, not for Mrs. Starbury or Mrs. Fetterman or Mr. Piscotti, but for the United States of America. There was lots to read on the walls while she mopped: "Loitering and Soliciting in the Building Prohibited," "Notice of Rewards for the detection of burglary, bombs or explosives, theft of mail." There were large posters labeled WANTED, with pictures of mean-looking men, in full face and profile, staring down at her.

The other employees were mostly white, but they were all very pleasant. They all sat down together in the "lounge" during the "break," eating and talking and playing cards. Miss Piper, the supervisor, made Rannee sit beside her because Rannee was new. Miss Piper was an elegant white lady in flowing scarves who spoke in stiff sentences that spread out around her like a starched skirt, so different from the sloppy, slouching speech of both races in the South and the harsh jagged speech of the North. Not even Mrs. Starbury sounded like that, and certainly not the white women or Mr. Piscotti in the factory. It reminded her of the language in *The Book of Knowledge* long ago. She listened carefully and tried to copy it. Miss Piper never said "ain't" or "I is" or "he don't." She said "expensive" instead of "espensis" and "children" instead of "chirren." She put different endings on words: "Chap*el* Street" instead of "Chap*er*" and "library" instead of "liberry" and "care*ful*." Sometimes she put endings where none had been before: "an*d*" and "goin*g*" and "husb*and*." Sometimes, she left them off: "people(s)" and "policemen(s)." Rannee knew that for mopping floors and sewing buttons it didn't matter how she spoke—or whether she spoke at all. But she kept listening and trying just the same, whispering words at night in her room at Beet's with the door locked—"I *am*," "child*ren*," "*ex*-pect"—and reading right through Spencer's newspaper.

Sometimes, instead of talking during the break, Miss Piper read a book which she carried back and forth in her purse. "I couldn't survive that dreadful bus ride without it," she said. Rannee wished she had a book too, to read during the break and on the bus and in bed in her lonely room at Beet's. It never occurred to her to *buy* one. She was saving all her money for Christmas presents for her children: coloring books and Woolworth cars and trucks and candy canes. There would never be an empty shoe box for any of *her* sons. She did not even buy a newspaper. She read the posters on the walls instead.

Sometimes, in the evening, between jobs, she ate downtown at a counter all alone—a bowl of soup or a dish of Jell-O—and stared at the ads: "Soup Sandwich," "Beef B.B.Que," "Toasted English." But the pictures of pretty young white women smiling over their Coca-Cola made her feel lonely. She thought of Mama who always ate alone with her sugar. But the Jell-O was sweet enough. It didn't need any sugar.

Sunday she went to church, as always, though she no longer had much faith in the stern white God of Simms Quarter. She went, mainly, to hear the music and sing the hymns and to sit quietly among colored people for a little while. Whenever the Reverend Hampton began to shout about "ee-vill" and "Chris-tee-en," she took off her shoes and closed her eyes and thought of Uncle Floyd who might be preaching in a church up here this very minute, a small gentle man who let God's message pour out of him, thick and slow and sweet, like syrup from a can. She closed her ears and heard him whistling "Only Believe." If only she could find him, she thought, she might just begin to believe again too. Until then, she behaved as if she did. She needed something in this cold climate. She even taught Sunday school, helping little colored children to color in pictures of old white patriarchs, helping them to keep the crayon inside the lines and off their Sunday clothes.

In the afternoon, she fetched Carter from Bay's and walked slowly downtown, pushing him in his stroller and looking into store windows. She saw stiff, sneering, white mannikins with their heads high and their shoes half off. She saw reflections of herself in a blue dress with a white collar, a city dress, not like the coarse drab cottons she had worn at home that hung straight as laundry on the line. She smiled at the mannikins, and her face, with the matching features, no longer seemed, as Grandma Sukey had said, like an empty plate. For now it held a garnish of happiness round the edge. For the first time in her life, she did not have to rush back home to be questioned or scolded or whipped. Often, getting ready for bed, she found herself singing again: "Sometimes I'm up/Sometimes I'm down/Sometimes I'm almost to the ground." She let her voice bounce up to the ceiling and off the walls and out through the cracks around the windows. She forgot to worry about needing Uncle Floyd's bass to keep her steady.

One night, when she was working in the mailroom, she noticed a new man sorting letters. He was a tall, very thin young colored boy with black-rimmed glasses and a tense look. He was sorting letters so fast he might have been dealing cards. She watched him in fascination. "Hi," he said and smiled, but kept sorting. "Name's Wesley." He was neatly dressed in carefully pressed khakis and loafers and carried a comb in his hip pocket.

During the break, he sat in a corner drinking 7-Up and reading a big book which Miss Piper said was about chemistry. "Studying to be a doctor," she said, nodding approvingly. "He'll be going back to college after the Christmas vacation." She sighed. "I hate to lose him. He's a gem, that boy."

He rarely spoke, as if all his energy went into sorting letters and studying chemistry. "Scuse me," he said one evening as he rushed past Rannee during the break, carrying his 7-Up and his book to the chair in the corner. "Got to learn to be a doctor fast," he said. "So my daddy can retire. He's a doctor too. But he's all tired out from all those night calls." Rannee was surprised to learn that doctors made night calls. She thought of the nights she had spent in the hospital waiting for the doctor. The baby usually came first.

Wesley must be smart, she thought. Only a boy and about to become a doctor. She loved to watch him sorting letters, so fast he might have been reading the addresses with his finger tips. It was an important job too. If a letter got lost, it could never be replaced. It was the only one of its kind in the whole world. She had missed Berthadell's funeral and had, perhaps, lost Uncle Floyd forever, because of a misplaced letter.

One evening when she was sweeping and humming in the lounge, she saw his big, fat book lying open on the table. She swept her way across the room and stood leaning over, looking at it. It was almost all numbers with a few letters sprinkled in among them.

"Interested in chemistry?" Wesley said from the door.

"This chemistry?" she said. She remembered that she had had something in high school called chemistry but it was mostly measuring things in little jars. "Can you read this?" she said.

"Not for reading," he said. "It's for *studying*." He sat down, opened his 7-Up, and picked up his book. Miss Piper came in, sat down, and opened her book. Rannee sat down, put her hands in her lap, and stared at the picture of Atlas Scruggs who was WANTED by the FBI. After a while, she was quite sure she would know him anywhere, on any dark night, full-face or profile. He reminded her of Jarvis. She gave a slight shudder.

Wesley looked up. "Like something to read?" he said. He got up and pulled a book from his jacket pocket. "Just finished this coming to work on the bus tonight," he said. Everyone, she thought, seemed to read on the bus. "Read it for Lit. 202," he said. "Try it." He held it out.

She thanked him and took it carefully. It was called *The Heart Is a Lonely Hunter*. She opened it and read: "In the town there were two mutes . . ." She had no idea what "mutes" meant, and she was too embarrassed to ask. She felt hot with shame. Miss Piper looked up for a moment and smiled. Wesley raised his eyes and smiled too. Then they all bent their heads to their books.

"You saved?" Shubah asked her in the factory one morning.

"How you mean, saved?" Rannee said.

"You receive the Holy Ghost?"

"What for?"

Shubah was shocked. "You a Christian?" she said.

"Course I'm a Christian."

160

"You baptized?"

"Course I'm baptized."

Rannee remembered the night when she and Beet and Bay and the cousins were given white gowns and taken to Perkins Pond to be baptized by Mr. Tubal Tuttle who did all the baptizing around the Quarters. He was very tall with long arms as if he could reach right down to the bottom of the water to see if any old sinner had gotten stuck down there. Rannee stood on the bank, waiting her turn, expecting something special to happen, something that would help her to find the Lord and walk in His ways and sit quietly in Sunday school. Opposite, she could see Beet and Bay, sopping wet, with their hair hanging straight down like shoelaces. They didn't look saved at all, just cold. She was scared.

She clutched Mr. Tubal Tuttle's arm and took a deep breath. She had planned to keep her eyes open down there to watch her sins swimming around on the bottom. But before she knew it, she was standing, cold and wet, on the other side with the "saved." The sky and the pond looked exactly the same. She was exactly the same too, except for her hair. It was all beautifully straight now, but she knew that as soon as it was dry, it would go all fuzzy again. She hadn't really changed at all. Tomorrow, she would go on fearing not the Lord but Mama and Grandma Sukey. She would never be able to find Jesus and walk in His ways. She would be much too busy washing and sweeping and cooking and chopping. Someday, she had thought, when she was grown and living up North with Uncle Floyd and didn't have to work so hard, she would have more time to look for Him.

"You baptized in Jesus's name?" Shubah said now.

But Rannee couldn't remember what Mr. Tubal Tuttle had said.

"You baptized in *water?*" Shubah said sternly.

"Course," Rannee said. But it occurred to her now that perhaps that short rinsing had not been enough.

"Ain't enough," Shubah said. "You gotta be baptized with the Holy Ghost."

Rannee was impressed. "Where does it say that?"

"Acts, 1:15. Ain't you never read the Bible?"

"Course I read the Bible." But the truth was that she never really had. She knew only snippets, read aloud from the pulpit, mostly about Moses and the Children of Israel and the Lord giving orders. She had never heard anything about the Holy Ghost.

"You goes to church?" Shubah said.

"Sure I go to church. Been going since 'fore I was born. I even teach Sunday school."

"You like church?" Shubah said. "You feel peaceful and happy and raised up in church?"

Did she? She pictured the Mount Zion Baptist Church where every week she sat among strangers, mostly women and a few old men, while the preacher shouted, spraying saliva all over his congregation. He lived in an enormous house in a white neighborhood and drove around in a long black car like the candy man. His wife played the piano in church and his mistresses sang alto in the choir. Reverend Hampton spent most of his time shouting about the Children of Israel as if he'd never gotten past the first five books of the Old Testament, while Rannee thought of *her* children: Carter living with Bay and the others still home with Mama. She was a woman who couldn't keep her own children. She had no right to sit in church, and certainly no business teaching other people's children.

"You needin somethin in your life, chile," Shubah said. "You wanna come to my church sometime? Holy Light Pentercoster Church over to Bewler Street?"

"No, thanks," Rannee said. "I'm a Baptist. I go to the Mount Zion Baptist Church on Newcomb Street."

"You ever think what's gonna happen when you pass?" Shubah said.

"When I pass?"

"When you gone from this world. When the writin in your book a life is done."

"I've got lots of time 'fore I need to start worrying about *that*. And lots of other things to worry about first."

"You never knows," Shubah said. "Ain't you been tellin me you has trouble breathin right now?"

"That's nothing but the asman," Rannee said. "From working in the laundry next to the cemetery. I'm much better now." But she felt slightly worried. She saw Shubah bend and start the sewing machine, saw the stitches appear so neatly, one after the other. But whenever Shubah lifted her foot again, the stitches would stop. She heard her own breaths coming, one after the other, one after the other. But someday, God would lift a finger and her breaths would stop too.

"Is a wonderful feelin, knowin you is saved," Shubah said. "No more worryin bout dyin or hell fire or what all you gonna be doin for the resta eternity. Cause you know you be shoutin an singin an walkin down that smooth, smooth road with Jesus right beside you. You needin somethin in your life, chile. That's clear. You needin *Jesus*. You come on long to the Holy Light Pentercoster Church over to Bewler Street. Anytime. An give the Lord a chance. Let Him walk into your life."

"I'm a Baptist," Rannee said. "My parents and my children and my sisters and brothers are all Baptists. I go to the Mount Zion Baptist Church on Newcomb Street."

"You won't never find Him there," Shubah said.

That night, between jobs, Rannee picked her way through the litter of trash and discarded consonants in Beet's house to her room, thinking of what Shubah had said. She felt ashamed and afraid; ashamed at how little she knew and afraid of death. She saw herself walking recklessly, blindly, down a long road, not knowing that someone was walking beside her, counting her steps. She sat quietly for a long time, staring into the yard at the scrawny trees holding out empty branches and the dusty bushes sprouting scraps of paper. Shubah was right. She needed *something*. Friends? Lovers? The northern colored girls were loud and bold. They jangled. The men were merely smoothed-down versions of Jarvis. Cruelty lay beneath their

163

shoulder pads and their walk was full of greed. Except for Wesley. And he was only a boy.

"What do I have to do to be saved?" she asked Shubah the next morning.

"Be filled with the Holy Ghost."

"How do I do that?"

"Ain't nothin *to* do," Shubah said. "Is a gift. A gift from the Lord. All you gotta do is believe. An live a good Christian life."

"How do you do that?"

"Like the Scriptures says. No smokin or drinkin or fornicatin."

That was just plain old Baptist talk, Rannee thought. "What else?"

"No lyin or swearin or drugs."

That wasn't hard, Rannee thought. She never did any of those things anyway. "Anything else?" she said.

"Ain't *positively* require. But most saints mostly don't go to no movies or dances or bars or parties. An no TV."

Me neither, Rannee thought. She was halfway to being saved already. "What *do* they do?" she said.

"Goes to church, mostly."

"What do they do all that time in church?"

"They has Bible class an choir practice an missionary an prayer. They prayin an singin an praisin the Lord. Sometimes they cookin an cleanin too."

But Rannee knew she couldn't stand being in church so much. Even after a little while, the muscles in her legs started to jump. And she had all the cleaning and cooking she wanted at Beet's. "What else?" she said.

"They has Revivals an Homecomin an Gospel singin. They prays for sick peoples in hospitals and starvin peoples in Africa an ole Mrs. Honeywell, so bad she can't lift nothin, not even her own head. Saints takin care a her roun the clock an writin letters for her to send to her son in Rocky Hill State Prison. Saved peoples on call all the time. If someone needin prayer an you called, you jes stop whatever you doin an git down on your

164

knees an pray. You at work, you stop that work an pray. You in bed or the bathtub, you gits right outa that bed or outa that tub an down on your knees an prays."

That was much harder, Rannee thought. She wondered what Mrs. Starbury would have said if she had found Rannee on her knees beside a bucket of soapy water, praying instead of scrubbing. She wondered what Mr. Piscotti and the United States Postal Service would say. She decided she couldn't afford to be saved just yet.

"Thank you very much," Rannee said to Wesley one evening, handing him his book and speaking with care.

"Finished already?"

She nodded. She had read it steadily on the bus, in bed, at meals.

"Like it?"

"Oh, yes." She had figured out what "mutes" meant and was full of sorrow for Mr. Singer and admiration for Mick, who reminded her a little of the young Rannee, except that Mick was much bolder and braver and smarter than Rannee had ever been. She was horrified at what happened to Willie, a colored man, and was surprised that a white woman should know so much about colored people and write it all down in a white book. She wondered if Uncle Floyd had ever been in prison.

"Like another one?" Wesley said.

"You *have* another one? That you're not reading?"

He grinned and handed her *The Catcher in the Rye*. "Finished this just in time," he said.

It was a strange title, Rannee thought.

After the break, she went back to washing the floor. Near the letter boxes, she noticed a new poster tacked on the wall. "Examinations," it read, "for Carriers and Clerks." She stared at it for a moment. After that, she watched Wesley sort the mail as often as possible. One night, during the break, she tried it herself with old envelopes.

165

"You gotta give it more wrist," Wesley said from the door. He came in and showed her. She practiced every chance she got. Wesley helped her and even wrote down the abbreviations of the states for her: New Jersey, N.J.; Maryland, Md.; Virginia, Va.; Maine, Me.; Missouri, Mo.

"I'm gonna recommend you for my job when I leave," Wesley said. "But while I'm still around, what about a movie?"

"What about your chemistry?"

"Can't study chemistry *all* the time."

"Why do you want to take me to the movies?"

"Why not?"

"Why not someone your own age?"

"What's age got to do with it?"

"A lot. How old are you?"

"Nineteen. And you?"

"Twenty-four. Old enough to be your older sister."

"Well, I'd like to take my older sister to the movies."

She was about to say, "No thanks," when Wesley suggested they meet at the library. "Library? What library?"

"Public library. On Maple Street."

"All right," she said. "But I have to be home early. I live with *my* older sister and she's very strict."

Wesley grinned. "I gotta be home early too," he said. "I'm in training."

"Training? To be a doctor?"

"No I'm *studying* to be a doctor. I'm in training for basketball. Got a basketball scholarship."

She had no idea what that meant. "What do you do in training?"

He grinned. "It's what you *don't* do," he said. "You don't smoke and you don't drink and you don't . . ."

"I know." She smiled. "I'm in training too."

"*You* in training? What for?"

"A quiet life."

"We'll go to a quiet movie," he said.

166

# 13

"How you stand this mess?" Rannee asked, picking her way through a tangle of stockings and bras and bread crusts and apple cores. It was the first time Rannee had seen Beet in weeks.

"Not standin it much longer," Beet said. "I cuttin out."

"Cutting out?"

"Cuttin out. Leavin. Quittin. Splittin. Pickin my clothes up offa that floor an puttin them in a suitcase an walkin out that front door. Tha's what I mean."

"You leaving Spencer?"

"You damn right, I'm leavin Spencer. Tha's *egg-zackly* what I'm doin."

"You leaving your *husband?*"

"You damn right I is. I leavin this husbin an this town an this here mess."

"What about those children?"

"What about them?"

"You leaving them too?"

Beet shrugged. "Some of them's Spencer's, don' forgit."

She left Rannee a closet full of clothes—satins and sequins

167

and velvet pants and spiked shoes. But all Rannee took was an old pair of sneakers with the laces gone. The little girls stood silently, surrounded by rubbish, and watched Beet go.

Rannee was leaving too. Mama was ailing. She had to sit down most of the time now and take care of her pressure instead of her grandchildren.

"You go put yourself on Welfare," Shubah said, "an git those chillun back. You bin away how long? Two year? Tha's too long."

"We need statements," the Welfare lady said, "testifying that your mother is unable to care for your children." She wore pants and a jacket like a man, with a great golden bug crawling up the lapel. "Married?" she said. She was wearing six rings but none of them were wedding rings.

Rannee took a deep breath and tried to speak very slowly and very carefully. "A long time ago," she said.

"Widowed? Divorced? Separated?

"Separated," Rannee said. "And I want to keep it that way. Don't tell him my address. I don't want him around."

"If he's the father of your children," the woman said sternly, "he's supposed to contribute to their support."

"Him? He contributes nothing but pain and trouble." The thought of him was still like a knife in her brain. The slightest jolt and she could feel the point.

Her children, the Welfare lady said, would be sent by Travelers' Aid. "Be sure and pick them up," she said. As if they were packages, Rannee thought.

That night she warned Bay. "Jarvis ever come looking for me, don't give him my address, hear? Don't tell him anything about me. Don't let him near me. Otherwise, I'm clearing out. Outa this town, outa this state, outa this country."

Between jobs, she began to look for an apartment for her children.

She met Wesley at the library on Saturday night. He spent his days studying there when he wasn't at the Y shooting bas-

168

kets. His house was too crowded and too noisy: his father's patients kept the phone and the doorbell ringing, his sister practiced football cheers, the baby banged his head against the wall, his older brother was forever on his own personal line to Las Vegas, and his mother ran the vacuum steadily to drown out the other sounds.

Rannee had never been to the library before. She was amazed at the number of books, even more than in Mr. Fetterman's den, walls and walls of books. She wondered how long it would take to read them all.

Wesley was sitting at one of the long tables, all hunched over. He raised his head for a moment, smiled at her and dropped it again. He seemed to forget all about her. She didn't mind. It gave her a chance to look at the books. She wandered around, not quite daring to touch them. The librarian, a scrawny white woman wearing two sweaters and a pencil in her hair, came up to her, eager to help. She pulled a book off the shelf. "You'll enjoy this," she said.

Rannee thanked her and opened it at random. "That ain't the kind of love I understand, old lady," she read. "What you reckon he do . . . ?" She looked up. "This by a *good* writer?" she said.

"One of the best. James Baldwin. A *famous* writer."

Rannee had no idea who James Baldwin was, but she didn't think he wrote good English. The librarian handed her another book. She opened it and read: "Nigger, yuh sho better be damn glad it wuz us yuh talked t' tha' way. Yuh're a lucky bastard cause if yuh'd said tha' t' somebody else, yuh might've been a dead nigger now." Rannee closed the book. "This by a famous writer too?" she said.

"Richard Wright," the librarian said. "You can't get much more famous than that. Not in this country."

Rannee looked at it sadly. It could not teach her what she wanted to know.

Wesley rushed up, full of apologies. He had forgotten all about the time. He was studying History 101. It was the longest history in the whole college. "Let's go," he said. "Unless you want to take that out."

"Take it out?" In the library of the Chawnee High School for Negroes, no book ever left the building.

"Sure, all you need is a card."

"How do I get that?"

He took her over to the desk. "Now would you like to take that out?"

She looked down at Richard Wright. She was glad he was famous. She hoped he was rich too. He must have been pretty poor when he wrote that book. "No thanks," she said. But she did not tell Wesley why.

It was too late for the movies. Wesley bought her an enormous hot fudge sundae instead, and watched while she ate it. She had never tasted anything so good in her whole life. She thought of Mama who loved sweets. But even Mama wouldn't have to put any sugar on this.

Wesley stirred his root beer. "Training," he said, grinning into the glass. "Next week we'll go to the movies and I'll watch you eat popcorn." Walking home he recited important dates: 325, 410, 787, 1571. Rannee wondered what they meant.

At her door he turned. "I could kiss you good night," he said. "Wouldn't be breaking my training if I kissed you good night."

"Be breaking mine," she said.

The next day, after the factory, she went back to the library. The librarian was standing behind her desk, staring at the door. A sign in front of her said MISS DE PALMA. She was still wearing two sweaters and the pencil in her hair. Like Daddy and his hat, Rannee thought.

Miss de Palma looked up. "Glad to see you're back," she said. "Hope you find something you like this time," she said. "We have 55, 972 volumes, not counting the interlibrary loan."

"Please, Miss de Palma, ma'am," Rannee said timidly. "Do you have any books in *good* English?"

Miss de Palma stared and moved her pencil to the other side of her head. "Go see for yourself," she said. "See what you make of Jane Austen." She waved toward a bookcase and shook her head. Her pencil bobbed.

Rannee walked over to the As and found Jane Austen. She read: "About thirty years ago, Miss Maria Ward, of Huntingdon, with only seven thousand pounds, had the good luck to captivate Sir Thomas Bertram, of Mansfield Park, in the county of Northampton, and to be thereby raised to the rank of a baronet's lady, with all the comforts and consequences of an handsome house and large income." It was, Rannee supposed, closing the book, very good English, but she didn't think she wanted to read about Miss Maria Ward who sounded a bit like Merleene. She tried again: "Emma Woodhouse, handsome, clever, and rich, with a comfortable home . . ." Emma Woodhouse, Rannee thought, didn't sound very exciting either. She imagined her like Mrs. Junius back home, a rich white lady who sat on her front porch drinking lemonade and fanning herself and shouting orders to her colored maid in the house behind her without even turning her head.

It was time to go to work. She still had *The Catcher in the Rye*— she had only gotten as far as page thirty-eight—but she wasn't enjoying it. She wasn't really interested in those rich white boys and their fancy school. They had a whole room just for two people in that school and private showers between the rooms. But the boys swore at each other and complained all the time anyway. She felt sorry for the boy writing the story though he swore worst of all and didn't like anyone (not up to page thirty-eight, anyway) or anything, not even the steak and mashed potatoes on Saturday night.

She walked past the loan desk, conscious of her bookless arms and Miss de Palma watching her go. She could almost feel the point of that pencil poking into her back.

She found an apartment on Jewel Street in the colored section called, for some mysterious reason, the Hill, though it hardly rose above the railroad tracks and was more like an ugly bump on the backside of the town. Jewel Street was short and crowded with small, scrawny houses on one side and the county jail on the other. Walking past, Rannee saw black arms and black legs and black faces sticking through the bars. The prison, she learned, was always full. "Stuffed with niggers," Mrs. Puglisi, her landlady, said.

She was the only white woman on the block. She lived down-stairs and worked in the jail across the street and listened to police reports on the radio when she was home. There was no Mr. Puglisi in residence. She had probably locked him up long ago, Rannee thought. She showed Rannee an apartment at the top of the house. It had a living room and a kitchen with one corner curtained off for a toilet and shower. "Output right next to input," Mrs. Puglisi said. "Very handy with kids." There were two bedrooms with bunk beds and a rope to throw out the window in case of fire. The only radiator was in the kitchen. The rent was forty dollars a month. Welfare paid her ninety dollars.

"There'll be *five* of us," Rannee said.

"I know," the Welfare lady said, handing her vouchers for three towels and four blankets. "And no employment while receiving payments."

At the shirt factory, Shubah kissed her good-bye. "Praise be the Lord you takin your chillun back into yo life," Shubah said. "Now all you gotta do is let Jesus in too."

Rannee said good-bye to Miss Piper and the United States Postal Service. They all crowded around, telling her to be sure to come back, officially and unofficially. "We'll save our best commemorative stamps for you," someone said.

"Overnight delivery."

"No 'Postage Due.'"

"No 'Addressee Unknown.'"

"All junk mail returned to sender."

Rannee, whose mail was limited to letters to and from Mama, was delighted.

Saturday night, his last in town, Wesley took her to the movies. They met in the library again. Rannee got there early.

Wesley, bent over his book, did not see her, but Miss De Palma did. She smiled, nodded, and dug her pencil more securely into her head.

This time, Rannee began with the Bs. She had no idea what *Clayhanger* meant, but *The Old Wives' Tale* sounded promising. She read: "These two girls, Constance and Sophia Baines, paid no heed to the manifold interest of their situation, of which, indeed, they had never been conscious. They were, for example, established almost precisely on the fifty-third parallel of latitude." Rannee closed the book in despair.

Sadly, she wandered along the Bs until she saw a title that caught her eye: *The Pilgrim's Progress*. She had heard about Pilgrims in school. They had crossed the Atlantic in a tiny boat and shot wild turkeys and lived with the Indians and invented Thanksgiving. They sounded interesting. She opened the book and read: *"As I walked through the wilderness of this world, I lighted on a certain place, where was a Den; and I laid me down in that place to sleep; and as I slept I dreamed a Dream."* She read on. She was still reading when Wesley came up. "Time to go," he said. She took *Pilgrim's Progress* with her to the loan desk. Miss de Palma looked at the book carefully. *" 'The Pilgrim's Progress,' "* she read, *" 'From this world, to that which is to come . . . his dangerous journey.' "* She smiled. "Good luck," she said, stamping the book and handing it back to Rannee.

In the movies, Wesley held her hand. She stiffened. In a little while, he was asleep. She relaxed, slipped off her shoes and recited to herself: Louisiana, La.; North Dakota, N.D.; Vermont, Vt. After the states she went through the dates: 325 and 410 and 787 and 1571.

When Wesley woke up he was full of apologies. "It's that Holy Roman Empire," he said. "It wasn't holy and it wasn't Roman and it wasn't an empire. But it sure is a pain in the neck. It's ruining my social life."

"Never mind," she said. "It was a terrible movie." Over her sundae she made him explain those dates.

"Be back for the summer," he said at her door. "And I won't be in training then." He grinned. She let him kiss her good-bye.

She would miss him, she thought, getting ready for bed. He had taught her a lot, though he was only a boy. Thanks to Wesley she had a library card in her wallet, and all the abbreviations of all the states and some of the most important dates in the history of the world in her head.

She went to bed with *Pilgrim's Progress* and read far into the night. She was fascinated by the plight of the man dressed in rags with a book in his hands and a great burden on his back who wept and trembled and cried out, "What shall I do?" She wrote down the difficult words to look up in the library— "Slough" and "Despond" and "Obstinate" and "Pliable"— and slid quickly over "the children of my bowels." She felt great sympathy for poor Christian hoping to find the Celestial City as she had hoped to find Uncle Floyd. In the meantime, she kept *Pilgrim's Progress* within easy reach in the kitchen and renewed it regularly.

"Never allowed children in this house before," Mrs. Puglisi said, looking down at Rannee with her four sons strung out on either side of her like spread wings. "Never wanted them. Don't want them now. Any trouble, out you go." And across the street to be locked up, Rannee thought. Mrs. Puglisi, born Brody, had learned to adjust.

She had a round, flat, white face that looked as if it had been rolled out, with a fringe of bleached blond hair like a pie crust. She had six brothers-in-law, all muscular men with strong stomachs and strong opinions who all owned property on the Hill: a liquor store, two bars, a grocery store, a department store, and several worn-out tenements. One brother was a cop and another a "mortician." One brother killed you, people said, and the other buried you. No one could eat or dress or even die on the Hill without making some Puglisi a little richer.

The other tenants kept to themselves. Old Mr. Caliph lived all alone and was terrified of being robbed. He never went out except to the grocery store on the corner at different times each day, taking his most precious possessions with him: his trousers and topcoat over his pajamas, his pipe and two 75-watt electric light bulbs in his pockets, his extra shoes in a paper bag, and a three-legged dog on a leash. Mr. and Mrs. Lambert, the young couple on the floor below, were always out or asleep. They looked very much alike—same height, same short, curly hair, same black trousers and black jackets. They both worked at the same hospital but were never seen together. She worked from eight to four, he worked from four to twelve. Rannee knew they were home from the sound of the television that ran all day. After a while, she could tell from the programs which one was home and when they were home together. Then there would be raised voices and shouts and the sounds of the channels being yanked back and forth.

Mrs. Puglisi kept the thermostat down very low so the heat never rose to the top floor. Rannee's pipes froze and the plumbing broke down regularly. Mrs. Puglisi always blamed the children. "We don't put garbage or newspapers or old socks down the toilet," she told Rannee regularly.

"Neither do we," Rannee said.

The boys gave her no trouble. They were still so little, satisfied to hold on to her skirt or her sleeve or a free finger. They loved to go downtown with her, to ride on the bus and see the gulls and the people on the Green: the lady with the bird cage on her lap, feeding her canary with a tweezer; the young man in an Indian headband and fringed jacket, standing barefoot and still in the cold, holding a one-man vigil for the Indians of North America. And the stores! The little boys had never seen such stores. "Don't touch," Rannee warned. "And don't ask. We're just *looking.*"

She was still terrified of the stores. She stood paralyzed in the middle of the huge self-service shops, not daring to help herself. But the way her sons looked wrung her heart. She bought them colored pencils and plastic spoons and rubber bands and packs of Life Savers at Woolworth's. She stocked up on chicken parts—legs and wings and thighs—whenever she could. None of her children, she promised herself, would ever have to make do with a whiff of the tail. They had had so little—even less than she who had had Mama *and* Daddy in the next room and Uncle Floyd right up the road—and not even a yard or a porch or woods to play in. The only parks were far away at opposite ends of the town, where the white people lived in big houses with enormous gardens full of tables and chairs, like huge living rooms that no one ever used. In the ghetto there was nothing but an old dusty cemetery. Sometimes, to save bus fare, she took the children there to picnic on potato chips and Kool-Aid. It reminded her of her own school lunches, leaning against Mr. Bumpus in the graveyard where she had last seen Uncle Floyd.

On rainy days, she took them to the library and let them look at the picture books in the Children's Room while she browsed among the Cs and the Ds, though she kept on reading *Pilgrim's Progress* too. There seemed to be an endless supply of books. She found a whole row by someone named I. Compton-Burnett. She opened one at random. "It is a pity you have not my charm . . . ," she read with delight, and she tried it on Bay the next Sunday.

"How come you talk so funny?" he said.

One day Lance pleaded with her to let him stay and finish "reading" his book.

"He can take it home," the children's librarian said, and made out a card for him. After that, Rannee read to him whenever she could. Sometimes, when she was sitting at the kitchen table with her book, he would run and get his and sit down beside her with his head in his hands like her, staring into his book like her, turning the page whenever she did. Every now and then he would lean over and ask, "What that say there, Mama?" as if he had read all the rest, as if that were the only passage that gave him trouble.

When she was home, she kept the children indoors, for the neighborhood frightened her: the constant group of men swaying on the corner outside Big Joe's with their coats open and their arms flapping, shouting words she could not understand. They were always there, as if they'd been put out with the trash. There were the Ledbetters, five doors down, who fought every Friday, a slow night on television. Mrs. Ledbetter ran out in her nightgown with Mr. Ledbetter right behind, beating steadily till the cops came and took him away. As soon as he was gone, Mrs. Ledbetter stumbled up the stairs, bathed and dressed and invited the neighbors in. It was, she explained, the only chance she had. Often, Rannee saw a police car parked on the corner with two enormous cops, their guns slanted in their holsters, tipping down a sagging porch: one of the Gomez kids being picked up again. The Gomezes never had a full house. There was always a Gomez doing time somewhere. The ambulance came constantly for births and deaths and attempted suicides and, once, for a newborn baby found buried in a flowerpot. The police came regularly to the bars around the corner on Market Street, to the sound of sirens and smashed glass and occasional gunshots. And sometimes, in the middle of the night, Rannee heard the sirens from the jail across the street and imagined long dark men squeezing between the bars and climbing silently up her front steps.

And always, even in the ghetto, she was aware of the white people watching. White policemen drove around in shiny cars with big white eyes rolling around on the roof and Mrs. Puglisi spied on her even in her own house. At school, white teachers stared down at the little colored children over folded arms, or asked questions from the other side of the desk.

She took Lance to school the first afternoon—he went only in the afternoon—with high hopes. The school was called simply the Abraham Lincoln School. Good, she thought, remembering the Chawnee Primary School for Negroes. But the Abraham Lincoln was an old square stone building with rusty fire escapes and peeling walls and a cement playground and a huge staircase with high steps going up to the front door. "That it?" Lance had whispered, clinging to her hand and looking way up. "That the *school?*" The children, Rannee realized, were all colored. When she saw the white teachers, she felt better. Good, she thought, remembering the Misses Nora and Dora French. Lance would be *taught*, like white children, instead of *whipped*. For Lance, she knew, was smart. At home, she often found him alone in the kitchen with his book or staring at the letters on the calendar or the coffee can. His big sad eyes seemed to search out meaning everywhere, even in the linoleum on the floor. He was growing fast now. He would be tall like Ward.

He hid behind Rannee's left hip that first day and stared up at the tall, stern white lady with a long pointed nose who was saying things he couldn't understand. Rannee remembered her own first day at school. Daddy had taken her on the mule, right up to the schoolhouse door. He had lifted her down and kissed her good-bye and told her not to worry. She had lots of friends in school, he said, pointing to Beet and Odette Peters and Marbelle. But Lance had nobody. He clung to her hand and stared at her with his huge frightened eyes, and she felt she was deserting him once again. But this time she was leaving him with a total stranger, a *white* stranger, who knew nothing at all about him. He was just another colored child whom she would not recognize or even understand.

Walking home with the other children, Rannee realized that the colored school was right on the edge of the ghetto. White families lived just across the street. White women stood in their doorways clutching their babies and staring angrily at the little colored children marching, two by two, into the building. Rannee felt her sons clutching her. "Where Lance at?" they said. "Why we not bringin Lance home?"

Near her house, she saw a car stuck in the middle of the street with a colored couple inside and a white policeman beside it. It was Officer Puglisi, a huge man who looked as if he could pick up that battered old car all by himself and dump it inside the jail. He was shouting and the woman inside the car was shouting back. Finally, Officer Puglisi opened the car door and began to drag the woman out. She screamed and a crowd gathered. Rannee grabbed her children and hurried home. But not before she heard shouts and the sounds of smashed glass behind her. She spent the rest of the day inside. The streets here, she learned, were dangerous places where white policemen rode around looking for colored people to fill up their jails. Sometimes clashes broke out; sometimes people got hurt or even killed, ordinary people just walking by or looking out of a window or standing in front of a store, ordinary people with black skin.

When she picked up Lance that afternoon, he looked more frightened than ever. At home, his face quivered. He put his hands over his small, delicate ears and began to cry.

"What happened?" Rannee said. "She whip you?"

He shook his head. "Don't have no whippin in that school. Just hit you on your hand with a ruler."

"She hit you?"

"No."

"Then what?"

"She say Lance not a real name. She say no such place as Bammer where Granny live. She say I never only six year old. I too big. She say how come I kin read so good. She say you not *spoze* to teach me to read. I tole her you never taught me. I *tole* her." He was crying and shaking harder than ever. "I tole her not your fault I kin read."

Rannee sat down in the rocker and pulled him into her lap. "Hush," she whispered, kissing and rocking him. "Hush. Don't you mind. Don't you never mind. It's gonna be all right. Everything's gonna be all right." But she felt a stab of fear. She had failed him, she thought, had provided no protection, instilled no safeguards. She had not prepared him as Mama and Grandma Sukey and Simms Quarter had prepared *her*. When his sobbing finally subsided, she stood him up between her legs. "Now," she said sternly, in the voice of Simms Quarter, "did you sass that white lady?"

"No, Mama. I *never* sass that white lady."

"You ask foolish questions?"

"No, Mama. I never asked *no* questions."

179

"Now you listen to me," Rannee said. "Don't never ask *anything*, you hear? They ask you something, you answer as best you can. Otherwise, you keep your mouth shut. Understand?"

"Yes, Mama."

"And you mind your manners and you never talk back to white people. Hear? And you always say 'Yes, ma'am' and 'No ma'am' at all times. You hear?"

"Yes, Mama." He climbed back into her lap and put his face in her neck. Poor Lance, she thought, rocking him again. He would attract anger and hatred for being so gentle, so mild, just as she had attracted it for being aloof and sullen and even defiant. But she had been tough, not like poor Lance who was always so scared, as if the gunshot that had killed his father before he was even born had frightened him for life.

The next afternoon, she put on her Sunday dress and her Sunday shoes. "We goin to church?" Flash said as they started out.

"We are going to *school*," Rannee said, clutching her purse and stressing her consonants. "To fetch Lance."

At school, Lance was watching for her, staring through the fence of the playground. Across the street, she noticed, the big white boys were home from high school, bouncing balls, throwing stones at passing cars, and hurling sticks and jeers at the fence of the playground. She was frightened. She took the children inside and left them near the door with orders not to move and not to say a word till she came back. Then, with her head high and her heart beating hard enough to knock the buttons off her dress, she marched down the hall.

The white lady hardly bothered to look up from the papers on her desk. "Yes?" she said, marking something with a pencil.

Rannee took a deep breath, straightened her back and marshalled her English. "It's about Lance Peters, ma'am," she said. "That's his rightful name, ma'am. *I* gave it to him. Out of a book. Not his fault, ma'am."

The teacher nodded and turned a page.

"He's really only six years old, ma'am. That's the truth. He's just big for his age. I got his birth cer-tif-i-cate right here." She opened her purse. "His daddy was very tall too."

"I really don't understand," the white lady said. "Is there something you wanted Mrs. . . . . Peters?"

"Lyle, ma'am. Peters was my first husband. Lance's daddy. But he's dead now and . . ."

"Yes. Well. I'm terribly sorry but I'm really awfully busy. Unless it's something . . ."

"I just wanted to explain about my boy, ma'am, Lance Peters. I never taught him reading, ma'am. He just learned by himself. And he really was living in Alabama, ma'am, with his granny. That's the truth."

"Yes, well, I'm afraid I really don't see . . ."

"I just wanted to explain about my boy," Rannee said quickly. "Thank you, ma'am." She hurried out.

That night Lance had a nightmare again, but this time it was not about Jarvis but about Mrs. Sperling, the first-grade teacher, who stood in the middle of a narrow hall with an enormous net in her hands. Whoever went up or down that hall would be caught in her net and locked up in a box with rats and spiders and prickly plants, to be studied with the other specimens. Rannee, sitting beside him while he shouted and cried in his sleep, knew there was nothing she could do to help him, only pray that somehow he would manage to slip through the tiny holes in that net. When he finally awoke and looked at her with his huge teary eyes, she was reminded again of her own nightmares of the slaughtered animals of Simms Quarter whose eyes had paved the road beneath her feet.

She kept to herself, surrounded by her children. The neighbors spoke of her as "the lady with the little boys." Whenever they saw her, she was herding her children down the street beneath the barred windows of the jail, past the discarded men on the corner.

Sometimes some of the neighbors left their children and their pets with her. "You not workin," they said. Even Bay and Merleene brought their new baby for Rannee to keep while

Merleene went to her new job, writing down appointments for a colored doctor. "That child so spensive," she said.

"I got four," Rannee said between clenched teeth.

"I pay you for your services," Bay said. But he never did. Instead, he came on Sundays with Merleene and the baby to take Rannee's children for a ride and a Good Humor. Rannee never went. It hurt her to see Bay with his hair greased and his big-ringed hands splayed out on the wheel of that fat, shiny car. And she knew Merleene would make her hold that new baby— hot and cranky and leaky—all afternoon. Rannee preferred to stay home alone with her shoes off and a library book in her hands, reading and practicing her vowels.

# 14

One very cold afternoon, when all the heat in the house stayed crouched down on the first floor, Rannee's doorbell rang. It was Mrs. Voncia Watkins, who lived next door. "I see you through my winder," she said, "settin in that kitchen in coats and blankets an I know that Puglisi's furnace broke down agin. So, you all come on over to my house. I got a real good furnace. My son bought me a real nice furnace. It sendin up heat like the prayers o the faithful. You come on over 'fore those sweet lil boys freeze up like popsickles."

She was a widow with a son on the police force, but she went out to work just the same, cleaning the big white houses on Wellington Place. She took to dropping in often on her way home to visit Rannee, with the remains of her lunch in a paper bag and a newspaper which she always left for Rannee. Rannee used it to line her garbage can. She never read it. She did not want the world in detail anymore. She preferred books that kept their distance.

Voncia would sit at Rannee's kitchen table with her hat on and her feet resting on top of her bumpy shoes and her large crooked fingers wrapped around a cup, and talk: about God and Jesus and her son, Officer Watkins, known as OW, a friendly young man who, she said, was sometimes *too* friendly. He had, out of sheer good nature, married—in rapid succession—an alcoholic, a lesbian, and a mother of five. Now he was single again. Like most people up North, Rannee thought, all separate men and women, bouncing around on their own.

But Voncia was very proud of him, the only colored policeman in the whole neighborhood. "Everybody love OW," she said. "You a nice sweet girl, Lyle. He never seed a nice sweet girl like you that growed up on a farm, nice an quiet. An purty too. A nice quiet kind a purty." She stared at Rannee for a moment. "Time you was married agin, girl."

"No thanks," Rannee said. "I've been married twice already. I'm finished with marrying."

The first time she saw OW, he was wearing his uniform. He had stopped in on his way home to pick up his mother. But Voncia had already left. He stood in her doorway with his hat under his arm, a handsome young man with his face and his buttons shining.

She stared. She had never seen a colored policeman before. Suddenly, she became conscious of her old Chawnee dress and Beet's old sneakers with the laces gone. But he didn't seem to notice. He was gazing down at her face like a man staring into his teacup, trying to read his fortune.

He smiled and introduced himself. "How do you do?" he said.

Not "Hi," she noticed, or "How ya doin?" or even "How do?" But "How do you do," smooth and careful and beautifully shaped, like words from a cookie cutter. His fingers closed firmly around her hand. She felt a tingle right down to her knees. "Good afternoon," she said softly, smoothing her syllables. She was glad she had been practicing her English so hard for so long. "Never had a policeman in my kitchen before."

He grinned. "Nothing to worry about," he said. "I'm off duty. Besides, I don't like making arrests. I'm more interested in preventing them." He smiled again. "You ever need that kind of service, just let me know."

184

"Oh, I will. I certainly will," she said. After he left, she spent ten minutes sitting at the kitchen table, just breathing.

The next day, he dropped in on his way to work. He had, he explained, just broken up with a shoplifter who had left him most of her loot: four Mars bars, a bottle of Arpege, and a police whistle. "To protect yourself," he told her. "Four men and one woman, you are at a distinct disadvantage." He grinned at the children, peering at him from behind the couch. "You just blow this," he said, "anytime you need protection. Small boys are my specialty." He swung his billy. "I can crack their heads like eggs and lay them out like omelets. You just let me know." The little boys giggled wildly.

"I don't think that will be necessary," Rannee said very carefully, "Officer Watkins."

He grinned. "Name's OW, Mrs. Lyle."

She grinned back. "Name's Rannee, OW." She had never said that to anyone before.

"Well, keep it in mind." He smiled, saluted them all with his billy, handed Rannee a packet of peppermint-flavored toothpicks, and left.

The square of linoleum where he had stood, Rannee noticed, looked newly polished.

The next time Voncia Watkins stopped by on her way home with her newspaper and her personal garbage in a paper bag, she told Rannee all about Mrs. Homer Huntington, a worrying white lady on Wellington Place. She worried about her hair color and her hemline and her weight and her sunburn. She worried about her son who was getting married and her daughter who was not. She had terrible troubles, Voncia said, but refused to try Jesus.

Voncia had tried Jesus quite often, it seemed, and talked about Him a lot. She told Rannee how He had saved her from dying, right there on Jewel Street. "I so sick *everybody* give me up," she said. "I know cause ole Doc Teeters even send for that ambulance to fetch me to the hospital. An I know once I git in that there hospital ain't no one but the undertaker gonna fetch me out agin. I lyin on that bed, prayin an beggin the Lord not to let them take me. An then I seen Reverend Moses comin through the door. He the new preacher then, a sweet-faced man with the mark o the Lord right on him, smilin an noddin an askin would I like him to pray with me. He kneel down an take my hands an spread them on the cover. 'You believe?' he say. 'You believe the Lord kin save you? Kin heal you?' Then he lift my finger, one by one, an I feelin the strength comin back, finger by finger. When he finish I fast asleep. When I wake up agin, he gone an I feelin so strong I git up an dress and gwan out. Time the ambulance come, I kneelin in the church, praisin the Lord and waxin the floor. An I never been sick agin to this day. That Reverend Moses a good man *an* a good preacher. But he gone to Columbus, Ohio, doin missionary work. He from way down South somewhere. But he leave there long ago. Got no home, no wife, no chillun, no family. Only the Lord. He movin roun all the time, doin the Lord's work. He say that why he called Moses."

Like Uncle Floyd, Rannee thought, who had no home and no wife and no family either. She imagined him in his black Sunday suit and his big head stuffed with chapter and verse, reading the Lesson in Columbus, Ohio, answering questions and saving souls and whistling "Only Believe."

Voncia loved to talk about her son, OW, too, who was always after her to stop working and rest. "But I tell him I can't stand too much settin. I gits the pain in my legs. Muscles gittin all locked up from all that settin. Besides, what I gonna do if I stop workin an the next day he go out an git married agin? The kinda woman he choose. Besides, he supportin too many womens right now." She stopped and smiled at Rannee. "But he a good man," she said. "A good husbin an a good friend."

"A good son, you mean," Rannee said.

"He like you, Lyle. He like to come an see you."

"Let him come," Rannee said. "Let him see. But that's all. Because I'm finished with men. For good."

She had her sons, she thought, locking the door behind Voncia. Turning, she saw Voncia's newspaper lying, as usual, on the kitchen table. Ever since OW's first visit, she had been reading Voncia's newspapers before using them for the garbage. She read them aloud to herself, practicing how to say long words like "gubernatorial" and "executive" and "investigatory," and even looked them up in the library dictionary.

Now she saw a huge picture on the front page. It showed a few scared-looking colored children in front of a school, surrounded by a mob of angry whites and two rows of soldiers with pointed guns. She sat down and studied it.

Later that evening, OW came to the door. He was wearing his uniform and holding his hat in one hand and a huge carton of ice cream in the other. "For the men of the house," he said. The buttons on his tunic glowed at her.

"The men of the house," she said carefully, "are fast asleep."

"For their mother, then."

"Bad for my asman," she said.

"On the contrary. *Good* for your asthma. Very good."

"Good for my asth*ma*?" she said, and repeated it to herself: "asth*ma*."

"Yes, madam," he said. "Guaranteed. But it's dripping." He grinned.

She smiled and opened the door wider. He came in, put the ice cream in the refrigerator, his hat on the table, and sat down. "Can you spare a cup of coffee for a hardworking policeman?" he said.

"Doesn't that hardworking policeman have to go to work?" She filled a cup.

"Not for another hour. Besides, it's good for me to relax first. In fact, it's necessary." He paused and stirred his coffee. "It's a lonely business being a policeman," he said.

"Lonely? With that whole big station full of great big policemen?"

"*White* policemen, don't forget. I should say it's lonely being a *Negro* policeman. But it's nice sitting here. *Very* nice." He leaned back and stared at her. She was sitting quietly with her hands in her lap.

187

"What's the matter?" she said.

"You. Never knew anyone like you. Pretty and peaceful both." He grinned and shook his head. "A pretty woman who doesn't push or publicize or even paint herself. Never knew a pretty woman before who could be so still. Still as a picture on the wall." He was staring at her as if he longed to take that picture down and carry it off in his arms for himself.

She saw his hands stretched out on the table in front of him, strong, smooth hands with long, straight fingers and no rings, no gold anywhere. She imagined them reaching out to touch her. She looked away and saw Voncia's newspaper folded on the counter. "Ever hear of something called integration?" she said.

"Yes."

"What does it mean?"

"It means that the schools have to stop crowding Negro children into rickety old buildings with bad teachers and not enough heat and not enough books."

She nodded. Like the Chawnee Primary School for Negroes, she thought.

"It means that all children, Negro and white, go to school together, to the same schools with the same conditions."

"You mean white people send their children to school with *colored* children?" she said.

"It's the law," he said.

She got up and showed him the picture in the newspaper of the little colored school children, surrounded by a crowd of screaming whites and soldiers with pointed guns.

"Like that?" she said. "Is that integration?"

"That's the South," he said.

"In Lance's school, all the children are colored and all the teachers and the principal are white. Is *that* integration?"

"No," he said angrily. "That's just discrimination. They hire white teachers and send them to Negro schools for practice—or punishment. And that white principal is just waiting to get transferred."

Poor Lance, Rannee thought. She was glad that colored children went to school for only half a day up North. She wondered where OW had gone to school and how he had managed to learn so much. She noticed he always said "Negro" instead of "colored." She must remember to say "Negro," too.

Suddenly there was the sound of raised voices from downstairs. "Lamberts must be home," she said. "Both of them."

The voices grew louder and mingled with the sounds of television channels being yanked about. After a while there was a crash and the sound of knocks and bumps as of objects banged against the walls. Soon there was a knocking on Rannee's door. Mrs. Puglisi stood outside, breathing heavily. "That nigger cop here?" she said. "Well, why the hell don't he *do* something? Sitting in my house drinking coffee like he's the commissioner, letting those damn niggers bust up my place."

"Not my beat," OW said. "Call the station."

"Why the hell should I call the station and wait half an hour while they break up my house when I got a cop right on the premises? In fact, I oughtta start chargin you rent, practically livin in like you are. A regular live, live-in cop. That is, if there really is such a thing as a *colored* cop."

"I'm a cop, all right," OW said softly.

"Then why the hell don't you act like one?"

"They're just having a little family beef," he said. "Leave it alone and it'll be over soon. No one's getting hurt and nothing of yours is getting broken. That's just their own furniture they're throwing around. I don't hear any windows being smashed or ceilings coming down. But if you want the cops, call them. This isn't my beat."

"And you sure as hell ain't no cop. They're down there committing breach of the peace and disorderly conduct and destruction of property and criminal mischief, and you sit up here doin *nothin*. Well, you can stop hanging around here. I don't like strange men hanging around my property, in or out of uniform." She turned and glared pointedly at Rannee. "You hear me?"

189

"I hear you," OW said. He stood up and put on his hat. "OK, I'll take a look." He winked at Rannee and left.

Locking the door behind him, Rannee realized that she was scared. She knew from the newspapers that up North, even policemen were sometimes shot and killed. And OW was a *colored* policeman. She clung to the kitchen chair and prayed that OW would be all right. Lifting her head, she noticed *Pilgrim's Progress* in its usual place on the kitchen counter, between the clock and the ketchup bottle. Between the bangs and crashes from downstairs, she heard the sound of the clock, like Christian's heart, beating loud and fast, as if he were scared too.

Suddenly, the noises stopped. She opened the door and saw OW, smooth and shining and completely unscratched, coming up the stairs.

"What happened?" she said.

"Just what I thought. A little family beef."

"What did you do?"

"Took off my hat, sat down, and watched."

"And they stopped?"

"They stopped. No fun having a little family beef with a stranger in the room. Specially if he's a cop."

Mrs. Puglisi came shouting down the hall. "You didn't arrest em?" she screamed. "You didn't get em out of my house? You didn't do *nothin?*"

"I stopped the fight. Isn't that what you wanted?"

"I want the law on em. That's what I want. For disturbing the peace and creating a nuisance and destroying private property." OW put on his hat, bowed slightly, and started down the stairs. "You won't do it, I'll get the law on *you*," she shouted after him. "Dereliction of duty. In fact, the law's on his way up here right now."

Rannee, watching OW go downstairs, saw a strange man coming up. He was a big white man, big shoulders, big ears, big nose, and a big head paved over with smooth black hair. There was no room for him to pass OW on the narrow stairs. But he kept coming up anyway. And OW kept going down. "My brother-in-law, Joe Puglisi," Mrs. Puglisi shouted over the bannister. "*Officer* Puglisi to you. Having trouble with this here nigger cop, Joe," she said.

On the stairs, the white man kept going up and the black man kept going down. "Yeah?" Puglisi said. "I can believe it."

Now the two men were one step apart, Officer Puglisi looking up and OW looking down, the white man looking up to the black man and the black man looking down on the white man. "Looks like *I'm* gonna have trouble with him too," Puglisi said. The men stood still, each on his own step, and glared at each other.

The front door opened. It was old Mr. Caliph back from his daily trip to the corner grocery store with his paper bag and his three-legged dog beside him. He stared at the two men immobilized on the steps, at the white man looking up at the black man looking down. He could see the gun Puglisi carried in his back pocket. On duty or off, Puglisi always carried a gun. "Evenin all," Mr. Caliph said. He winked at OW behind Puglisi's back and jerked the leash. The dog began to growl softly.

"Get that filthy mutt outa here," Puglisi said without turning.

"Yessir," Mr. Caliph said. "Only he *live* here. He jes hungry. He be all right soon as I can git him upstairs an feed him. Soon as you gentlemen finish goin up an comin down." The dog growled again, tugging at the leash in the direction of Puglisi's ankles. Puglisi stiffened. "Matta fack," Mr. Caliph went on, winking at OW again, "white po-liceman out front ticketin a big black car right now, license JLP."

"Jesus," Puglisi said. "Another dumb cop. Town's full of em. OK. I'm goin. But I'll remember you," he said, pointing a fat finger in OW's face. He turned and began to go downstairs. "An you," he shouted at Mr. Caliph, "you get that filthy mutt outa my way."

On the landing, Mrs. Puglisi watched with fury while Officer

191

Puglisi made a wide circuit around the dog and hurried out. OW turned, tipped his hat to her, and smiled at Rannee. Then he continued down the stairs. "Thank you, sir," he murmured to Mr. Caliph, and stopped to pat the dog.

The children got bigger and the Welfare check got smaller. After a while it seemed to shrink till it could no longer cover the month. Rannee stopped going downtown. She stopped buying chicken parts. She longed to buy in bulk as they did at home: huge sacks of flour and sugar and meal. But without a car, she was forced to shop at the small store on the corner where everything was measured out in tiny packages. She came home with mostly wrappings: cardboard and cellophane and plastic. Mr. Rodriquez, the new owner, was a devout Catholic who kept his windows full of large figures of agonized saints with their eyes turned up as if trying to see their own halos. At their feet were rows of dusty bottles in different sizes and colors, with pictures of more saints on the labels. "For the good fortune," Mr. Rodriquez explained. But Rannee had no money for good fortune. The rest of the stock looked small and expensive and stale, as if it had all been delivered years ago, with the picture of Pius XII still smiling above the cash register. Mr. Rodriquez lived in a tiny room at the back.

He had escaped from Cuba in a fishing boat and kept telling Rannee that Americans didn't know how lucky they were to be free. He talked a lot about being free but kept his credit tight. It was not his store, he explained. It belonged to Mr. Sal Puglisi. "Very hard man," he said. "Very high rent." Whenever Rannee wanted to charge anything, Mr. Rodriquez lapsed into Spanish. She walked home past the men stuck on the corner and the men stuck in jail. The last two days before the next Welfare check, she diluted the milk and diced the bread. The children stared when she said there was no more. "Why don't we work the patches?" Flash said. One morning there was nothing left but Karo-flavored water, half a loaf of bread, and OW's peppermint toothpicks.

That night, after the children were in bed, Mrs. Puglisi came up to tell Rannee that she couldn't wait for the rent any longer. "Ten days late already and I got a real nice sheriff from Watertown ready to move in. No pets, no children, not a single living relative except his wife waiting it out in the Seaside Convalescent Home. *And* a family-size Cadillac. Says he hates driving alone." She patted her hair and adjusted her bosom. "And no nigger cops hanging around."

Rannee locked her children in and ran all the way to Bay's. Like the night she ran across town to Aunt Vee's, she thought, with Jarvis right behind her. There was something else behind her now.

Bay looked bigger than ever and his apartment more crowded. There were brand-new lamp shades and couches and big white chairs and a pink-and-white bassinet, with Bay's brand-new baby inside, all wrapped up in plastic. The couch crackled when Rannee sat down. Merleene, stretched out on a love seat, was wearing an extensive line of "lounge clothes" all at once: pants and blouse and jacket and stole, and scarves and bracelets and beads dripping down her arms and breast.

"Sure, Tink Baby, sure," Bay said. "Too bad you come at such a disadvantage time." He peeled three fives off a roll and handed them to her. She stared at them and thanked him. She would never ask Bay for money again.

At home, she sat in the dark of her living room and thought of that northern family who had sat down to an empty table three times a day and said grace over their empty plates. But after the "Amen," Preacher Brown had said, there was always a knock on the door. Someone was always standing there with his arms full of food. But no one except Mrs. Puglisi and the Watkinses ever knocked on Rannee's door. Perhaps because she didn't really believe enough, she thought, remembering Uncle Floyd's favorite hymn, remembering him whistling it over and over, "Only Believe."

The next afternoon, Voncia dropped by wearing her hat, with her apron under her coat. Rannee poured out her tea and stood staring down into the cup. "I'll take jes a drop of sugar like always, Lyle, honey," Voncia said.

Rannee turned to scour the sink. "Sugar's gone," she said.

"How bout jes a drop a milk then, honey?"

There was a pause.

"You got a squirt a lemon handy?"

Rannee shook her head.

Voncia looked at the empty table with nothing on it but her cup. "Never mine," she said. "I be gittin my supper soon. You go right ahead an fix yours, Lyle, honey. I know those boys'll be wantin their supper. Don't mine me. You go right ahead an fix it."

"Nothing to fix," Rannee said into the drain.

Voncia put down her cup. "Course there ain't," she said. "Not with you tryin to live on Welfare like you do. Ain't no one ever tole you it can't be done?"

"Then what am I supposed to do?"

"Get you some supplementer income."

"What's that?"

"A job, girl. A job."

"And lose my Welfare? I can't afford to lose my Welfare."

"Who say anythin bout losin Welfare? Jes make a lil extra to feed your family between checks is all. A lil part-time job."

"Doing what?"

"Cleanin house. Same as me. I kin git you a job. Through the church. White peoples always callin the church wantin saints to come scrub their toilets."

"What church?"

"The Holy Light Pentercoster Church. Down to Bewler Street."

It was the second time Rannee had heard that name. "I kin git you a job any time," Voncia said.

"What about my children?" Rannee said.

"They ain't in school yet?"

"Just Lance and Flash. I can't leave the little ones alone."

"Well, you can't leave them starve neither."

Rannee walked to the window and leaned on the sill. "That Welfare lady will stop my payments soon as she finds out."

"How she gonna find out? You git your pay in straight cash. How she gonna find out?"

Rannee stared out the window at the bars of the jail across the street. "It's the law," she said.

"Everybody breakin that law," Voncia said.

Later that evening, there was a knock on the door. It was OW with his arms full of groceries. He wore a tan suit and a tan shirt and a tan tie. He looked smooth and suave and soothing, like some special blend made to order. He knew all the best restaurants in town, he said, and had toothpicks to prove it— multicolored and multiflavored. "Fifty-seven varieties," he said, offering them around. The little boys looked at her.

"Not now," she said. "It's bedtime now."

"Then I'd better stay on duty right here," OW said. "You might be needing some assistance. This gang looks pretty dangerous to me." The little boys put their hands over their mouths and giggled with pleasure.

"No thanks," Rannee said. "That's a job for a *mother*, not a policeman."

"Doesn't this mother ever go off duty?" OW said.

"No. Never," she said firmly. But, closing the door behind him, she wondered where he was going, and thought how nice it would be to be off duty with Officer Watkins.

Later, after the children were in bed, she sat in the dark in her nightgown and stared at the lights of the jail across the street. It was an old jail that had originally been built in the next state. Condemned there, it was carried, piece by piece, down the river and set up in Jewel Street. There were rats big as rabbits in that jail, Mrs. Puglisi had told her, and the cells stank from the unflushed, leaky toilets. It was always cold in those cells, she said, and dark all day, but at night the lights shone steadily. Mrs. Puglisi liked to talk about the prison which, she said, was called a correctional center now. The lockup downtown at police headquarters, she said with relish, was even worse.

They wouldn't have to bother to take her downtown, Rannee thought, staring at the dark building across the street. They wouldn't even have to send a patrol car. They could just *walk* her across the street with her children watching from the window. What would happen to them if she went to jail? She could feel their hands clutching her and their breath in her face. "You can't leave them starve," Voncia had said. But I can't leave them alone either, she thought. "What shall I do?" she moaned, like Christian contemplating the burning city. But her only answer was the siren on Market Street.

# 15

Voncia's newspaper lay on the kitchen table. There was a picture of Freedom Riders—white men being beaten by other white men in Mississippi. She thought of Uncle Floyd and the white man from the North who had been killed by the white men in the South. She wondered what would happen if the Freedom Riders came riding through Jewel Street.

But there was enough violence already up North, and even worse, right in her own town. GUNMAN KILLS SEVEN IN BUS DEPOT, the headlines said: "'Only passengers south of Atlanta,' killer tells police. 'I don't bother nobody else.'" Rannee was hurrying to lock the door when Mrs. Puglisi appeared. "Phone for you," she said. "But make it snappy. I'm expecting a call from Sheriff Caldwell and he's allergic to busy signals."

Rannee ran down the stairs. "Someone here wantin to see you, Tink," Bay said.

"Who?"

"Guess."

She could think of no one who would want to see her.

"Your husbin."

"Jarvis?"

"Right. He sittin right here in my livin room, in that bran-new green lounge chair, right this minute."

"Well, you keep him right there."

"He wants to see you."

She thought of the gunman at the bus depot. "Only passengers from Chawnee," she imagined him telling the police. "Only women and children from Chawnee."

"No," she said. "And don't be giving him my address. Please, Bay."

"Don't worry," Bay said. "He just wanna talk to you."

"No."

"He say he wanna see the children."

"No."

"He say he wanna give you some money."

"I don't care if he wants to give me the whole entire Bank of America."

"Just for a minute, Tink. Else I'll never git him off that green lounge chair."

"You can buy another one."

"Please, Tink. I promise. I won't give him no address, not even the street name. Nothin."

"All right. But it's gonna be the shortest conversation this phone company's ever seen."

"Hi, Doll," Jarvis said. "How you?"

She swallowed. He sounded as if he had someone's fist down his throat. "What you doing here?" she said.

"Workin in Nuffield. Over to the Sanitation Department. I took the truck after work and drove me up here. To see you and the chillun."

"No."

"Jes for a minute, Doll. Please."

"No."

"Then you give me your address so I could write to you some time?"

He sounded weak, a big man squeezed down to fit through a wire. She clutched the phone. "No!"

"I give you *my* address," he said.

"Don't bother. I'm not planning to write."

"I took a big chance," he said, "drivin that department truck all the way from Nuffield. To see you and those chillun. I could git arrested. Or fired. How come you so hard, Doll? You didn't used to be so hard."

He sounded weaker and weaker. He might be bleeding from the mouth, bleeding his past away. She wet her lips. "Please do me one favor," she said.

"Sure," he said. "Sure. Anything you say, Doll, I be glad to do it. Anything. Jes aks me. What you want me to do?"

"Go away," she said slowly. "Far away and don't ever come back. Other words, don't ever bother me again."

There was a long pause. "That make me very sad, Doll," he said.

"OK," she said. "It's your time to be sad. I had mine. So, please. Go away an stay away an don't *ever* come back." She hung up and wet her lips again. They tasted of blood.

The next day she added another bolt to her lock. She was glad OW lived next door.

One Saturday night, OW dropped in. To see how his men were getting on, he said. He lined them all up, examined between their toes, turned them upside down, and lined them all up again. Then he shouted in a loud, fierce voice:

> "Speak roughly to your little boy
> And beat him when he sneezes:
> He only does it to annoy,
> Because he knows it teases."

The children climbed all over him, begging for more.

Later, he sat in Rannee's kitchen, a clove toothpick poised elegantly between his lips, and talked. Rannee went on working, cleaning her refrigerator, scouring her pots, scrubbing her stove.

"We could go to dinner at Lin Fu's," he said.

She kept rubbing.

"We could go to the movies at the Strand," he said. "John Wayne."

She wrung out the cloth. "We could go to church."

"Church? On Saturday night? Where?"

"Holy Light Pentecostal Church. You can go there every night in the week. A continuous performance. Down on Beulah Street."

"You go to church?"

He grinned. "Not every night. But I go. You may not believe it, honey, but you're looking at a full-fledged, paid-up ex-saint. I've been saved twice already."

"*Twice?*"

"I backslid. I was what you might call 'premature.' A premature saint. But I'm still in good standing. I can be saved any time I want. But I'm not ready yet. I figure after thirty-five is time enough." He grinned.

"You know an old black woman in your church, name of Shubah Leonard?" she said.

"Ask Mama. Mama knows everybody. She's so saved, she talks in tongues even on the telephone." He laughed and stretched and twirled his toothpick. "How about it? Some nice Chinese sweet 'n' sour with lots of soy sauce and just you and me, real quiet and peaceful imbibing our tea?"

"What about my boys?"

"Mama'd be glad to mind them. She told me so. I think maybe she thinks you're going to save me again."

"I'm not saved myself. Not even once. Besides, I've already had my supper."

He kept coming, sitting in her kitchen, talking and twirling his toothpicks and inviting her out. She liked having him there, liked to look at him, a strong, handsome, yet gentle man, a combination she had not met before. He made her feel safe and scared at the same time. But she liked to look at him. And she liked to listen to him too, to those smooth words, bright and firm and tidy as the buttons on his tunic. It was a change from listening to her children, she told herself.

One night, he noticed her old library copy of *Pilgrim's Progress* on the counter, fenced in between the ketchup and the clock. He picked it up. "Are you reading *this?*" he said in surprise.

She nodded. "You know it?"

"God, yes! My Aunt Lilla made me read it to her every night when I was a boy. Luckily, she usually fell asleep after ten minutes. Lord, how I hated that book. But then, I hated everything about Aunt Lilla. Including her smile. What about you?"

"Oh, I like it. But then, I never had an Aunt Lilla. Only I'm terribly slow. I have to keep renewing it. And I have to keep running to the library to look up all those funny names."

"Names?"

"'Delectable' and 'Apollyon' . . ."

"Have you found *me* yet?"

"*You?* I don't think so." She grinned. "Unless you're Mr. Worldly Wiseman."

"Come on, girl. That's not only slander, that's *un*christian. I'm Mr. Faithful, of course. Every Pilgrim needs one."

"I haven't found any Mr. Faithful yet," she said.

"You will, girl," OW said. "You will."

The next time he came, he brought her a paperback dictionary and a brand-new copy of *Pilgrim's Progress*. "So you can leave the library copy in the library and give the other readers a chance," he said.

Finally, one night, she agreed to go to dinner with him while Voncia stayed with the children. It was the end of the month. A strictly economy measure, she told herself.

"Mrs. Watkins is going to stay with you tonight," she told the boys.

"Why?" Reed said.

"Because Mama's going out—for a little while."

"But it's nighttime out," Flash said.

"Sometimes mamas goes out at night," Voncia said.

"Not *this* mama," Reed said. "Not less she takes us too."

"This mama never goes *nowhere* less she takes us," Flash said.

"Well, this time she is," OW said. "This time she's going out and she's staying out. With me. I'm leaving you men in charge here. You're going to take care of *my* mama and I'm going to take care of *your* mama. And you're going to keep those beds nice and warm and those blankets tucked in while she's gone."

"How long she be gone?" Reed said.

"Long enough to tell me all about certain boys who might need a whipping," OW said. "By the name of Lance and Flash and Carter and Reed."

The boys squirmed and giggled. "That *too* long," Flash said.

"Lyle, honey," Voncia said. "You jes go 'long now an put on your hat an coat an cut on out. Cause these boys an me got things to do." She marched them into the bedroom. Rannee, getting ready, strained for sounds of anger or tears. But all she could hear was Voncia, reading from the Old Testament. "So Joseph died, being an hundred and ten years old; they embalmed him, and he was put in a coffin in Egypt." Rannee put on her coat and fled.

OW took her to a Chinese restaurant and told her about the crimes on his beat. Just last week, a sixteen-year-old boy shot his father in the stomach for not letting him use the family car. And yesterday they found a child with nothing on but a dog collar, leashed to the newel post of an empty house. Rannee thought about her own children and Voncia who entertained the Holy Ghost. He might even visit her in Rannee's kitchen tonight, with its ragged dish towel and no milk for the tea.

"You're not listening," OW said. "Or eating. You don't like Chinese?"

"Oh, no. I like it fine. Only I guess I'm not really hungry now. Maybe I could take it home and eat it later?"

"Sure, Sweetie, sure. Whatever you like. Next time we'll go to the Golden Slipper since you're not much on eating. Do you like to dance?"

"No."

"We could go to the Strand Palace. Do you like the movies?"

"No."

"Hockey? Basketball?" He grinned. "Pool?"

She smiled back. He was a nice man, she thought, a kind

man, like Jarvis before he turned so mean, only much better-looking. The other women on the block were always oiled and polished with their lips moist and their blouses fluttering whenever OW was around, eager to be taken into custody. Even Mrs. Ledbetter, who specialized in meter men, said she wouldn't mind being detained by Officer Watkins. But Rannee was afraid of the hair ready to grow on his upper lip and the glint of gold which might someday appear in the back of his mouth and the toothpick forever stuck between his teeth. He smiled again and put his hand over hers. She felt her own blouse begin to flutter. She thought of the little boys at home, hearing about Joseph embalmed in his coffin. What was Voncia reading to them now?

"It must be church, then," OW was saying. His hand tightened on hers and she felt a warm spot inside her, opening like a fist.

"What must?"

"Where you get your fun. Like Mama. She doesn't dance or sing or relax either. Except in church. She hardly even *eats* anywhere else. Like you, maybe. You're not even tasting your fortune cookie."

"I don't need a *cookie* to tell me my fortune," Rannee said. But she took home four extra cookies along with her dinner in a doggie bag. She wondered how the boys would like Chinese food.

The next morning, Voncia appeared. "Those real fine boys you got, Lyle, honey," she said. "But they growin up heathen."

"How do you know?"

"Never mind *how*. I jes *knows*. I jes looks at the back a their necks an I *knows*. I know your chillun needin religion. They needin Bible study and baptism an . . ."

"They've *been* baptized."

"Not proper, they ain't. Not right. Not in Jesus' name. Ain't no real baptism less it in Jesus' name." Rannee stared, remembering what Shubah had said.

"Tell you what," Voncia said. "How 'bout if I come here Saturday mornins and give those chillun some Bible lessons?"

"Why should you? They go to Sunday school regular. Every Sunday."

"An they ain't learnin *nothin*. You know very well they ain't."

It was true, Rannee thought. Just as she had learned nothing. "All right," she said. "But how am I supposed to pay you?"

"The Lord will pay me," Voncia said.

She came every Saturday morning and sat in the living room with the children around her. They picked their noses and their scabs and bit their nails and listened. Rannee, ironing in the kitchen, listened too. She was surprised, even frightened, at how much she didn't know. All about Death and Hell and the souls that were cast into the lake of fire. She had never really thought about such things before, as if she expected to go on forever in Beet's old sneakers. Preacher Brown at home had never preached about the soul but about Abraham and Jacob and Noah, country people like the people around Chawnee. And Reverend Hampton spent his Sundays wandering around in the Wilderness with the Children of Israel. Even reading *Pilgrim's Progress* hadn't affected her, except as an adventure story, like the story of Ulysses in *The Book of Knowledge*. She knew nothing at all about her own soul. She thought of it— ignored, neglected, starved, shriveled down to the size of a peanut, so small she might have passed it long ago, along with her morning tea. She thought of Miz Zophara, making them all drink hot lemon juice to keep their souls nice and clean and shrunk down. What if she had made Rannee's soul disappear completely, with all that lemon juice and that evil eye? Rannee imagined a cavity inside her where her soul should be. When she died, she would be nothing but a dead body with a hole inside for the dirt to fill.

That night, after the children were asleep, she opened *Pilgrim's Progress* and read: *"Now at the end of this Valley, was another, called the Valley of the Shadow of Death . . . 'A wilderness, a land of deserts, and of pits, a land of drought, and of the shadow of death, a land that no man* (but a Christian) *passeth through, and where no man dwelt.'"*

She shuddered and closed the book. Was she a Christian? She thought of her baptism and remembered how she had promised herself that when she was grown she would go up North and find Uncle Floyd and Jesus and walk in His ways. But she hadn't found either of them. She hadn't even looked. She had found OW instead.

Every night, after supper, she would read for a while and then sit alone in the dark, doing nothing, thinking nothing, just sitting. Like Mama on the back porch, she thought. Sometimes, after she had been sitting there for a long time, she began to have the strange sensation that something else was sitting there too, just across the room. She couldn't see it or feel it, but she knew it was there. She began to dread being alone at night.

The next Friday, she let OW take her to the movies. She let him buy her four bags of popcorn and hold her hand. He began to massage her wrist and palm with strong, gentle fingers. Soon, she was aware of nothing but his hand and her body spreading out beneath it, soft and limp, with the edges dissolving, ready for him to form her into any shape he wished. She jerked her hand away and gripped her purse and tried to concentrate on the tombstone face of John Wayne. But he reminded her of Jarvis. She wondered if he would ever try to visit her again. What if he were there, at home, right now? Or what if the Holy Ghost dropped in unexpectedly and Voncia began to talk to Him in tongues? She would frighten the children. Rannee stood up. "You stay," she said. "But I must go home to my children."

OW said nothing, just helped her on with her coat and carried the four bags of popcorn. At the house, he turned to face her. "I'll just take these up for you," he said softly. He ran a finger along her cheek and down the side of her neck. "And make sure those little boys are dreaming correct, regulation dreams, and let Mama go on home." His finger was traveling lightly around her neck and throat and along the top of her blouse, stirring that warm spot inside until it flowed all through her and threatened to run out between her legs. He had gentle fingers, soft and light as the tip of a feather. But she was afraid of them. Jarvis's had been soft and light in the beginning, too. OW's might someday clench into fists or curl tightly around a clothes hanger. Sooner or later, she warned herself, they might want to curl around her and her children, squeezing until the little boys' eyes popped with fear, squeezing until they forced another baby out of her. She stepped back. Then she took the popcorn, thanked him, and said good night on the doorstep.

The next Sunday when Bay came to take the children out, he gave Rannee a letter from a hospital in Nuffield. Her husband, Jarvis Lyle, the letter said, was being treated for acute alcoholism.

"They dryin him out," Bay said. The letter assured her that they would do the very best they could for him. She was not to worry. After Bay left, she read the letter again. They might dry the alcohol out of him, she thought, but they'd never get all the meanness out. She tore up the letter, stuffed it into the garbage, and went out.

She walked quickly past the jail. Jarvis had never been a heavy drinker, she thought. When had he become an alcoholic? "Hi, babe," a voice called softly. It was a gentle, pleading voice. "You slow down a minute an say hi?" She looked up at the barred windows. She could see nothing but a black hole and a black arm hanging out, no face, just that thin black arm. He began to whistle softly. Suddenly, she thought of Uncle Floyd. What if *he* were in there, for cussing a white man or talking back to a white cop? She remembered the stories of the rats and the open toilets. "Good afternoon," she called back.

She kept walking, past boarded-up grocery stores and open bars, past crowded houses and empty lots filled with garbage and old mattresses and two-legged chairs, past hallways with no lights and cars with no wheels. The streets were empty of people but littered with smashed cans and broken glass and torn paper, like a deserted battlefield strewn with wreckage, waiting for the war to begin again. She passed the row of burnt-out tenements. It had caught fire last week, in the middle of the night, and the Negro residents had been taken to a white church five blocks away. But a white crowd gathered, jeering and shouting obscenities. They threatened to attack unless the Negroes were removed. Staring into the black, empty doorways, Rannee wondered where they had gone.

Turning the corner, she heard the sound of music: drums and piano and cymbals and saxophone. It came rushing to meet her, like Daddy at the bus station whenever she had gone home from Montgomery. She felt tired, as if she had come a long way, which, in fact, she had, all the way to Beulah Street and the Holy Light Pentecostal Church. The music was the sound of saints, come to greet her and welcome her in. She walked slowly into the church, sat down in the last row, and watched and listened. After a while, she slipped off her shoes. Soon she was gripping her seat to keep from jumping and singing and dancing and shouting with the others.

# 16

Beet came back one Saturday night wearing a red wig and red pants and red shoes. And not much else, Rannee thought.

"Hi, Tink, honey," Beet said.

"You back already?" Rannee said. "You homesick for this here town already?"

"No, honey. I jes plain tireda Florida."

"Didn't take long," Rannee said.

"Too much sun," Beet said.

"I see it turned your hair red."

"Yeah. Too much sun not good for the scalp. I fixin to stay up North for a while."

"Where you staying?"

"Over to Bay's."

"Bay's? He can't squeeze another goldfish into that house."

"I know. I curled up in the broom closet with the vacuum and seven attachments. But listen, honey, is borin as hell over there. His wife sittin in front a that TV, lookin to see what else can she buy. An Bay runnin out every night, working for the gas company along with the phone company so's he can pay for it. How 'bout you an me goin down to the Cougar Club?"

"You crazy? That sun burned your brain along with your hair? What would I do at the Cougar Club?"

"You do like everybody else. You drink an dance an have yourself a real good time for a change. I think *you* must be goin crazy sittin here alone every night of your life, watchin your nails grow. But tonight, honey, you gonna swing."

"And what am I supposed to use for money in your Cougar Club?" Rannee said. "I've got just enough for one quart of milk and a box of rice. And no Welfare check for another four days."

"I loan you some."

"Oh, no you won't. Because I'll never be able to pay it back. Besides, I am *not* going to that Cougar Club. Not me."

"I warnin you, Tink. Somethin teerbul gonna happen to you, you go on settin here every night with nothin but those four walls an those four boys. An I know zackly what it's gonna be too. You gonna wake up someday an fine you is somebody else. Like that woman in Fort Lauderdale, Florida. Thought she was the Virgin Mary. Went aroun in a ole blue curtain an wouldn't eat nothin but peanuts an punkin seeds. Carried a ole gin bottle wrapped in a blanket an said it was the Lord Jesus come agin, right there in Fort Lauderdale. They took her away on Good Friday while she tryin to git to heaven from the top a the post office buildin. Know what she had?" Beet paused and glared at Rannee. "*Re*-pression. That's what she had. Paper said so. A bad case a *re*-pression."

"Well, you can stop your worrying," Rannee said. "I do not have any repression. Just a little asthma . . ." And concern about OW. She had not seen him since the night she left him standing on her doorstep like a salesman peddling something she refused to buy. "And all those children," she went on. "What am I supposed to do with *them* while I'm swinging at the Cougar Club?"

"They sleepin now, right? Well, let em sleep. Ah, c'mon, Tink. Jes this once. Jes till I git goin in this here town agin. Then I won't never bother you agin. I promise. Besides, this here my birthday."

"You never had a birthday in November before," Rannee said.

"Never jes blew in from Florida before."

Rannee hated it. She sat sweating in Beet's yellow satin dress and sipped water and thought about her children, sleeping peacefully while the house burned down around them. "Left them to be turned into chipped beef," she imagined Mrs. Puglisi saying.

Rannee felt the colored lights turning her purple and green and blue while the music threaded her like a needle. "Hi, Jacko," Beet shouted suddenly to a tall man in a black turtleneck sweater. "I waitin on Trinidad. But this here my sister. She love to dance with you." He looked big and black and sleepy, Rannee thought, as if he'd just stepped out of a dark closet.

"Hi, babe." He held out his arms. Beet kicked Rannee under the table. She got up. He smelled of bourbon and bubble gum. He smiled and grabbed her by the neck while his hips and knees gyrated around her. When the music stopped, he remained standing in the middle of the floor, holding her neck. He danced three times without letting go. Then he smiled and said, "Thanks, baby. I be back here next week. See you then."

Not me, Rannee thought. This was the first and very last time she would ever spend an evening with her neck in the hands of a stranger and her children locked up alone. But when she got home and undressed, she found a twenty-dollar bill down the back of her dress. She stared at it. Just for dancing?

She stood looking at it for a long time, turning it over and over, studying the picture of the big house on one side and the old man on the other. She walked around the room, still holding it, admiring it, the pictures and the decorations and the four 20s on each side. Twenty dollars just for dancing! A present, she told herself. No Welfare lady could stop her checks for *that*. When she finally went to bed, the bill was propped up like a photograph on her bureau with the picture of a man named Jackson looking slightly annoyed.

On Monday, she paid Mr. Rodriquez five dollars and took the children to Woolworth's. On Friday, the food supply was low again. On Saturday, she went back to the Cougar Club with Beet. But Jacko wasn't there. She sat waiting with her eyes on the table and her body clenched tightly inside the yellow dress, refusing all other invitations. Beet danced with everyone who asked her and disappeared around ten o'clock. Rannee went on sitting. She would wait till eleven, she thought. At ten-thirty Jacko arrived. He darted toward her, yanked her up like a weed, and grabbed her around the neck. "You get my little present?" he said.

"Yes, thanks. My children thank you too. Three pairs of shoes and a chicken leg each."

"That's cool, baby. That's real nice an cool. Just remember, there's lots more in my hip pocket. You just be here nice an easy on Saturday night when I hits town and it's all yours." He kept her dancing till the band stopped and the place closed. Then he led her to his car.

"I live on Jewel Street," she said. "Number 37."

"Uh huh." He slammed the door and started the engine.

"This isn't the way to Jewel Street," she said.

"You right, baby. You one hunnerd percent right. This here the way to heaven. Only shut your mouf cause I can't stand no yakkin on the road."

She sat rigid with fear. They drove to the Jack Frost Motel and he pulled her out of the car. "Whassa matta, baby? You scared? I tole you ain't nothin to be scared a. We just on our way to heaven. A nice easy roll into heaven with a nice big admission fee for you. Cause I pays my way, baby. I always pays my way. You just remember that. Jacko always pays his way. Less I find trouble a course. But I can deal with that too."

On the bed, she closed her eyes and forced herself to take inventory—three winter jackets, two pairs of boots, four blankets, rent money, utility bills—while Jacko rammed his way into heaven. He drove her home through a smudged dawn with fifty dollars in her purse. She sat stiffly, staring at the silent, empty streets, streets without name signs and houses without numbers. And though the neighborhood was familiar, she knew she was riding through strange territory inside a woman she no longer recognized, a woman who had allowed a strange man to push his way into her life as he pleased, using her like a sink. She put her fist in her mouth.

"You be here for Christmas?" Jacko said.

"Christmas?"

"Yeah. Comin soon. You be here?"

Christmas. Except for Jacko's money she would have almost nothing until January, nothing for rent or clothes or Christmas. Nothing at all for Christmas. She still remembered that morning when she had knelt beside an empty box.

"Yes," she said finally, licking the blood off her knuckles. "I'll be here for Christmas."

She went back to the Cougar Club often after that, though Beet disappeared for good with a tall, thin mulatto with blond hair who was on his way to New Mexico. "A chance to see some a them foreign parts," Beet said. So Rannee went to the Cougar Club alone in Beet's yellow dress, with her knees clamped together and her knuckles raw. Sometimes Jacko took her to dances and jazz sessions and private parties. But they always ended up in the Jack Frost Motel. She never let him come to the house and he never knew her last name.

Whenever she passed the Watkins's house, she wondered what OW was doing. She had not seen him for weeks. He was probably out courting right now, she thought, with John Wayne and fortune cookies and his own light touch.

At the end of February, she decided to stop going to the Cougar Club. The children were fairly well clothed and spring was on the way. She went one last time to cover any possible ear infections. But Jacko was not there. She decided to wait until eleven.

"Would you care to dance, Mrs. Lyle?" someone said. She looked up and saw OW standing in front of her in a dark suit and a white shirt and a smile that seemed to cover the table like a cloth. She looked down quickly, hot with shame. "No, thank you," she said, standing up. "I'm leaving. Right now."

"Then allow me to take you home," he said, tipping his smile like a hat.

But first he took her to the Rooftop Café high above the city, with the lights of the buildings below and the stars above and the NO EXIT sign reflected in red across the sky. He bought her a sweet emerald-colored drink that rested smoothly on the back of her throat. He told her about the men he found in the parking lots, sleeping beneath empty cars all winter with their feet in cardboard boxes. "They'd be warmer in jail," he said. "But I figure they prefer it that way." He never mentioned the Cougar Club at all. She sat listening, warm with gratitude, with the thick, sweetish drink soothing her throat and his voice stroking her cheek. At her door, he kissed her good night. Upstairs, she cut up the yellow dress and stuffed it into the trash.

The next Saturday night, he arrived with Voncia and a carton of peppermint-stick ice cream. He took her to dinner in a quiet place and ordered food she had never heard of while the waiters stood around and watched them eat. Once, she began to reach for the sugar like Mama back home. But she was not like Mama, she remembered: She was a long way from home, eating strange food in a strange place, with a strange man who could charm her just by the way he ate his meat, using his knife only to cut, balancing his fork gracefully by the end of its long handle. He was smiling at her above the veal scallopini. She left the sugar where it was and smiled back.

He told her about his life before she met him. He was born in Bildad, Mississippi, with no daddy and no schools for Negroes past the sixth grade. Voncia sent him to Trenton, New Jersey, to live with his Aunt Lilla and go to high school. He hated Aunt Lilla who was fussy and light-skinned and called him Orville. She made him wear a white jacket and pass the cranberry juice on a tray whenever she had company. The rest of the time he had to wear dark suits and carry her bundles and her umbrella when she went out. The other children made fun of his clothes and his accent and his name. When he was sixteen, he ran away and joined the army. He preferred a uniform to a white jacket. He told Rannee about the striped waters of the Adriatic and the palace in London with a real live queen inside, and the streets of Paris, so wide you could sail a battleship down the middle. He learned to shoot guns—though not to use them—and to talk fast, to say "good night" in several languages and to pay in several currencies, to walk through strange streets that curved and circled and squared away to enclose gardens and parks with flowers and benches for the living and memorials to the dead. In his spare time he was often alone, reading books and observing the signs and tempos of strange cities.

When he resigned, he switched to a different uniform with a badge on his chest and his own beat where no one told him what to do or when or how. And no one knew that he had ever worn a white jacket or that his name was Orville.

He came regularly, bearing gifts: cartons of groceries and candies and cinnamon-flavored toothpicks. He brought presents for the children: police cars and fire trucks and badges and caps, and a special detective kit for Lance, as if to make up for Jarvis. Sometimes he took the boys to the station house and put them into handcuffs and took their fingerprints. "Better mind your mama now," he said. "We've got you on record."

"Yes, sir, Mr. OW," they said, staring with delight at their own smudges.

"How come you're not married?" Rannee asked him one night. "Have children of your own?" The boys were in bed and OW was sitting beside her on the couch with his jacket off, his tie loosened, and a lazy smile. He looked sleepy all over. He put his arm around her. "Been married," he said, and kissed her.

She did not move but her insides dived down behind her kneecaps and her breath fled to some far corner. It took several seconds to yank it up again. "How come you never *stayed* married?" she said.

"Never found the right woman. Some women are like the army. All right for a short hitch. But I never planned to spend

214

my life in the barracks. And right now, I think that maybe I've found a place of my own, a permanent place." He kissed her again. "Why don't *you* marry me?" he said. "And save me from the barracks."

She stared at him. "*Marry* you? You want me to *marry* you? With all those children?"

"Why not? You need a husband and those boys need a father and I need a family," he said. "Seems like the perfect arrangement."

"What about all those girlfriends?"

"*Ex*-girlfriends, you mean," he said. "And they're going to stay that way. I want a *wife.*" He put his arms around her again. *"You."*

She grabbed the arm of the couch as if hanging on for dear life and turned her head to the wall. "I'm finished with marrying," she said.

"Why? What are you afraid of?"

She turned and forced herself to look at him, carefully, critically. The scared boy in the white jacket was gone completely. Was there any hint of Jarvis coming to take his place? She examined his features: the smooth upper lip and the teeth, straight and even as his sentences. There was no need for gold in that mouth. It was a beautiful mouth, she thought, as he leaned forward to kiss her again. It never occurred to her that she might still be married to Jarvis.

That night she dreamed she was pregnant again. She got bigger and bigger. On the street, people pointed and laughed and tried to push her over to see if she would bounce. She was being punished, at last, for the Cougar Club and Jacko, for all the children she had not allowed to be born. Now she was carrying them all, all at once. She became enormous, too big to wear anything but Pa Peters's old army coat. But she kept on growing until, finally, she was too big even to get through the door. Yet she ate nothing at all. Everything she sent down came up again, as if she had dozens of hands inside her pushing it all back. But still she kept growing, filling the house, squeezing her

215

sons into the corners, pressing their faces into the walls until the blood ran.

The next time OW came, she avoided his touch. When he left, he stroked her cheek. "Be seeing you," he said. "Let me know if you ever change your mind."

But watching him walk away, swinging his arms and tilting his head toward whatever was coming next, she knew he would not wait around. She knew he was walking out of her life into someone else's. There would never be any empty patches in OW's path.

She avoided the couch and slept knotted up, her teeth, her hands, her thighs clenched, her head rammed into the darkness. Saturdays and Sundays disappeared. It got colder and colder, outside and in, and the children were always sick. There was always someone coughing or vomiting or running a fever.

"Where OW at?" the children asked. "How come he not comin any more?"

"Yes," Lance said. "Where is he? Why doesn't he come to see us? What did you do, Mama?"

What had she done? Even Christian had been glad of the company of Faithful. ". . . *He suddenly stumbled and fell, and could not rise again, until Faithful came up to help him. Then I saw in my dream, they went very lovingly on together.*" But she had doomed herself to go on alone. And doomed her children as well, especially Lance.

He became increasingly quiet, withdrawn. He grew taller and thinner. He spent his free time at the kitchen table, reading books from school or the public library, reading the newspapers left by Voncia and the handbills left by the mailman, trying to figure out the print on cans and coins and the bills in Rannee's purse. At night, he slept with OW's detective kit under his bed. Like me with that empty candy box, Rannee thought. He was completely different from the other boys. He had had a different father, after all. She could hardly remember Ward, that slow, silent, country boy, except that he was nothing like Lance, who could read so well and talk so smoothly. Lance, she realized suddenly, was more like OW's son. And now he had lost his father again.

# 17

The next winter was worse than ever. The wind tore at the buildings as if to make them tip their roofs in greeting and the snow poured down like salt. Icicles coated the bars of the jail and snow wadded the streets and climbed the steps and stopped the doorways, bandaging the whole neighborhood. Pipes burst and furnaces blew up. Around the corner on Market Street, Puglisi's Café caught fire. Some of the customers, it was reported, began to help themselves. The police arrived before the firemen and began to shoot at the looters. One of the Gomez boys was hit in the shoulder, but no one was killed. "Lousy shots," Mrs. Puglisi said, collecting Rannee's rent in a ski mask. "I'll bet it was Lover Boy Watkins. Best friend a criminal ever had. My brother-in-law Joe says he hasn't made an arrest since he's been on the force. Just sits around taking the taxpayer's money for drinking coffee." Carter, terrified by the ski mask, began to cry.

Down the street, the Ledbetters were evicted. First the movers came and took the furniture: the fridge with its door flapping, the huge double bed reduced to a few sticks and carried easily by one man with a leer, a few old, maimed chairs with their heads down. The gas man came and the electricity man and, finally, the telephone man. One afternoon, after they had taken everything else, they came and took the Ledbetters, with Mrs. Ledbetter clinging to the rail. Then the doors and windows were boarded up. Rannee thought of Cousin Travers at Simms Quarter who had been allowed to "fit in" till he died.

In her apartment, she could see her own breath. The price of fuel went up and her rent went up with it. She put the older children in bed together for warmth and took the little ones in with her. In the morning they were stiff with cold. The next night she put them to bed in the kitchen with the oven on and sat beside them, wide-awake, to make sure they weren't gassed. Rats came from the jail and the empty lots. She spent the night with the lights on and a frying pan in her lap. One after the other, the children got flu and earaches and stomach upsets. She thought of Mama's "tea" and her "fever cure" and longed to wrap her children in a leaf for warmth. But nothing grew in the North. Everything had to be bought. The children lived, intermittently, on Karo and dried milk and bread and rice. Even OW's toothpicks were gone. The Welfare checks were always late, as if the United States Postal Service had frozen up too. Lance and Flash tried to get jobs shoveling snow but nobody bothered about the snow. They just let it lie there. Rannee could never get used to it, so white, so beautiful, making the streets silent, secretive, dangerous. At night the sirens sounded louder than ever.

She saw almost no one that winter. She had long since stopped going to church to save the bus fare, and she did not see the Watkinses at all. Voncia was probably too weak to go out in such weather and OW was probably too busy courting; it was certainly far too cold for crime. Bay had moved to the suburbs and was working weekends as well as nights to pay for the new house. Rannee saw no one but Mrs. Puglisi, in mittens and boots, collecting the rent.

Rannee gave up reading *Pilgrim's Progress* with Christian locked up in Doubting-Castle and persecuted by the evil Giant

Despair. She was locked up too, locked into the ghetto with strange unpredictable black men and violent white policemen and a vicious white landlady, locked up alone with her children.

One afternoon, Lance came home with blood all over his face. From a snowball, he said, thrown by one of the big white boys across the street from the school.

"No *snowball* did *that*," Rannee said.

"That snowball gotta have a stone in it," Flash said.

Rannee felt a sense of panic. She remembered the picture in the paper of Negro children surrounded by screaming whites and soldiers with pointed guns. But that was the South, because of "integration." This was the North. There was no integration in the Abraham Lincoln Elementary School. Only Negro children and white teachers and a white principal waiting to be transferred. She wished she could transfer her children. "OW will hear about this," she said, bathing Lance's face.

"He can't do anything," Lance said.

"Why not?"

"Not his beat." He looked at her. "Besides," he said softly, "the police right there all the time."

"What did they do?"

"Kept on directing traffic."

"What police?"

"Officer Puglisi."

She knew that Lance was right. There was nothing OW could do. He was only a *Negro* cop, after all. And it wasn't even his beat. It was Officer Puglisi's beat. OW couldn't protect her children. *She* would have to do it. Looking at Lance, she felt as if she had rammed her own fist into his face. The older children refused to let her walk them back and forth to school, but she followed them anyway, keeping out of sight but keeping them in view. She dared not leave them alone.

One day, when there was nothing left in the house but a box of rice and half a bar of soap, Rannee went to see Mr. Rodri-

219

quez. Inside his store, she hung around, admiring the little colored bottles with the pictures of saints on the labels and the bath oils inside that promised to make the user clean and fragrant and fortunate.

"You like some?" Mr. Rodriquez said. He was wearing gloves and earmuffs and stamping his feet. "Is holy water," he said. "Is blessings for you. You like some?"

"Sure I'd like some," she said. "Me and my children sure could use some blessings and some fortune. You got some free ones, Mr. Rodriquez?" He stared at her and she stared back. He had grown a beard, she noticed, and remembered that he had come to America in a small boat all the way across the ocean because, he said, America was free. He looked cold and his shop was empty and unheated. He looked thinner and paler except for his new black beard. Had he come to America to grow a beard? "You giving those blessings away free?" she said. "Otherwise, never mind. Same with that shank bone and those greens. You're a free man now, right, Mr. Rodriquez? Other words, you're free to give all that away, right? Whenever you want."

He was still staring at her, his breath making a curtain between them.

"This is a free country, right, Mr. Rodriquez?" she went on. "Isn't that what you're always telling me? Some people are free to eat and some *not* to eat, right? They free like that in Cuba, Mr. Rodriquez?"

"OK, OK," Mr. Rodriquez said, raising his hands. "But you no tell Mr. Sal Puglisi, yes? Is *his* store. You see, no heat. Last week, he turn it off. Maybe next week, no light." He shook his head and came out from behind the counter. He gave her some bones he had been saving for his dog—good soup bones, he said—and some broken crackers and half a loaf of bread and some sliced baloney. After that he saved things for her: bits of meat from the grinder, overripe fruit and vegetables, scraps of cheese, heels of salami. Once, he even gave her a bottle of bath oil with a picture of a dragon on the label. She wondered which saint that was.

Finally, she let Voncia find cleaning jobs for her, in spite of the Welfare lady and the bars of the jail gleaming at her across the street and the white boys throwing stones, in spite of the school system which took two of her children in the morning and two in the afternoon. She worked part-time for she was still afraid to leave them alone. Carter and Reed were too young and Flash was too wild. Only Lance was responsible. She worked mornings, leaving him with Carter, and rushed back in time to see them off and be there when the other two came home.

She worried about them all morning, phoning whenever she could, bringing Lance down to Mrs. Puglisi's hall phone. "Don't worry, Mama," he told her. "I can handle it. Any trouble, I'll just call OW." But OW worked on the other side of town. Lance told Carter stories about the wallpaper and the names in Mrs. Puglisi's old phone book, stories full of long descriptions of elaborate meals. Carter loved to eat. Lance even gave him lunch. Like a father, Rannee thought: as if Lance had turned himself into his own missing father. He spent more and more time reading, but the books he brought home from the library seemed strange to her: not stories with pictures, but solid print telling of real events and real people who lived long ago in strange places with complicated names, like the parts of *The Book of Knowledge* she had always skipped when she was a girl.

He must go to college, she told herself, climbing into the bus. The other children, she thought, settling herself into a center seat, would be all right. Flash could play ball and Reed could fix things and Carter could be a cook. He was a fat, good-natured little boy, probably from all the sweets Merleene had stuffed into him when he was a baby. Only Lance worried her. She had deserted him when he was so young and he was growing up with a scared, lost expression.

Every morning she rode the bus to Terraces and Drives and Circles and Squares to clean houses big as railroad stations with closets big as rooms and carpets that covered the floor like grass. Just vacuuming took half a morning. Some of her employers were fussy, some friendly. One woman padlocked all the phones, another kept the silver and the liquor and the stamps locked up. Each paid what she pleased, by the hour. If Rannee missed work for any reason—sickness or snowstorms or holidays when the family didn't want her around—she didn't get paid. Some gave her carfare, some didn't. No one gave her a paid vacation. If her employers were away, she was simply laid off, except that she was sometimes expected to water their plants and check their locks and forward their mail.

But housework was easier in the North, she found. She could get off her knees occasionally and use a broom or a mop. Most of the houses were empty most of the time, and she liked being alone with no one watching, working in her bare feet, humming hymns to the rhythm of the mop.

She liked working for Dr. Charles Leighton who had fifteen pipes and lived alone with a phone in every room including the bathroom. She hardly ever saw him, only his clothes, waiting for her on the bed. He was a big man with the biggest wardrobe she had ever seen outside a department store. But the styles changed so quickly that he was forever buying more. He left the old ones—hardly used at all—for her. She found jackets with back vents and side vents, with wide lapels and narrow lapels; trousers with and without cuffs; fat ties and skinny ties; turtlenecks and crew necks and ski suits and track suits. "For your boys," his notes would say "When they are grown to man's estate." They would have miles of elegant clothes, twenty years out of style. He also left little packets of extra cash at odd times, carefully labeled: "For Ground Hog Day," "For Lent," "For Trotsky's Birthday."

But Mrs. Samantha Stewart was the friendliest of all. She was the friendliest woman Rannee had ever met. She was a Friend of the Library and a Friend of the Symphony and a Friend of the University Art Gallery and a Friend of the Historical Society. She was even a Friend of the UN. She was a tall, slender young woman in smartly cut suits and with blond hair in a neat, shiny bun like a buttered roll. She was very friendly to

Rannee. "Oh, Mrs. Lyle," she said the first morning, "how good of you to come," as if welcoming her to a party. She ushered Rannee into the kitchen, made her sit down at the table, poured out coffee for both, and sat down opposite her. "Tell me," she said sternly. "Why do you do it?"

"Do what, Mrs. Stewart?"

"Call me Sam." She put her elbows on the table and frowned fiercely. "Clean other people's houses. You're young, attractive, intelligent. So why? Because you're Negro?" She nodded. "Of course. From the South? Of course. They break the spirit down there. Well, things are different up here. Like voting. I hope you're planning to vote."

Rannee looked into her cup and stirred. She would avoid calling her anything, she decided, but thought of her as Mrs. Sam.

"Because you *can* vote here. You *must*. Vote for Ryan. I'll give you some literature." She went on to talk about the NAACP and the ACLU and the UF and the Committee of Concerned Citizens.

Rannee had no idea what any of it meant. She slipped off her shoes, rubbed one foot on top of the other, and glanced at the clock. The kitchen counters were covered with dirty dishes and there were pots soaking in the sink. An overflowing trash basket stood in one corner and an ironing board heaped high with clothes in the other.

"You should join the CCC," Mrs. Sam was saying. "We're demonstrating tonight. Against Moncrieff's. For racism." Moncrieff's was a very expensive department store which Rannee had seen only from the outside. No Negro, she was certain, had ever been inside, either to buy or to sell. "Get there around seven," Mrs. Sam said. "There'll be a march through the store and then a glorious tearing up of credit cards right in the president's office. God, it'll be wonderful! Wish I could be there but I've got a United Fund dinner. You can tell me all about it. Don't forget to take your credit card."

What credit card, Rannee wondered.

Mrs. Sam jumped up. "My God, I'm late for the VN board meeting. And I've got a YWCA Award Luncheon so I won't be back before you leave. I left a list of jobs on the bulletin board. But I don't want you to work too hard. Remember that." She leaned on her hands and looked intently at Rannee across the table. "I mean that. None of this," she waved her hand around her dirty kitchen, "is really important. Remember that." She straightened up, dashed into the hall, and came back with a suede coat, an enormous shoulder-strap bag like a mail pouch, and an armful of leaflets. "These are for *you,*" she said, shoving them at Rannee. "For your friends and neighbors. Also to distribute around, to stores and schools and churches. You know." She swung her pouch onto her shoulder. "Bye. See you next Monday. Don't forget to tell me all about Moncrieff's. And don't forget your credit card."

Rannee opened her mouth.

The door slammed.

Rannee closed her mouth and looked at the list of jobs. It was very long and surprisingly explicit: "Kitchen: floors, fridge, stove (including oven), sink, counters, dishes, trash; all bathrooms: floors, walls, tubs, mirrors; ironing; Venetian blinds in sunroom; vacuum . . ." Rannee stopped reading. She could never get through that list in a month of Mondays. Next week most of the items would have to be done again. It was past ten o'clock already. She looked at the list again. Her eye caught "corners," "tiles," "cupboard," but not a word about wages. She looked all around the kitchen, in the study, the bedroom, the hall table. But she could find no sign of a check or an envelope with her name outside and her wages inside. Mrs. Samantha Stewart would not be back until long after Rannee was gone.

She was late leaving for home. Flash and Reed would be back before her. Sitting on the bus, passing the park, she saw white women on the benches with their hands in their laps, watching their children grow.

One morning, long after Mrs. Sam had gone and just as Rannee was about to put her shoes on and leave, the doorbell rang. She was late again, looking for her check again, which she did not find again. A white policeman was standing on the doorstep. He took Rannee with him in his police car to identify the body of Jarvis P. Lyle, who had come to town two days ago with nothing but a wallet and a book of matches in his pocket. Last night, at six in the evening, he had jumped from the seventh floor of the Y. The policeman was young and businesslike and seemed to be in a terrible hurry, as if afraid of missing his lunch.

He did not show her the body, for the face was too smashed to identify. Perhaps, she thought, he figured that all Negroes looked alike anyway. Instead, he rushed her into an office and handed her a worn wallet done up in oilcloth, the only thing still recognizable on the dead man. It held a bus ticket, two dollar bills, and a snapshot of a man and woman on a street corner, holding hands. Rannee thought of those long strolls all over town with Jarvis, before they were married, when their hands had been stuck together with fat from the fish fries and the peace of a Sunday afternoon. The man had a tiny mustache underlined by a broad smile but the woman's face was covered with blood stains. Rannee did not remember the picture at all. She certainly didn't remember that smile. What she remembered was the gold watch and the belt and the snarl. Where were they? Jarvis was certainly not the kind of man who would carry a photograph of an angry, runaway wife in his pocket for so many years. Jarvis was not the kind of man who would jump out of a YMCA building on a Sunday evening just when everyone else was sitting down to supper either. But that was the old Jarvis. Had he changed again? She remembered his visit to Simms Quarter when he had given the children ten dollars and left with a sad smile for them all and with his new soul, Mama said, shining through the lining of his jacket. But the smile in the picture was not sad and there was no soul she could see shining anywhere, unless it was on the slab in the morgue under all that blood. Actually, there was nothing at all left to identify Jarvis except a couple of dollar bills. But a man cannot be recognized by the money he carries, even when it is soaked in his own blood.

The policeman was waiting impatiently, rocking back and forth on his heels. She stared at the picture. "How come you so hard, Doll?" Jarvis had said that day on the telephone. "You didn't use to be so hard."

She had refused him then but she could not bring herself to deny him now. "Yes," she said at last, handing back the picture. "That's my husband. That's Jarvis."

The policeman went on rocking for a second as if giving her a chance to cry. Then he landed firmly on his soles and gave her the small oilcloth bundle, the remains of Jarvis P. Lyle. She burst into tears.

At home, she said nothing to her children. She would go to the funeral alone and grieve alone, like a good widow, while they buried a faceless man. But she would give him a face, not the face of the man with the belt and the knife and the wire hanger, nor even of the young, handsome, good-natured Jarvis who glittered in so many places. Instead, he would have the sad, subdued face of Jarvis, the prisoner, with the gold all gone and a sprinkling of gravel dust in his hair. It was a face she could mourn.

Toward evening, Mrs. Samantha Stewart phoned. "I understand the police were here," she said. "I understand they dragged you away in your bare feet. Well, don't worry. I know *the* best civil rights lawyer in town. In fact, he's a *very* good friend of mine. I can't talk now. I'll call you tomorrow. Not to worry."

Rannee opened her mouth.

Mrs. Sam hung up.

Rannee fed her children. She bathed the younger ones and put them to bed. The older children put themselves to bed, so quietly that she never heard them. She went on sitting there, thinking of Jarvis, thinking of him standing in the window of the Y, standing there, perhaps for hours, all alone, while everyone else was eating supper. Perhaps he had changed since the day she had made Mama send him away. But she had only meant to push him out of her life, not out of a window.

She had pushed them all out now: Jarvis and Jacko and OW. She was completely free. Which was, she realized, just another way of saying she was completely alone. She thought of Simms Quarter where she had never been alone. She remembered how she had longed to run away to the cities of the North, to escape from working in the fields and cleaning white people's houses. She was still cleaning white people's houses. Only now she was colder and hungrier and lonelier than ever.

She went on sitting there in the darkness with her shoes off and her hands limp in her lap. Slowly she became aware of that hole inside her, growing and growing, pressing against the sides of her body as if her entire being were opening, reaching out for something. The emptiness would split her apart. "That's what prayer is," Voncia had told her once. "A longin an a yearnin an a reachin out." But Rannee could not pray. She longed for Shubah or Voncia to come and stand beside her and pray for her and never stop until the emptiness was filled. But they were home praying for themselves. She was all alone. "You needin somethin more in your life, chile," Shubah had said. "You needin Jesus."

"Help me, Lord," Rannee whispered. After a while, she became aware again of that strange presence just beyond reach. She stretched out her hand. But she could not find it. She went on sitting there until she fell asleep.

She dreamed that it was very late and the house was empty. She was sitting up, waiting for the boys to come home. In her dream they were big boys who came and went as they pleased, and all in different directions: Flash to the gyms and playgrounds all over the city, Lance to the libraries, Reed to the bars and nightclubs, and Carter to the Gomez house on the corner. No one stayed home anymore. Fun was far away, beyond the threshold, noisy and expensive and dangerous. The trees shook and the dead lay hidden beneath the snow. She dreamed of young men in black jackets and older men in overcoats and women in pants, all reaching out, reaching for her sons with guns and razors and knives handy as handkerchiefs.

In her dream, she heard the clock on the Green striking the same hour every fifteen minutes. Where were the children? Finally she got up, a tired, aching old woman, to find her sons: in the bars and nightclubs, through the parks and playgrounds where she could see Flash's smile retreating from one basketball court to another, as soon as he saw her coming. "I see ya, Mama," he whispered. darting behind a tree. "Poor ole Mama." She walked for hours while the shadows grew more and more deformed and the moon flickered and went out. In the end, she was forced to go home alone and wait. Staring out the window, she saw Lance's face staring back through the bars of the jail. The clock struck again.

She awoke with a start and hurried to the bedroom to look at her children. They were all there, all sound asleep, safely tucked in. Their feet were still quite a way from the bottom. Even Lance, tall as he was, did not quite fill the bed. She still had a few years left.

In spring, the neighborhood looked entirely different. Porches and cars and storefronts and people emerged suddenly, throwing off the snow like dust sheets. The children looked bigger and the sidewalks cleaner and the houses seemed to pull themselves together and stand a little straighter in the April sun. Even the air seemed fresher, as if, during that long winter cycle, it had been washed and rinsed and spun dry.

OW came back in May looking brand-new too. He dropped in one night after work, wearing a dazzling smile with his buttons bright as butter. Looking at him, she realized that she remembered every angle and wrinkle and fold. She got out the ironing board.

He sat at the table, in the exact center of the kitchen. But wherever he was, she thought, would always be the exact center. She shifted the board and looked at him out of the corner of her eye.

He grinned and held out a toothpick. "Licorice," he said. "Newest, sweetest flavor on the market."

"No thanks." Nothing, she thought, ever got stuck between her teeth. She bent her head, pressing on the iron.

"How are the boys?" he said.

"Sleeping," she said firmly. "And they're going to stay that way."

"Sorry I wasn't around much lately," he said. "But I've been mighty busy."

"How come you got unbusy?"

"She left town." He grinned.

She pressed down on the iron.

"Had to get busy *some*where," he said softly. "Seeing as how I wasn't exactly welcome around here."

She looked up and felt his glance shoot through her, right down to her soles. She unrolled a shirt.

He began to invite her out again: to jazz at the Arcadia next Saturday, a basketball game at the Arena on Friday, and Chinese and Italian and Greek dinners anytime.

"I'm too tired," she said. "I work now. You find yourself someone else."

"I want *you*."

For a moment it rained starch all over Lance's shirt.

"What about church?" he said.

"What about it?" She was smoothing a wrinkle.

"We're having a Revival. Had a real good time in church last night."

She looked up. "A good time in *church?*"

"Uh huh." He leaned back, smiling at her, with the toothpick at a jaunty angle and the badge like a shield over his heart. "A real good time. Everyone was feeling the spirit and enjoying themselves. It was nice, real nice, being in church and enjoying the Lord."

A good time in church? Enjoying the Lord? She had heard that phrase before, from Uncle Floyd long ago. He had been talking about Cousin Travers in *heaven*. But OW was talking about enjoying the Lord on *Beulah Street*. She put down the iron and thought about that Sunday afternoon when she had sat in the back of the Holy Light Pentecostal Church and watched people singing and dancing. She remembered how she had felt, with her feet and her fingers and her shoulders beating time, how she longed to get up and join them. But she had been soldered to the seat. She could not imagine herself shouting and swaying and clapping that way. She could not imagine herself doing anything but working and sleeping and sitting alone in the dark.

"How about it?" OW was saying. "Want to come to church with me some time? Say tomorrow night? They're having special Revival services all week with a special preacher all the way from Columbus, Ohio. Reverend Moses. Mama swears he saved her life once. Maybe he'll save ours too." He smiled and reached for her hand. "What do you say? Mama says she'll be glad to stay with the boys."

"I'll think about it."

"I'll be here around seven. It's Saturday night, after all."

She double-locked the door behind him but she knew she had not locked him out.

Going out the next night, they heard Mrs. Puglisi on the hall phone. "Better get the hell over there fast, Sal," she was saying. "Rodriquez's store's on fire. Looks like another arson job. Make it snappy before they rob you blind."

OW ran out of the house with Rannee beside him and Mrs. Puglisi right behind. They ran past the row of small skittish houses to the tiny store on the corner with its saints still in the window but its rump in the dust. The rear end of the house had collapsed as if it could no longer stand up straight. Mr. Rodriquez's end, Rannee thought.

There was a small crowd in front and a small blaze still burning away in the back. As they approached, they saw someone run out of the building. "Stop him!" Mrs. Puglisi shouted. "Stop that bastard." But Rannee could see that it was only Mr. Rodriquez wearing his apron. He disappeared around the corner. A man carrying a brown paper bag came running out behind him. "Stop them, damn you," Mrs. Puglisi screamed again. "Stop them!"

A big black car drove up with SOP on the license plate. Sal Puglisi jumped out with his gun drawn. "Get em, Sal," Mrs. Puglisi shrieked. "Get em!" Puglisi shouted something and began to fire. There was the sound of broken glass. One of the saints in the window fell forward, its halo still intact, and the man with the paper bag dropped to the ground. It was old Mr. Caliph. He lay still with his three-legged dog beside him and his paper bag in his arms.

"Get that fuckin honky," someone shouted. The crowd yelled and began to attack the store, hurling stones, smashing windows. Mrs. Puglisi screamed, "Kill the bastards, Sal. Kill em." But before he could fire again, OW knocked his arm so that the bullet went wild. Someone grabbed Puglisi from behind. There was a short struggle and the sound of a single shot. Sal Puglisi lay bleeding on the ground, killed by his own hand with his own gun, with Mrs. Puglisi beside him. The smashing and the looting had stopped. The crowd was gone. Only Rannee, OW, and Mrs. Puglisi were left. Behind them was the wrecked store with the saints broken in the window as if they had suffered a second martyrdom.

Rannee knelt beside old Mr. Caliph lying dead in the doorway with his dog licking his socks and the paper bag in his arms. Inside were his extra shoes and a can of tomato soup.

OW had taken off his coat and was covering Sal Puglisi's body with it while Mrs. Puglisi sat on the ground beside it, sobbing. "Like a brother to me, he was. A real Goddam brother." For a moment, Rannee pitied her.

OW crouched down beside her. "I know," he said softly. "I'm sorry. Very sorry."

She raised her head and glared at him. "Fink! Murderer! *Nigger!*" she shouted into his face. "They'll get you for this. You can count on it. The Puglisis'll *kill* you for this."

# 18

Rannee lay in bed thinking of OW. Tonight, instead of going to church, he had gone to a fire and two murders. She wondered how many nights he spent like that. Finally she fell asleep and dreamed that OW was standing beside her, gazing down at her. He was wearing his uniform, buttoned up tight from throat to crotch. "Go away," she whispered. "You've got no business here." He moved closer. She could see the lines of his body under the jacket, the long, gentle slope from shoulder to waist, the slight, curving smile of the hips, the thick bulge between the legs. He was being crushed inside his clothes. "Go away. Go away," she pleaded. It was no business of hers that he was being squeezed by a uniform. *He* was no business of hers. He was danger and trouble and sin and sorrow. "Go away," she moaned. "Please go away." But he moved closer, smiling down at her. She could feel his breath on her face. She reached out slowly and began to undo his buttons. And then she heard a voice, a loud, deep voice, calling to her, commanding her.

She woke trembling. The room was completely quiet but she could still *feel* that voice as if it were right there behind her, waiting to speak again. She got out of bed and stood on the threshold of her room with her heart pounding. She was afraid to go on but she dared not go back to where OW was waiting, ready to fill her emptiness. She felt a cold wind in her face and remembered the voice in her dream, a soothing but commanding voice. "Isaiah 26:3," it had said. Still listening, she moved mechanically down the hall and into the living room. She turned on the light and saw Voncia's Bible on the table. She picked it up. It opened to Isaiah 26:3. "Thou wilt keep him in perfect peace," she read, "whose mind is stayed on Thee: because he trusteth in Thee." She sat down and read it again while her heart bounced like a ball. She sat there for a long time, holding the Bible, saying the words over and over: ". . . in perfect peace . . . trusteth in Thee." Finally her heart dribbled down and her whole body relaxed. She closed the book. She could go back to bed now. OW would not be there any more.

He came the next morning. She was ready. She could feel that void inside her spreading, reaching out. But now something outside was reaching in too. She stood with her hands pressed against her sides, holding herself together. "I've been thinking about going to church," she said. "I'm ready."

"You're ready? Great! Now?"

"Now." It was Sunday, after all.

She refused to wait for a taxi. She locked the children in and ran all the way, as if she were being pulled, with OW right beside her. Halfway there, it began to rain. She lifted her face, opened her mouth, and let the waters of heaven pour in.

The church was full of smiling people: Voncia from next door and Shubah from long ago, brown and skinny as a cigar, and friends Rannee had never seen before. It was, she thought, a real Homecoming. She sat down among them, slipped off her shoes, and looked around. Some of the windows, she noticed, had colored pictures. The one near her showed Jesus in a blue robe with His arms out and the words, "Love your enemies, bless them that curse you," beneath his feet. He seemed to be watching her, watching and beckoning. She shivered. It was raining harder now and thundering. She had always been afraid of thunder.

"Sister Elwina gonna preach tonight," Voncia whispered. "Sposed to be Reverend Moses but he too busy savin souls in Columbus, Ohio."

"The Reverend Moses who saved your life?" Rannee said.

"Tha's right," Voncia said.

"The preacher with no home and no family but the Lord?" Rannee said.

"Tha's it. Tha's him. A man o God. Jes a little bit of a man but he a mighty big preacher. That man got the sign o the Lord right on him. Yessir. Someday I gonna go to Columbus, Ohio, jes to hear that man preach again. But Sister Elwina a powerful preacher for the Lord too. Been preachin since she a tiny chile. First word she ever say was Je-sus. Yessir. Not Mama or Daddy but Je-sus. Right there in the cradle. Been preachin God's word ever since."

Sister Elwina was a tall woman in steel glasses and a white dress with a soft persuasive voice that seemed to slide smoothly among the pews and curl up in Rannee's lap. "Ain't too late," she was saying. "Ain't never too late to be saved. Ain't never too late to come to Jesus and be saved." Rannee could almost see those words hanging out in front of her like clothes on a line. They were just the right size and color and shape. She longed to slip them on.

"Ain't nothin you gotta do, nothin you gotta earn," the preacher said. "Is a gift, a free gift from the Lord. Is the gift of the Holy Ghost."

Rannee had never had any "free gifts." Just all those names and all those children, she thought.

"Is promised," the preacher said. "All you gotta do is receive. Just empty your mind and let the Lord Jesus walk in."

I'm empty already, Rannee thought. I've been empty a long time.

"Praise the Lord," Voncia shouted.

"Hallelujah," the others said.

234

Suddenly, across the aisle, an old man stood up and began to speak with his head back and his eyes on the ceiling, saying strange words in a strange voice as if he had swallowed the wind.

"He talkin in tongues," Voncia whispered.

He was one of the saved, Rannee thought. Not just a plain old man with a wobbly Adam's apple but a sanctuary for the Holy Ghost who might drop in at any time, surprising his wife at breakfast.

Rannee thought of her parents who had spent every Sunday of their lives in the Chawnee Immanuel Baptist Church, dozing through the Lessons and the sermons, understanding nothing, feeling nothing unless it was the taste of the food at Homecoming. Yet they had gone every single Sunday and taken their children and grandchildren to call upon the Lord in His House, certain that He was there somewhere behind the pulpit and the coattails of Preacher Asa Brown. Changing churches would be like changing gods to them. "You find a different church, Shoo?" Daddy would say, moving the hat around on his head. And Mama would rock back and forth slowly and fold her hands and her lips to keep from saying, "Fetch that switch, Sister." They would never take her to church with them again. Beet would shrug her skinny shoulders and laugh, and even Bay would look at her in disgust and back away as if she were diseased instead of anointed. If she found Jesus, she would lose them all.

She heard the wind dusting the roof and sweeping around the building. She thought of her children locked up in the empty apartment. If the Holy Ghost touched her mouth would He put His fiery finger on their lips too? She could not imagine her sons rounding their shoulders and bending their legs, night after night. "I don't wanna be saved," she had heard Flash tell Voncia. "Only ole, sad, sick peoples saved. I don't wanna be saved less the Lord's gonna save someone I can play with." Did she want to be saved without her children? Did she want to go anywhere at all where she could not take her children?

235

The preacher's voice was louder now. "'And suddenly there came a sound from heaven,'" she said, "'as of a rushing mighty wind . . .'"

"Praise the Lord," shouted Shubah.

"Hallelujah!" Voncia said.

The saints were strong inside their salvation, Rannee thought. They stood steady as mountains and moved slowly, as if counting the steps till Judgment Day. Anyone could tell, just by looking, that Voncia and Shubah were saved: by the way they held their heads as if listening for the Holy Ghost; by the way they smiled as if it were always Christmas, though they worked all the time—for white people during the week and for the Lord on weekends, for white people during the day and for the Lord at night. He must surely know their faces. But they enjoyed themselves with Him too. Rannee had not felt like dancing or singing since she was a girl. Would she be able to dance and sing for the Lord? She admired Shubah and Voncia, strong, self-sufficient women whose children were grown and whose husbands were gone and who had taken in Jesus to fill their lives. Would He fill hers too? For she needed something to put in that empty space inside her, like a room waiting to be let: something more than those four walls and those four children and OW tormenting her, twirling her heart like a toothpick between his lips.

"An the Holy Ghost waitin on you too," the preacher was saying. "He waitin to save you too. All you gotta do is jes open that door an let Him in."

If only He *would* come, Rannee thought, and push all the other men out forever. She remembered, with shame, the whole string of them, like signposts through her life, pointing the wrong way, the way she had never meant to go: Ward and Jarvis and Jacko—and now OW, still there, still waiting, still dangerous, sitting so quietly in the pew beside her. She did not want any man in her life ever again. "Only Jesus," she murmured, aware of Him standing in the window with his arms out, reaching for her.

Suddenly, she felt a strange silence in the church and realized that she was twitching and sliding and jerking in her seat. She couldn't stop. Everyone was watching her: the preacher and Shubah and Voncia and the people at the altar waiting to be saved. Even Jesus, staring through the window, was watching.

"Pray, church," the preacher called.

"Je-sus, sweet Je-sus," the others shouted. "Je-sus, Lord, help. Have your way, Je-sus. Have your way." And then the whole church burst into song, softly at first, then louder and louder, voices and piano and saxophone and cymbals, swirling around her and over her and under her, lifting her arms and her legs and her feet, lifting her out of her seat and up to the altar— past OW and Voncia, past a child swinging his legs, past an enormous woman shaped like a kettle, without touching any of them. She was standing at the altar in her stockinged feet, staring at a hole in her toe, surrounded by praying, singing, shouting people. After a while, the music died away and everyone else left. Only Rannee was still there, clinging to the altar as if stuck, with her head bowed.

"Is there somethin you wantin?" the preacher said.

"Prayer."

The preacher lifted her arms and prayed. But Rannee stood there helplessly with the Lord's fist in her back, staring at her naked toe.

"Is there somethin else?" the preacher said.

"Just prayer."

"I *been* prayin for you."

"Pray again," Rannee mumbled. The preacher raised her arms again and the music began again, loud and strong, like great wings that swayed and swooped and folded around her. She could not move.

Suddenly the music stopped and she heard the thunder again, crashing into hills, turning corners, rolling down toward the Holy Light Pentecostal Church like the thunder that had rolled down toward that tiny cabin in Simms Quarter. She longed to hide now as she had as a child. But the thunder kept

237

rolling, churning up the wind, knocking corners off the sky, hurling them at the roof of the church. "Listen!" Mama used to say. "That the Lord talkin."

"Listen, Daughter," Sister Elwina said, "the Lord is dealin with you. He been dealin with you since before you left your seat. That's why you can't go back. Let the Lord come into your life. He *callin* to you."

Rannee thought of that voice in her dream and felt the sweat on her scalp.

"He callin you right now," Sister Elwina went on. "Listen. He callin to you. You hear Him? He callin your name right now."

Calling her name? *Which* name? She had so many, she thought, recalling that long terrible list: Sister and Girl and Tink and Shoo; Peachers and Sweetie and Lyle and Doll. There were so many of her. Far too many. Too many to be saved. The Lord would never find the right name.

"Listen!" Sister Elwina called.

She listened and felt the breath stopped dead in her throat. It was very still now, as if *everything* had stopped: the rain and the thunder and the blood waiting in her ears and her heart like a great load in her chest, too heavy to beat.

"Listen!" the preacher shouted again. "Listen! Lift up your eyes and listen."

Rannee raised her head and saw Jesus in the window with His arms toward her. She could almost feel His hands on her shoulders. And now the thunder began again, rolling down the walls of the church, coming closer and closer. It hovered about her head and poured down over her shoulders. And then she heard a voice, loud and strong as a ramrod, calling her by name, a *single* name, the name nobody ever used, piercing her like a stake: "Saryanna!" She felt the breath leap in her throat and the blood spurt through her body and her heart began to turn like a giant wheel. "Saryanna," the voice called again, the name she had almost forgotten: "Saryanna," filling her like a rushing, mighty wind.

She opened her mouth to answer but suddenly there was a terrible noise, as if the thunder had finally crashed through the side of the church and exploded on the altar. The floor in front of her rose and the ceiling above her fell, covering one end of the church, covering the dais and the altar and Sister Elwina with her arms still raised, leaving a terrible hole at Rannee's feet, a hole which burst into flames, turning God's sanctuary into a fiery furnace. She felt the fire at her feet and reaching for her face. Behind her people were crying and screaming. And then OW was pulling her away, away from that burning spot where Jesus had spoken to her, had called her to the very edge of the pit.

Standing outside with the crowd, dazed and trembling, she stared at the half-burnt church. The rain and the thunder had stopped as if driven away by that bomb hurled into the peace of the Lord's Day when the streets were empty and His House full. Around her the crowd moaned and wept and knelt to pray, or stared fixedly at the building as people were helped out. "Where's my mama? my husbin? my sista? my son?" they called. Rannee was grateful that her children were safely locked up at home. Two choir members and Sister Elwina had been killed, Sister Elwina who had begun to serve the Lord when she was still in diapers. Rannee stood staring at the church. The windows were all empty now, like open mouths, except for the one with Jesus still holding out His arms and the words "Love your enemies, bless them that curse you," still left beneath His feet.

At home, Rannee checked on her children. She would never take them to church again.

"Why?" Rannee asked later that evening as Voncia sat in Rannee's kitchen in her Sunday hat, blowing into her tea. "Why?"

"On accounta Sal Puglisi."

"Sal Puglisi? He's dead."

"Tha's why. Peoples say that bomb throwed from a big black car. License have JLP on it."

"Joe Puglisi's car? Why would the Puglisis throw bombs at the Holy Light Pentecostal Church?"

"Didn't throw it at no church. Throwed it at OW."

At OW? And two hundred fifty Negroes besides, while the Lord watched from His window and told them to bless their white murderers?

"Wouldn't never happen if Reverend Moses was here," Voncia said. "The Lord wouldn't never let that happen, not with Reverend Moses preachin."

"Why not?"

"Cause that man a saint. That man a very special servant a the Lord. Yessir. You kin tell by lookin at him. Got the sign right on him."

"What kind of a sign?"

"Sign a the Lord. Long red sign. Like the Lord pass His fiery finger over that man's mouf."

Rannee put down her cup. "You mean he has a mark? A long red mark, right over his lip?" She was almost shouting. "Like a second mouth?"

"Tha's right," Voncia said. "That the marka the Lord. Right on him."

That's the mark of the white man, Rannee thought. "Is he small and thin with a big head stuffed with Bible verses and hymns?"

"Tha's right!" Voncia said. "Tha man know the Bible front to back an top to bottom, includin Leviticus an Numbers an Lamentations."

"He says words out of the Bible all the time and whistles 'Only Believe' all the time?" Rannee went on excitedly.

"Tha's him!" Voncia said. "Tha's Reverend Moses."

That's Uncle Floyd, Rannee thought. She could hardly believe her ears. Uncle Floyd wasn't dead or in prison or wandering, hungry and cold, through the streets. He was *safe*. "Thank you, Jesus," she murmured in spite of herself.

"Use to be right here in the Holy Light Church," Voncia

said. "A comfort to us all. But he gone now. Lef jes 'fore you come to live here."

She had missed him again. "Thank the Lord or he'd be dead now," she said. "Where did you say he went?"

"Columbus, Ohio. To the Mount Zion Free Will Baptist Church."

"Is that far?" Rannee said.

"Teerbul far," Voncia said.

Later that night, after Voncia had gone, Rannee sat alone in the dark, thinking about the church and the terrible hole that had opened so suddenly at her feet and the flames that had reached for her face. The menace she had felt growing around her ever since she came North had exploded, at last, right in front of her, right there in the House of the Lord, at His very altar; even, she thought with a shudder, at the sound of His voice. "Saryanna," He had called, summoning her not to salvation but to the very rim of death. She remembered her dream last night, when the Lord had saved her from OW in order, she thought, to save her for *Him,* "to keep her in perfect peace." But He was a white God who merely watched from the window while the white man bombed His church and killed His worshipers. It was *OW* who had saved her, who had snatched her from that fiery hole. And saved my children from being orphans, she thought. Would he be able to keep on saving her, and her children?

She thought of Simms Quarter with the tiny cabins crouched beneath the hill and the sky bending over them and the town far away at the other end of a long dirt road, where violence was kept beyond the borders, held off by Mama and Daddy and the uncles. It had never, in Simms Quarter, exploded right in her face.

But she had broken out of Simms Quarter, had pushed her way through the ring of tiny cabins to look for Uncle Floyd and to find Jesus. But they had both moved on—Uncle Floyd out of town and Jesus out of the ghetto. Yet she knew now that He had never really been there at all, had never set foot inside the

Hill section in spite of all those little churches like stores for Negroes too poor to buy anything else.

She went on sitting alone in the darkness as usual; only tonight she knew there was nothing in the room with her, nothing to reach out to, nothing but empty space.

# 19

Lance grew taller and thinner and had the fastest walk and the highest grades in the Abraham Lincoln School. It was an integrated school now, with black and white students, white teachers, and a white principal. But in the playground and the cafeteria, the school was always segregated. Gangs of tough white boys still gathered across the street and Officer Puglisi still directed traffic out front.

"Give it time," OW said. He was coming around regularly again, bringing all kinds of gifts for the children. "Equipment," he called it. He taught Flash to hit a mean ball and Reed to ride a bike and Carter to build huge towers, and he taught Lance various aspects of the law. Lance adored him, sitting at his feet, leaning against his chair, watching his face, asking questions.

"OK, sergeant," OW would shout. "Read the prisoner his rights."

Lance would snap to attention, arms rigid, chin up, eyes front, and declaim: " 'You have the right to remain silent. You have the right to a lawyer. You have the right to a reasonable bail. You have the right to a speedy trial.' What's that 'right to a reasonable bail' mean, OW?"

"That Lance is one very, very smart boy," OW told Rannee later that evening. They were sitting on the couch after the boys had gone to bed.

"I know." She grinned happily. "*Very* smart. I'm planning to send him to college. Somehow."

OW put his arms around her. "That's my girl," he said. "*We*'ll send him to college." He kissed her and went on kissing her as if he never intended to stop. After a while, she felt his lips begin to wander, felt his fingers unbuttoning and unzipping, and his hands smoothing and patting, preparing the way. She felt the terrain shift and slide and swell beneath him, willing him to find that secret entrance, willing him to raise his banner and stake his claim.

He became a regular feature of her landscape. He arrived every Saturday night and was always there for breakfast Sunday morning. She no longer thought of asking, "You carefer?," no longer worried about having babies. Thanks to OW, *she* knew how to be careful now.

She began to relax, to let go, to enjoy. She found herself singing in the kitchen and laughing in the bedroom and hugging and kissing her children anywhere. Not like Mama, who kept her singing for church and her kissing for infants, as if kisses were, like everything else in Simms Quarter, in short supply. But Rannee became reckless, as if her supply would never run out. She grew lazy too, sitting around on Sunday mornings in a bathrobe, letting the children stay in pajamas till noon. Instead of going to church, she sat on the sofa beside OW and read the paper or helped him do the crossword puzzle with the dictionary instead of a hymn book on her lap. OW didn't seem to care about church either. Had he gone just to please Voncia? He seemed perfectly content to stay home now—to please Rannee? He was always home when he wasn't working. The blouses on Jewel Street had stopped fluttering. But Rannee's bathrobe fluttered as he sat over the crossword puzzle. She felt a shiver just watching him fill in seven down.

She had wandered into Vanity-Fair, she thought one Sunday

244

morning, looking around the apartment with the new curtains and the new stove and a new bookcase full of books, like a piece of the public library, though she still kept *Pilgrim's Progress* on the kitchen counter between the clock and the ketchup; and the new rocking chair, all polished and padded, so different from Mama's; and the new plates with flowers all around the edges. But it was a messy apartment too, she thought, full of dirty dishes and unmade beds and undressed children and herself on the sofa in a bathrobe with OW beside her. "Glad my mama can't see me now," she said. "She'd tell me to 'Fetch that switch.'"

OW laughed and hugged her. "And my Aunt Lilla's probably churning the dirt up all over the Trenton Morning Star Memorial cemetery because of my 'slothful ways' and disturbing the residents. Why don't we get married and give the dead a little rest? Besides making our mamas happy? Not to mention me."

And me, Rannee thought, looking at him, longing to throw herself into his arms, to be buttoned up inside that snug tunic with his heart beating against her cheek, to curl up inside his life forever. "I'll think about it," she said.

"Any objections if I take up residence here in the meantime?" he said. "So those boys can get used to having me around?" The next night he moved in. But he went on asking her to marry him every other Thursday.

She longed to say yes. She knew she had married Ward out of despair and Jarvis out of loneliness. She would marry OW out of love. For the first time in her life, she was happy. She was not even cleaning other people's houses any more. She was stamping books in the library and putting them back on the shelves.

Miss de Palma, with her pencil between her teeth for a change, had called her over to the loan desk one afternoon. She stared at Rannee for a long moment, removed the pencil, and offered her a job. "Might as well," she said. "The time you spend here. You ought to be able to shelve those books in the dark. Very handy in a power failure." She smiled. "No overdue fines for employees," she said. "And first crack at the new books. But don't keep them out for more than nine months—to cover pregnancies—and don't read them in the shower." She smiled again and stuck her pencil back in her hair.

At night, Rannee no longer sat alone in the dark with the sense that the ghetto was coiling up around her, ready to choke her. Instead, she had OW's arms around her. They sat on the sofa, reading or making love. "The two most important activities in life," OW said.

"How about eating and sleeping?" Rannee said.

"Good. But secondary. Definitely secondary." He kissed her and, with his arm through hers, settled down with *Minorities and the Police*. He was reading more and more books about the Force. "So I can answer Lance's questions," he said.

He was practicing for the role of father more and more, she thought. He helped Lance with his homework, flew kites with Reed, threw footballs with Flash, collected bottle tops with Carter, and corrected everybody's English and everybody's table manners. Rannee no longer thought about finding Uncle Floyd or even Jesus. She sang duets with OW now: "No Hiding Place Down There," and "Company Store," and "Walking My Baby Back Home." His voice was deeper and stronger and steadier than Uncle Floyd's.

She settled down happily beside him and opened her book. It was James Baldwin's *Go Tell It on the Mountain*.

One Saturday, she heard OW talking to the children. He was telling Flash to tuck in his shirt and Reed to tie his shoelaces. "You men are going to have to shape up," he said. "Shoulders back, butt in. And keep these quarters clean. I want some order around here."

The next time he asked her to marry him, she said, a little faster than usual, "Not yet." Not till her children were grown, she thought. She didn't want any cop, however kind, however loving, policing her sons.

"Why not?" OW said.

"I like it this way. Let's just keep it this way."

"All right." He smiled and kissed her. "I can wait. But let me know when you're ready. I won't ask you again."

He might not wait much longer either, she thought, putting her arms around him, short, thin arms. They could never hold him.

They could hardly hold her sons any more. When they left in the morning, she kissed them and patted their cheeks and longed to keep her hands on their shoulders, to guide them, restrain them, protect them. But her arms would only be torn from their sockets. At work, she thought of the news she occasionally heard on OW's radio or read in OW's paper: stories of Negroes shot and buildings wrecked and crosses burning. At night, she dreamed she was wandering alone, looking for her sons down streets that ran like knives through the heart of the ghetto. OW went to work on the night shift again. She sat by the window for hours after he left, listening to the sirens, wondering where they were going and why.

There were incidents around the Abraham Lincoln School. Fights broke out constantly between blacks and whites. Windows were smashed, equipment stolen, skin torn. One black boy was taken to the hospital with a broken arm. There was garbage all over the playground and slashed tires and broken windshields in the parking lot. Finally, the grounds were kept locked before and after school, though the older white boys often climbed the fence anyway. Lance was frightened most of the time. He did his work and kept to himself. People said his father was a policeman. They left him alone.

On Wednesdays, he helped Miss Webster in the school library and was sometimes a little late getting home. On Wednesdays, Rannee worried. "You stay away from those white boys," she said.

"Sure, Mama. I always go out the back way, through the playground, so they won't see me. Nothing to worry about, Mama."

"I thought those big white boys climbed over the fence."

"Not till later. After Officer Puglisi goes home."

One Wednesday he was very late. Rannee remembered the time he had come home bleeding from a snowball with a rock in it. This time he might be bleeding from a knife or a gun. She rushed to school but it was all closed up, even the playground was empty and locked. She hurried home, planted herself beside Mrs. Puglisi's phone and began to call all over town: to friends and neighbors and teachers and Miss Webster, who said that Lance had left the library long ago. In between, she waited for a call. But none came. Finally she phoned OW on duty.

"Could be they've got him locked up downtown," OW said.

"Lance locked up?" her voice rose in panic. "*Lance?* What would Lance ever do to get locked up?"

"Not much," OW said. "If anyone needed a reason. But you're right, of course," he said quickly. "They wouldn't lock up an eleven-year-old boy without even . . ."

"He's tall," Rannee said. "He looks older." She hung up.

There were no buses at that hour. She did not wait to call a taxi. She merely opened the door and ran. She ran all the way, as she had that night in Montgomery. She thought of Lance sitting all alone in a cold cell with the darkness and the stench from the toilet stopping his nose and mouth. They had nothing but a hard metal bench in the cells in that downtown police jail, Mrs. Puglisi had said. No mattresses or sheets or blankets because of suicide. They even took away the prisoner's jacket and belt and tie and shoes to prevent suicides. Rannee imagined Lance shivering and scared in shirtsleeves and socks with the toilet leaking all over the floor, wondering how long he had been there and how long he would have to stay there, wondering if anyone would ever find him at all. She remembered his nightmares of Jarvis climbing out of the bureau to grab him and stuff him into the bottom drawer; of Mrs. Sperling, his first-grade teacher, catching him in a net and locking him up in a box for study. She remembered Lance declaiming with pride: "'You have the right to remain silent. You have the right to a lawyer. You have the right to a reasonable bail. You have the right to a speedy trial.'" But he didn't seem to have any rights at all now, except the right to remain silent.

At the station they told her that Lance had been taken to the hospital. She stared, turned, and ran again.

At the hospital she sat beside Lance's bed for hours, holding his hand, frowning at the bandages crisscrossed all over his head. He had, in a panic, rushed to the door of his cell. His frozen feet, in thin socks, had slipped on the wet floor and he had landed, face first, against the bars. "Thought I heard you coming, Mama," he said.

"What for?" she asked OW on the way home. "What did they lock him up for?"

"For walking through the playground five minutes after school closing time. Only they called it criminal trespass. And it wasn't *they*, it was Joe Puglisi, the bastard."

"Must be lots of kids cut through that playground before they lock it. Why pick on Lance?"

He was silent for a second. "Because of me," he said.

"What did you say they called it?"

"Criminal trespass."

She had heard that word before, long ago. Lance's daddy had been shot and killed for trespassing. Yet she knew that Lance had not trespassed any more than Ward had, Lance who was so skinny he hardly trespassed into empty space but lived with his ears and his elbows and his toes turned in, who even kept his eyes from wandering very far. Had she taken him out of Simms Quarter and brought him all the way up North to have him end up like his daddy? She felt as if she had led him right into that cell herself and smashed his face against the bars.

"I'll get that bastard, that pig," OW said. "I'll get that damn PIG-lisi."

"No!" Rannee said. "Please! Don't do *anything*."

"Don't worry. I can get him nice and legal," OW said. "I've got a real juicy list: false arrest and child abuse and . . ."

"No! Please. Don't mess with him. *Please*, OW. Promise me you won't do anything."

"But we can't just . . ."

"Yes we can. We *must*. Just let it be. For *my* sake," she said. For your sake, too, she thought.

"All right," he said grimly, shaking his head. "I'll let it be. This time. For *your* sake. But next time . . ."

There won't be any next time, she thought.

That night, after the boys had gone to bed and OW had gone to work, she sat alone in the dark again and stared out the window at the jail across the street, the jail that claimed so many young Negroes every day, as if it had a standing order. The jail downtown had almost gotten Lance. Someday, sooner or later, the jail would get them all, all her sons. They would be locked up there to fill the quota, for being poor and Negro and trespassing. For they were *all* trespassers, *all* Negroes everywhere who had broken out of the slave quarters and the Simms Quarters of the South. How could she have forgotten? That big tree had fallen across her path again, as it had in the woods back home, blown down for growing too tall, for reaching too high.

This time there was no Uncle Floyd to take her hand and help her over. Next time it might be worse. Next time it might fall right on top of her. Next time her sons might be burned up in church like Sister Elwina. Next time OW might be shot dead right out on the street like Mr. Caliph. There must never be a next time.

"You need a husband and those boys need a father and I need a family," OW had said. Yes, she thought, she needed a husband, needed OW more than ever, they all did, now that they were used to having him there all the time, their own personal security officer who had secured love and shelter and stability for them—but not, good policeman though he was, physical safety. For he was dangerous too, a tall, straight black man, a human target. Wherever he went, in or out of uniform, there would always be an Officer Puglisi, waiting. Wherever he went, OW would attract hatred and violence and death. And her sons, it seemed, only added to the threat. OW had been ready, even eager, to commit the rash, suicidal act of attacking Officer Puglisi in his own territory, because of Lance. However much her children and OW loved and needed each other, they were unsafe together. She dared not go on living with OW, dared not trespass on this town any longer. She must move on. But where?

Back to Simms Quarter, to the tiny cabin where Mama's youngest were still living, where her sons would sleep in the cold, wet, crowded beds in the back room; to the field with the sun frying their heads and the sweat dripping like grease into their shoes; to the Chawnee Primary School for Negroes with the cold pinching their bones and Miss French raising the switch? For nothing, she was certain, had changed in Simms Quarter. It was all still there as it had always been, as if the vines had, indeed, finally grown up over it, enclosing it, isolating it, *preserving* it. Her children would live her childhood all over again as if she had never left. No, she could not go back to Simms Quarter again. But she could not stay here either. She was like Christian, she thought, with the Ditch on one side and the Quag on the other. But where was the narrow way between?

She waited until Lance was well and school was out for the summer and she had saved a little more money. Then, one night in August, after OW had gone to work, she cleaned the house, washed and ironed all the laundry, and cooked enough food for a week. Then she rushed through the rooms in a panic, packing as fast as she could, though she knew there was no bus till morning. She remembered that night in Montgomery when she ran through that other house, stripping it bare, tearing and burning, leaving nothing at all but the wind and the dust. This time she moved quickly but gently, taking nothing but their clothes, though she allowed the boys one special item each. Lance chose his detective kit, and she took the paperback dictionary. At the last minute, she picked up *Pilgrim's Progress*. She read: "Then I saw there was a way to Hell, even from the Gates

251

of Heaven. . . ." She closed it quickly and put it back carefully between the ketchup and the clock.

When they finally left, the apartment looked exactly as always, except for the note taped to the refrigerator door.

She sat in the station, waiting for the bus, remembering all those other buses—from Simms Quarter and Chawnee and Montgomery. A permanent trespasser, she had spent her life moving on. But now she had her sons and a paperback dictionary moving with her.

The station was hot and dirty with litter on the floor and a harsh light overhead, lighting up torn posters and empty vending machines and Miss Hertz smiling at the overflowing trash bin. Toward morning, a group of people, Negro and white, began to collect in one corner. They were carrying signs that read: EFFECTIVE CIVIL RIGHTS NOW, END SEGREGATION NOW, INTEGRATE PUBLIC SCHOOLS NOW. They were going to Washington to march with Martin Luther King. She thought of that day in Montgomery when she had marched with Martin Luther King too, and a whole town of Negroes. That was a long time ago and they were still marching. But now white people were marching with them.

"We goin to Washington, Mama?" Carter said.

"No."

"*Where* then? *Where* we goin?"

"She *tole* you," Flash said. "She tole you a million times. We goin to Columbus, Ohio."

"But she never say *why*. *Why* we goin there?"

She looked at him, at all her sons whom she was yanking up once again, dragging away once again, to a strange place, to live among strange people, with the damp making strange new shapes on the walls. She gripped the dictionary in her lap. They had been asking the same questions all night, as if they could not accept the answers. But she had no others. They were looking at her the way she must have looked at Uncle Floyd sitting on the back porch at home. But she had no stories about the wonderful cities of the North, no swizzle sticks from the bars of Montgomery to give them.

"Why can't we stay here?" Reed said. "With OW."

"Yes, Mama," Lance said. "Why can't we?"

She looked at him. He was completely healed now, but she still remembered the pattern of those bandages crisscrossed all over his head.

The people with the signs were outside now, boarding their buses, singing and shouting and waving their signs. For a moment, Rannee longed to go with them, to carry a sign and shout slogans too, to be part of a crowd again, a strong, sure, friendly crowd, as she had been that day in Montgomery so that just walking home became exciting, was no longer merely walking but *marching*. She longed to be on a march again instead of just on the move.

Now she and her children were all alone in the station.

"Where's OW?" Reed said.

"On duty," Lance said.

"He comin after us?" Carter said. He was close to tears.

"Course he's coming after us," Lance said. "Right, Mama?"

"Maybe," she said.

"When?" Reed said. He was close to tears too.

"Soon as he's off duty," Lance said. "Right, Mama?"

"Maybe," she said again.

"Let's wait for him, Mama," Lance said. "He won't ever be able to find us by himself in Columbus, Ohio. Please, Mama. Let's wait for him."

He was crying now, and she saw those invisible scars all over his face. She would always see them.

"Yes, Mama," Flash said. "Why can't we wait for OW?"

"Yes, Mama," the others said. "Why can't we?"

"Because," she said once again, but slowly now, weakly, "we are going to Columbus, Ohio, to find Uncle Floyd."

"*Why?*" Reed said. "Why we goin to find *him?*"

"Who Uncle Floyd?" Carter said.

She stared at him, gripping the dictionary again, as if hoping to find a definition, a definition he would understand. Who is Uncle Floyd? Who is he? A preacher who might no longer be preaching? A tough, cheerful little man who might no longer whistle or even believe? He might be sick, too sick to take on a whole new family, or burdened with an old one, or locked up in jail. He might not be at the Mount Zion Free Will Baptist Church anymore. He might not even be in Columbus, Ohio, anymore. He might have moved on again, many times, for he was a trespasser too. He might not even be alive anymore. She closed her eyes and tried to picture him, a short, thin man in overalls with a big head and a scar like an extra lip. But, of course, he would not look like that anymore. Just as she was no longer a little girl in high-topped shoes and hair like a hooked rug, dreaming of escape with Uncle Floyd.

The wind rose, blowing the litter against their ankles, piling it up around them as if getting ready to sweep them out with the trash. It was more like the end of a journey than the beginning.

"Let's go home, Mama," Lance said.

"Yes, Mama," the others said. They were all crying now. "Let's go home."

"Home?" She stared at them. *Home?* She reached out and wiped their tears away carefully, one by one, with a gentle finger. Home to the ghetto and the Puglisis? Home to the guns and the bombs and the jail waiting right across the street?

"Let's go home to OW," Lance said.

She looked at him carefully for a long time. "All right," she said at last. "Let's go home—to OW." She stood up and led the way out.

On the street, she began to walk quickly, then faster and faster. Soon she was almost running. If they hurried, they could be there before OW got back.